PRAISE FOR *THE COURT MARTIAL OF ROBERT E. LEE* BY DOUGLAS SAVAGE

"A brilliant premise, superb characterizations, fine historical research and setting . . . [a]s good as *The Killer Angels* . . ."
—David Martin
Author of *Regimental Strengths and Losses at Gettysburg*

"Savage's creativity, eye for detail, and flair for character development make the book an irresistible combination of history, biography, and courtroom drama."
—Edward G. Longacre
Author of *The Cavalry at Gettysburg*

"It is a remarkable accomplishment."
—William Garrett Piston
Author of *Lee's Tarnished Lieutenant: James Longstreet*

"Here come to life are the personalities of the Confederate Government and military, and the forgotten figures in Lee's personal life ... Here is a powerful work of fiction that takes us into the life of the Confederacy ... [*Court Martial* is] a novel of deep fascination and literary rewards for the reader."
—*Wisconsin Bookwatch*

PRAISE FOR *THE GLASS LADY* BY DOUGLAS SAVAGE

"[A] technical masterpiece and a plain, old-fashioned, great story . . . There have been writers of the sea who were this good, but Douglas Savage has set the standard for the literature of spaceflight."
—Gordon Baxter
Contributing Editor, *Flying Magazine*

"[I]t is written with exquisite attention to creating realistic Shuttle operations, right down to detailing every switch and panel on the checklist . . . [T]he reader flies the mission . . . as it is really flown."
—Richard Berry
Editor-in-Chief, *Astronomy* Magazine

"To read *The Glass Lady* is to fly the Space Shuttle. The book is a remarkable achievement in the literature of flight."
—Allan Fritche
Editor, *STS Mission Profiles*

A MOUTHFUL OF DUST

OF DUST

A NOVEL

DOUGLAS SAVAGE

NORTIA
PRESS

Orange County, California

www.nortiapress.com

2321 E 4th Street, C-219
Santa Ana, CA 92705
contact @ nortiapress.com

**FT
Pbk**

Author photograph © 2011 by Elizabeth Gasper.

Stephen Crane photograph used with permission from the Special Collections Research Center, Syracuse University Library.

Library of Congress Control Number: 2012932106
ISBN: 978-0984225286

Manufactured in the United States of America

For Debra Savage Hurtt,
who knows that Mr. Chips was right

That was all it was to him—a spectacle,
something to be watched because he
might not have a chance to see such
again ... After all, you don't waste a war.

—William Faulkner,
Absalom! Absalsom! (1936)

What's the use of not being wounded if
they scare you to death?

—Ernest Hemingway
A Farewell to Arms (1929)

ONE

WHEN THE EXPLOSION LIFTED THE UNITED STATES ARMORED cruiser *Maine* out of the water last February, her keel broke as a heart breaks, fast and forever. The ship settled quickly, leaving only her crumbled white superstructure and masts above water. Now the two masts poked into the new morning at strange and ugly angles beside buoy Number 4. The sun painted tiny whitecaps red where the morning tide broke almost reverently over the wet grave of dozens of *Maine*'s 260 dead Yanquis whose bodies were not yet recovered for burial in Havana's Colón Cemetery. These bluejackets fed the fish inside 7,000 tons of steel.

The son, grandson, and nephew of Methodist preachers, the man on the wharf bowed his head to honor the decomposing sailors. Inside his fever-tormented brain, he heard the sweet, sad refrain of the hymn, which asks God—Who made the oceans which swallow men—to hear our prayers when we cry for those in peril on the sea. He had not thought of his minister father for months, nor of his mother. Neither of them would have approved of their youngest son becoming a camp follower of armies so he could turn their living and their dying into nothing more lasting than words on paper. On the battlefields of Greece and Cuba, he had learned that armies march by the regiment and by the division, but soldiers die one at a time far from home. He felt disappointment that he could hammer out a monument to their bravery and to their suffering no grander than ink scratches—what he called "only a little ink, more or less." These he knew would one day turn yellow, flake at the edges, and be forgotten.

He remembered that none of them knew the color of the sky two years ago when he was shipwrecked off the Florida coast in a shark-infested sea. The thin man on the Havana wharf opened his eyes wide. He wanted to know the color of the tropical sky. Daybreak this Thursday, December 8, rushed over his pale face and bathed his hollow cheeks in brilliant red.

The ocean of Havana Bay lapped softly against wooden piers, a gentle swish of dirty gray water against black rocks as if the sea had all the time in the world to dissolve the bloodied island. He had heard the sea roar in anger when its midnight waves had eaten his boat 23 months earlier. Even then, he understood that the sea meant no harm; she was only doing what she knew. Their ship *Commodore* opened her sides in wallowing submission. He remembered the gun-runner lurching under his feet, trying to pull him into the water's open arms. He remembered feeling that "he resembled a man on a sinking ship who appeals to the ship."

The low sun warmed his face when he felt a tug on his sleeve. He opened his eyes and blinked at the woman by his side. She looked at him with worried eyes.

"Perdido," the woman said. She held his arm firmly to keep the sea from sucking him into the gray water.

The woman pushed him away from *Maine*'s tomb. Behind them the post office on San Pedro Avenue in the Old Havana district west of the harbor glowed pink from the rising sun. Morning fog drifted over the Santa Catalina store houses in the middle of the harbor.

"You must write today, Perdido," the woman said in heavily accented English.

"Maybe," he said softly. "This war is over, Rosa. I need to finish writing what I saw."

"Are you a historian at home?"

"No. But I would like to have become one." He looked again at the hulk of *Maine*. "Historians are, as a rule, unsentimental."

The woman squeezed his bony arm as they followed cobblestone streets and alleys toward Mary Horan's. When he awoke this morning at Mary Horan's boarding house, his bedding gray as Havana Bay was wet with fevered sweat so he knew that today the yellow jack would skate up and down his spine on razors which felt like a "red-hot wire." His step hesitated whenever they passed doorways or low verandas where broken young men sat with bowed heads. First light made pustulating bandages glisten on brown or black foreheads, arms, and stick-thin legs. Some of the legs ended at bandaged stumps.

The woman pushed him faster when they walked too close to these wounded rebels who had survived the battle cry *¡Cuba Libre!* and the 30-year uprising against the Spanish fist. Half of these survivors, like half of Cuba, were descendants of African slaves. As a gun-runner and then as a newspaperman, he had come to Cuba many times to watch these wasted insurrectos fight and die. But he walked with the woman too close now to these hungry veterans. To the writer, the Cuban rebels always "looked like a collec-

tion of real tropic savages at whom some philanthropist had flung
a bundle of rags and some of the rags had stuck here and there."
He imagined that he could smell the gas gangrene eating the flesh
under their filthy bandages. In the jungle battlefields, it was not
so bad. Tropical wind blew some of the stench away. But in the
narrow alleys of Old Havana, the island's gravity made the taste of
rotting men hover like a thick cloud close to the earth.

The correspondent knew the battlefields of Greece and Cuba
even before he had seen his first. He had imagined them for a lifetime. Among the Greeks slaughtered by the Turks a year before
Cuba and in the Cuban piles of newly dead rebels and Spaniards
and then Yanquis, he saw what he had already seen in his writers'
mind when he had slept among the homeless in a New York City
shelter. "There was a strange effect of a graveyard," he wrote four
years earlier, "where bodies were merely flung." Only the smell after a battle he could not imagine.

Before Greece and Cuba he had loved his vision of war. When
he had closed his eyes as a boy he trod grim fields where the dead
men lay like clods of bleeding earth. Unable to become a soldier
in the real world, he retreated into his mind. He discovered that
novelists live in their day-dream world where only the heat of the
words can limit the passion in the writing.

Three years before Cuba he had invented Private Fred Collins,
a soldier like the writer had longed to be but could never become.
"He had blindly been led by quaint emotions, and laid himself
under an obligation to walk squarely up to the face of death." In
the flash of magic known only to novelists, the correspondent had
touched his pen to blank paper and the words had trickled out
in perfect order. Surrounded now by Havana morning and by the
decaying refuse of an army, his own words rang hollow and off-key
inside his war-numbed mind. Only six weeks into his 27th year,
already his literary future was behind him as he leaned heavily

upon Rosa Montoya's arm and inhaled the scents of frying fish and bubbling infection.

He heard the gritty sound of their shoes on the street. Looking up at the African, Indian, and mixed-blood faces of the wounded who watched him pass, he wondered why he could hear his feet on the street. From every balcony and open window, torn hungry men and starving children looked down with dark blank faces. The writer shivered when he realized that the wounded men were completely silent in their pain, as if their recent victory were cause only for mourning. The impenetrable silence of Cuban troops puzzled him. In June he had written of the Cubans he saw in the east, "He starves and he makes no complaint. We feed him and he expresses no joy."

Samuel Carleton stopped walking. When Rosa pushed him, he did not budge. He looked up at the cliff of open windows on either side of the narrow street. When the quiet army around him breathed out, he breathed it in. These broken, fevered bodies were the flesh and blood of the stories Carleton had come to write. Feeling their half-closed eyes upon him, he sensed himself shrinking. He glanced down at the crushed stones of the alley to see if any crack were wide enough to let him pass quickly into the Cuban earth. Rosa shook him from his stupor. He was grateful that she had grabbed him before he drained out of sight into the pores of the street. The reporter blinked and looked up at the yellow eyes and red bandages surrounding him and then he remembered Henry Fleming, another soldier created by his pen five years ago.

"The battle was like the grinding of an immense and terrible machine to him." The memory was Henry's, but the ink was the correspondent's. "Its complexities and powers, its grim processes, fascinated him. He must go close and see it produce corpses."

Turning away from the living corpses in the windows and doorways, he allowed Rosa to push him toward Mary Horan's.

When they arrived, Rosa climbed the flight of stairs to their one-room shanty and she closed the door behind her.

The American heard Rosa bolt her door as he knocked gently on a rough wooden door on the ground floor. He imagined warm, wary breath on the other side.

"María?" he said to the unpainted door.

A black eye and caramel brown skin peered around the door which slowly opened to reveal a young woman's face. She stepped back and opened the door only enough for Samuel Carleton to wedge his narrow shoulders inside.

"María Teresa," he smiled.

"Don Samuel," she said, looking quickly over his shoulder into the hallway as she closed the door.

The small room was stuffy with the single window darkened. There was no glass behind the unpainted shutter.

"From Rosa," he said, handing her two cloth sacks. "Beans and rice for the night if you have hunger," he said in slow, careful Spanish with a Newark, New Jersey twang.

"Thank you," she stammered in English.

Morning sunlight worked its way through the shutter lattice and touched the girl's large belly bulging in her ragged linen smock which reached her ankles above her bare feet.

"You and the baby are well this morning?" he asked cheerfully.

"We are. Today he moves much." When her smooth brown face smiled as she patted her belly with both hands, she looked not quite out of her teens. Samuel Carleton thought she was beautiful. Rosa had moved her into the boarding house before Carleton knew the older woman who waited for him upstairs. Once the girl had shared with him her fear of childbirth and he thought but did not say that she had never birthed a book whose agony of labor might last a year only to be stillborn after all.

"I am glad that you are well, María."

"When he comes the baby, you can tell me the names of other ships." She smiled and revealed the gaps in her fine bright smile where her pregnancy had dissolved four teeth.

When the American met the girl for the first time, he told her in his fractured Spanish that he had known a beautiful Spanish warship called *María Teresa*. The girl had smiled when she asked him where he had seen the great ship. "On a Cuban beach," the American had said. "Burned up."

He reached for the door latch.

"*Gracias*," María Teresa said.

"*Hasta luego*," he said to the door closing quickly behind him. He climbed the steep stairs and was breathing hard when he entered Rosa's home.

Carleton walked toward the open window and inhaled the December chill. Even in Cuba, winter mornings could be cool. He knew that by noon the day would be hot and beautiful. He picked up his pipe, lit yesterday's dried chewing tobacco, and drew hard to get it burning.

Inside a cloud of pipe smoke, the writer sat at a cloth-covered table in the center of the narrow room. His knees touched small wooden boxes arranged into a cube. The linen lay across the boxes. He turned to watch Rosa who stood at a dry sink in front of the window. She closed colorless shutters across the square hole in the wall and poured cold water from a pitcher into a basin. Its pottery rim was faded and cracked. Standing with her back toward the sitting man, she removed her white, peasant blouse. The man watched her smooth skin and muscles as she leaned over the basin and threw water into her face. She dried her face with a yellow towel. Then she lifted her firm arms one at a time and rubbed the moist towel across her armpits.

"Why are there no clean Cubans?" he asked without smiling.

"I am Cuban," the woman said.

"You are Spanish."

"No. I am Cuban now. I am sorry that you do not love Cuba as I do."

"No man should be called upon to report a war in a country that he loves."

Rosa turned and walked half-naked toward the writer. Looking up, he studied her finely angular face. Her face had been baked brown by 30-odd years of Cuban sunshine. But there was no Indian or African in her soft cheekbones and narrow nose. Her clear eyes were light brown like her long wavy hair that flowed down her bare back. Protected by her clothing, her smooth skin was white. She was *criolla*, purebred Old Spanish, and her European heritage showed.

The emaciated man closed his eyes, took the pipe from his face, and leaned forward until he felt her skin warm and fair upon his face.

Rosa took a step closer. Cradling his head in one hand against her breasts, she stroked his shaggy hair with her other. When he sighed deeply, she gently pushed his face away and smiled down at him. She stepped to a low dresser and opened a drawer from which she retrieved a pile of paper bound by string.

"Rosa," the reporter whispered.

"You must write today, Perdido. I shall be here for you when you finish."

The writer covered his mouth to cough. Rosa moved away and put on a clean blouse which she buttoned only half way. He watched her and smiled when she opened the shutters to allow in the Havana sunshine. The window had no glass. His pipe smoke felt like the calm eye of a whirlwind when he skimmed through the pages already written, filled with young men at war.

Samuel Carleton called himself the Correspondent when he wrote. He laid his cigarette stained fingers atop the taller pile of old newsprint. He breathed with slow, shallow breaths as his hand drew into his arm and through his shoulder his memoir that he had penned since early November. As a physician feels for a pulse, the writer's fingertips absorbed first faintly, and then strong, all that the correspondent had seen, felt, and inhaled since his newspaper's little boat *Three Friends* had been leased to the New York *World* to follow the white wake of *Panther*, which put 647 United States Marines ashore at Guantánamo, Cuba, on Friday, June 10.

Since the first landing of American fighting men on foreign soil in 51 years was unopposed, the Marines swam naked in the warm sea and cheerfully sang, "It'll Be a Hot Time in the Old Town Tonight." The next afternoon, a wall of Spanish bullets raised sudden little welts on the blue-green water. Marines wearing nothing but their cartridge belts ran firing and shouting up the little hill and pushed back the Spaniards. The correspondent heard sporadic gunfire all evening through his malarial chills and fever.

When Samuel Carleton's hand twitched on the pile of his memories, he felt vaguely his chest aching and his barefoot ankles throbbing from running through soft beach sand. As the tiny room in the boarding house dissolved around him and the licorice flavored pipe smoke smelled faintly of smokeless gunpowder from Spanish Mauser rifles, Carleton knew that he was almost where he needed to be.

With the writer's hand lying lightly on the manuscript, he heard a horse nicker in the alley outside. The correspondent shuddered. His own sour sweat overwhelmed the acrid pipe cloud and he felt the scent of regiments on Wednesday, June 22, climbing down from troop ships into small launches for a nauseating morning boat ride to Daiquiri beach, eighteen miles east of the city of Santiago. The boats aimed for the rusty old pier of the Juragua Iron Company. The hungry pony protesting beyond the window hole in Rosa's wall became the wail of horses pushed overboard 800 yards from the beach. Navy ships could not get closer. In his mind the correspondent heard cavalry horses screaming and drowning and buglers on the beach piping "Boots and Saddles" and "Fours Right" to steer the animals toward shore. All with American troops vomiting over the gunwales of their makeshift landing craft and then the correspondent was finally where he had to be—inside his story under his hand. He could live there now.

The correspondent's knees throbbed and his chest burned from climbing the mountainside opposite Santiago on Friday, July 1. Because he was on that hill at last, the correspondent knew that what mattered was how he felt then, not what he had learned since.

The all-day American seige at Caney, six miles east of his bloody hill, still crackled with distant fire and the desperate charge of the undaunted Americans beside him. The correspondent ached all over from walking with his legs bent, head bowed up that hill over the dead and around the wounded. At the crest, Richard and Harry waited for him. When the exhausted correspondent found them beside the little lieutenant colonel whose spectacles glowed like mirrors in the afternoon sunlight, the correspondent was too winded to speak. His trousers were still soaked from wading the river flowing pink from drained, floating American corpses.

Behind Carleton, Rosa turned toward him when his breath came fast and hard. Perspiration beaded on his forehead. He lifted his hand from the manuscript so he could rub his sore, wet knees. Rosa's worried face said nothing. She had watched him write for three months since he had slipped into Havana on September first. She knew that her gringo hunched over the shorter stack of blank paper was not really there at her table.

He held his pen above an inkwell and closed his eyes. To a writer, one blank sheet of paper is as empty and barren and wide as painfully white snow untouched by human footprints. He dipped the pen into the ink and waited for unnecessary words to drip back into the little bottle. Holding the pen above the paper, he waited for his story to come as silently as fresh tracks of wolf pups on new snow. He waited the way all writers wait—impatiently and terrified.

Richard Harding Davis liked to be called RHD and Sylvester Henry Scovel preferred Harry. They warmly greeted the correspondent at the top of the green mountain. Like weary old planets captured by the irresistible gravity of a garish new star, they hovered close to Lt. Colonel Roosevelt, whose brown trousers custommade by Brooks Brothers were dark with horse sweat from his mount Little Texas. Weary American regulars in sweltering blue uniforms mingled with Roosevelt's Rough Riders wearing First Volunteer Cavalry browns. When the little colonel took off his slouch hat, the correspondent saw the late afternoon sun glint on the pairs of spare spectacles which Edith had carefully sewn into the inside crown.

"Look here," Theodore Roosevelt shouted over the waning sputter of gunfire from Spaniards pulling back toward Santiago.

The correspondent and newspapermen RHD and Harry followed the lieutenant colonel between iron pots where Spanish beans and rice still simmered. American troops who called their bivouac Camp Hungry at the village of Sevilla now pushed tin cups into the kettles.

Roosevelt stopped beside a dead Spanish regular from General Arsenio Lenares's command. After General Lenares was gravely wounded in the American assault, General José Toral assumed command of the Spanish withdrawal from the hilltop.

"Got this one myself," Roosevelt grinned with his sweating face full of teeth. He patted the revolver on his hip. "Popped him myself with this pistol my brother-in-law—a damned navy man— salvaged from *Maine*, God bless her."

The three newspapermen glanced at each other and crouched

slightly in a too close volley of gunfire. Roosevelt did not even blink. He simply peeled off his blue polka-dot bandana—the proud non-regulation ensign of the Rough Riders—and he calmly wiped sweat and gunpowder from his spectacles.

"My crowded hour," Roosevelt said surveying his day's work: most of the 215 Spaniards killed and 376 Spaniards wounded on San Juan Hill and at Caney in the distance, where American infantry still clawed their way uphill through barbed wire defenses.

The three reporters turned and stumbled down the bloody mountainside.

At the crest of the ridge where they started down, they had paused respectfully at the corpse of Lt. Jules Ord, whose throat was raw bloody meat. His father was Civil War federal General Edward Ord.

They crouched on bent knees as they made their way over and around 89 dead or wounded Rough Riders. The correspondent recognized Rough Rider Captain Bucky O'Neill, one-time mayor of Prescott, Arizona, shot in the head. Nineteen months earlier, in Greece, the correspondent had seen another head wound. "One could have sworn that the man had great smears of red paint on his face," he wrote. "There was a dignity in his condition, a great and reaching dignity." As the red sun fell behind San Juan Heights, to the correspondent the back of dead Captain O'Neill's head only looked like a red melon dropped from a second-story window.

RHD hobbled with severe pain in his leg from recurring sciatica. Harry Scovel on one side and the correspondent on the other helped RHD keep his footing on soil wet with American blood and sweat.

Black troopers—dismounted cavalrymen from the 9th and 10th Colored Cavalry regiments, the battle-hardened Buffalo Soldiers of the Wild West—tended to their own dead and wounded. The Spanish bullet which plowed through black Private George

Stovall's heart stopped in Private Wade Bledsoe's black leg. The white boys in blue still called these veterans of the Indian Wars "the Nigger Ninth." But to RHD, Harry, and to the correspondent, they were the bravest of the brave, and the reporters were proud to call them friends.

By the time the three reporters returned to El Pozo Hill, they were far enough from San Juan Hill and Caney to enjoy a quiet tropical night. They heard only small crackling campfires between exhausted Americans. The correspondent watched Cubans shuffle barefoot between the dozing Yanquis. The Cubans were busy stealing rations from the haversacks left behind by the Rough Riders who still clung to Kettle Hill and San Juan Hill to liberate this new nation of midnight scavengers. Around them, the Americans were stripping off their sweat-soaked blue tunics and laying them carefully atop ant hills. The ants ate the army's lice. At least the lice were not as ferocious as the fleas Carleton remembered from Greece, which made him write that their bites were like "a fleet of red-hot stove lids."

Cuban lice made Samuel Carleton scratch at his wet armpits. The army he loved called the dreadful pubic lice "Rough Riders." Imagining that he itched everywhere, the writer laid down his pen, out of words now. Crossing his arms upon his fresh memories, he put down his head to close his blurry eyes for only a moment. In the dim yellow glow of his oil lamp damped low, he heard Rosa sleeping quietly and warmly. With his forehead on his arms, he had to rest.

TWO

SAMUEL CARLETON LIFTED HIS HEAD FROM THE PILE OF PAPER on the ragged linen tablecloth. A knock on the door woke him to the sudden daylight of Friday morning. He had fallen asleep on the pile of blank sheets of paper. His hand and cold pipe rested on the dozen sheets of cheap newsprint which he had covered with words before falling asleep at 3:00 in the morning, the way a child falls asleep over his toys. The woman walked toward the door. She had liberated the paper on which he wrote from one of the Havana newspapers which Spanish Governor-General Valeriano Wyler's loyal Voluntarios had burned to the ground on January 12, eleven months ago. The stack the writer used as his pillow was blackened at the corners. Pulling back her long hair tightly from her morning face, Rosa Montoya adjusted her frayed blouse as she leaned against the closed door.

"*¿Sí?*" she said to the peeling paint touching her smooth face.

"Doctor Hernández, señora,"

Rosa unbolted the door, opened it an inch, paused, and opened it wide.

Samuel Carleton looked up at a round, light-faced Cuban in open collar and baggy dark trousers frayed and shining at the knees. He carried a small leather bag. The writer's eyebrows raised when he saw that the visitor wore real shoes. Carleton stood. When he took a breath close to the man, he returned for an instant to the camp he had left on the table's pile of newsprint.

"You are unwell, Señora Montoya?" asked the fat man with the wet face.

"I am well," she smiled tightly.

"And the girl?"

"Her ankles are swollen," Rosa said, "but such comes with the child. I asked you to come for my friend."

The American caught up with the Spanish and he looked at Rosa.

Without a word, Dr. Hernández took three strides toward Carleton. He laid his bag on top of the writer's short stack of blank paper and he stopped nose to nose with the writer who tried to inhale only through his mouth as the stranger breathed into his face.

The physician's warm clammy finger pulled down Carleton's left cheek beneath a yellowed eyeball. The same moist hand raised Carleton's chin. Then the doctor, as round as he was tall, laid his sunburned ear upon the American's chest.

"*Respire.* In with the air," the stooped man said toward Carleton's shoes. "Out with the air, señor."

The American remembered reading about slave auctions as he stood dumbly beside the iron stove.

"*Muy bien.* Enough, señor."

Carleton regretted inhaling through his nostrils when the doctor straightened at the American's right side. Placing his left hand on Carleton's sore spine, he pressed his right hand hard under the American's ribs on the right side.

Dr. Hernández stepped back and reached for his bag. He pulled out a few dirty pills.

"*La quina*," he said. He spoke rapidly in Spanish to Rosa.

"Quinine," Rosa translated. "For the malaria; only enough for a few days. It is all he has."

"*Gracias*," the American mumbled, looking down into his open palm.

"*De nada*," said the physician with a slight bow. He took Rosa gently by the elbow and steered her five paces to the shabby room's far corner. They stood whispering beside the low unpainted bureau with their backs to Carleton, who watched them in a small chipped mirror standing in a wood frame atop the bureau. All he could see were the squinting, sad black eyes of the doctor as he whispered, very slowly shaking his head. Samuel Carleton knew that mirrors always tell the truth except about faces. So he returned to the table and sat while Rosa and the doctor turned toward him.

Dr. Hernández picked up his bag, bowed toward Rosa, and nodded toward the American. She closed the door behind the little man who walked into the dim hallway.

"Thank you," Samuel Carleton smiled. "I feel better already."

"You need fresh air."

"I prefer to stay in La Habana."

Rosa looked into his eyes until Carleton had to look down at his night's work where he had crossed the red creek at Bloody Bend and had climbed a mountain before fitful sleep on a little hill called El Pozo.

Rose turned toward a familiar gentle knock on the door. Looking first through the door opened two inches, she admitted María Teresa. For a cheerful hour, the American and the two women enjoyed a meager breakfast of hard-crust Cuban bread and stale rusty water pumped by hand in the hallway downstairs. Then María followed her round belly toward the stairwell.

Carleton started to read what he had written during the night. Another firm hand on the door interrupted his work.

"Rosa?" said a man's voice in the hallway. "*Rosita mía.*"

The woman nearly pulled the door off its creaking hinges. Carleton was standing by the time Rosa rocked in the arms of the tall man who embraced her at the doorway.

Carleton's English ears could not make out the muffled Spanish blowing through Rosa's thick hair. She pulled the stranger inside by his hands, then pushed him to arm's length so she could study him.

Standing beside the table, Carleton saw a man with gray hair and gray stubble on his face. His skin was pulled so tightly across his skull that the cheek bones looked as if they might burst through his thin skin if Rosa rubbed the weary face too hard. Rosa turned toward the writer and she spoke breathlessly.

"Samuel, this is my brother Francisco. By God's grace, he has come back alive to me."

The tall skeleton in beggars' clothing stepped into the little room. A dirty gray cord cinched Francisco's baggy trousers to his shapeless frame. Rosa closed the door behind him.

"Paco, Paco," she whimpered, pulling his long arms around her shoulders. "Thank God you are alive."

Beside the table Carleton stood motionless like one more piece of rough-hewn wooden furniture in the sparse cubicle. He brushed his hair from his face, wiped the sleep from his blue-gray eyes, and waited. Rosa pulled Francisco a step closer to the American.

"Paco, this is Samuel Carleton," she said while Francisco studied the young man. "Samuel keeps me safe from the Spaniards."

Francisco extended his hand. Carleton took it, felt the meat-
less bones in the man's fingers, and released his grip.

Rosa pushed a second chair toward the table. Francisco sat
and the American joined him when Rosa gently touched Carleton's shoulder. There was no other place for Rosa to sit except the
rumpled, dirty bed. She remained standing in the narrow shaft of
fresh clean daylight streaming through the room's single window.

Carleton estimated Francisco to be twenty years older than
Rosa who admitted 35 years.

"Paco is five years older than me," she said in her lilting English heavy with Castilian instead of Cuban accents. "My brother
is my one true love," she said, looking straight at the American.
Stifling a sniffle and touching her sharp nose quickly, she moved
barefoot to a tiny iron stove close to the wall. Its rusted chimney
pipe entered the clear morning air through a ragged hole in the
clapboard. She struck a match and tossed it into sticks of kindling
inside the door. When the wood caught, she closed the stove door
and set a cold kettle of water atop the burner lid and a small kettle
of milk beside it.

"We'll have coffee in a few minutes." She lifted her arm and
wiped her darkly lined eyes with her sleeve.

While the two men watched, Rosa opened wider the two shutters of the window. Sunshine exploded in their faces. Francisco
raised his right hand as if in salute to shield his yellowed eyes.
Sunlight revealed the yellow half-moons of his fingernails.

"We're a family again, Rosita," Francisco said when the woman
turned toward the two seated men. When Rosa's brother spoke,
the American could smell the tall man's breath. Carleton felt suddenly too close to something terminally rotting.

"Almost a family," Rosa sighed. She sat on the bed, five paces
from her two men. Rosa looked down at her brother's feet blotched

with purple bruises. Black toenails protruded from straw sandals wrapped in rags.

"I walked fifty miles, Rosita."

The woman nodded.

"I saw Alfonso two weeks ago." The tall man studied his sister closely. "He looked hungry but well."

"Then he really is alive?"

"Yes, Rosita."

"I have many blessings this Sabbath," Rosa said as she crossed herself.

Francisco watched the American. Carleton busied himself by taking the dozen sheets of paper newly full of brave and frightened American boy soldiers and arranging them carefully on top of the ink-filled pile of paper. The writer placed his night's work under the blank sheets and pulled the string around the six-inch pile of charred newsprint. He tied a lopsided bow with his shaking hands. He could feel Francisco watching him.

"Cuban fever," Carleton smiled.

"Yes," Francisco said. His accent was more Cuban than Rosa's. "I have had the malaria it makes ten years."

Carleton nodded. He forced a smile to show his appreciation for Francisco's English.

"I like the English," Francisco continued. "I have not been able to use it in the east."

"Did you escape?" Rosa asked in Spanish. The writer listened carefully, leaning his gaunt face slightly closer to Francisco.

"They let me go. Two months ago. When word came that General Toral had given up Santiago de Cuba to the Yanquis. They released me three times in the last five years. God is with me always."

"It is a blessing to see you, Paco," the woman said. She leaned forward, stretched out her arm, and reached for his face where the bones strained against the creased yellow skin. She moved closer to the stove. "Tell me of Alfonso."

"He was wounded again at Santiago. He served with General Linares at San Juan. He was taken prisoner by the Americans," he glanced at Carleton, "and was treated very well. When he healed, they released him after Santiago surrendered. He was walking toward Havana when I saw him. I told him that I did not know if you were still in the city and to leave word for me with the abbot. I only found you from Papá's people who still live here."

Steam rushed out of the water kettle on the stove. With a rag wrapped around the handle of each kettle, she moved them to a cooler corner.

Walking toward the table, she laid out three china cups. They were delicate and finely painted with European flowers. But each cup was different from the others in size and pattern. Not one of the cups had a rim which was not chipped. Carleton watched her hands as she set the table. Her gentle touch on the cups told the writer that these must be remnants from better times.

She reached for a scrap of linen stained black. She tied it like a tourniquet around the spout of the coffee pot. She filled each cup a quarter full with rich black drink, filled the cups to the rim with hot milk from the second kettle, and added a pinch of salt. Rosa unscrewed the lid from another glass jar and carefully measured a teaspoon of sugar into each cup. She turned the jar upside down to put the last grains of sugar into Francisco's cup of steaming, light brown, Cuban café con leche.

"I saved the last of the sugar for this day," Rosa said.

"This will be wonderful, Rosita," the brother said. The sister smiled and touched his sunken face. She lifted her cup and sat on the edge of the sagging bed.

Francisco wrapped his long, bony fingers around his cup, lifted it to his face, and closed his eyes. He inhaled deeply. His smile cracked his tight skin into deep furrows around his eyes. He touched the cup to his lips very carefully and allowed only a sip to trickle in.

"There's more, Paco," Rosa said softly.

Samuel Carleton lifted his cup and swallowed slowly. He broke a sweat across his upper lip, which he wiped dry with his sleeve.

Francisco put his cup upon the tablecloth. A smile crossed his thin lips.

"Paco?" Rosa leaned forward.

"I was thinking of Alfonso. What would he think of me drinking coffee with his mother and a gringo."

"Alfonso's war is over, too," Rosa said. She touched the corner of her beautiful eyes with a dirty sleeve.

"My nephew thinks a new war is just beginning." Francisco lifted the coffee cup. He looked into Carleton's emaciated face. "The boy will fight the Yanquis until Cuba is free of them. He fears that this island will become an American colony now that it is no longer a Spanish colony."

"I am nothing more than a writer, Francisco." Carleton laid a hand atop his pile of paper. "Cuba is only a story to me. I have no politics."

"You have been in Cuba long, Señor Carleton?"

"Please call me Samuel. I have been here, on and off, for two years. I wrote for some American newspapers. But I don't do much of that now. They don't even know where I am."

"How did you get through the Spanish authorities without being arrested?" Francisco sounded interested.

"I came into Havana without permission from anybody. I simply came in. I did not even have a passport. I was at a hotel while the government was firmly imprisoning nine correspondents on a steamer in the harbor. But no one molested me."

"I see." Francisco spoke very slowly in English, as if he had to translate his thoughts one word at a time from Spanish. "Do you hate the Spaniards like we do?"

"No. It was not my war. I don't hate any Spaniards. At Santiago, I saw them fight and die bravely. I don't believe they wanted to be here for all these years. Do you?"

"I did not give it thought. I only saw what they did to Cuba and my people. Especially what Governor Wyler did. Many times I was in his concentrado camps. I saw the starving and sick Cubans there—men, women, children, old people. May God forgive me, but I hate Spaniards. It is all I can do not to hate those Cubans who joined the Spaniards." Francisco glanced sideways toward his sister. She avoided his sunken, weary eyes.

"I'm sorry," Carleton said. "I can't hate Spaniards. The worst I can say of them is that Spaniards are liars. In that ability, they have impressed me."

"Yes?" Francisco's hollow face brightened. He leaned across the tablecloth toward the American. "How so?"

"Catch a Spaniard in a lie," Carleton said, "and he fights you off with the unthinking desperation of a cat in a corner. He will never admit it—never—never. You can only get a confession out of him by killing him and then journeying to Hell to wrest it from his spirit."

Francisco blinked at the American's sudden passion. He smiled.

"Señor Carleton—Samuel—we shall make an insurrecto of you yet."

"I take no side. I just want to write in peace."

Francisco put down the cup and looked at his sister. His eyes narrowed. When he spoke rapidly in Spanish, the American could not follow.

"I am pleased that you have found a friend, Rosita, but I would have expected you to take up with a revolutionary."

Carleton looked away from Francisco's suddenly hard face. The American's gaze met Rosa's across the tiny room. He raised an eyebrow.

"Paco says that his heart still burns with *¡Cuba Libre!*"

The American turned toward the brother whose face lost its sudden chill with another sip from his cup.

"Forgive my lack of passion, Francisco." Carleton sighed and his frail body visibly deflated. He looked even smaller than his five-foot, six-inch, 120-pound frame. "I have seen too much of war. My wars are over."

Francisco nodded and lifted his cup. He drank it dry.

Rosa stood and touched the coffee pot.

"It is cold. I have to go down the hall for more wood."

"I'll go," Carleton said.

"No," the woman said firmly. "You men talk. I'll be back."

Before either man could protest, the woman opened the door and closed it quickly behind her.

"I think she cannot listen long to talk of the war," Francisco said. He toyed with his empty coffee cup. "She has lost much and suffered much."

"To a woman, war is a thing that hits at the heart and at the places around the table." The American's face darkened. "She doesn't speak of it to me. I knew nothing of Rosa before I came to the city four months ago. Did the war touch her, too?"

"Touch her? Yes, it touched her." Francisco laid his hand atop the little table. "I lived with the rebels. Her son fought with the Spaniards against us. And the war killed her husband five years ago."

"I knew her husband was dead."

Francisco spoke softly toward his empty cup.

"Rosa's husband was weak. He had no politics, either." Francisco lowered his head as if it were too heavy with memories to hold up. "He had a tobacco business here in the city. He never chose sides: he needed the rebel farmers to grow his crop and he needed the Spanish authorities to ship it off the island to Europe and America. Then it came time for him finally to choose."

"Was he killed?" the American asked.

"Yes."

"How? Why?"

Both men turned when they heard the door latch creak.

"He died for me," Francisco whispered as his sister entered the boarding house hovel. She carried an armload of kindling which she let fall to the floor beside the stove. Kneeling, she rebuilt the little fire.

Francisco smiled weakly toward his sister's protector while Rosa worked her fire.

"I am glad that Rosa has you. La Habana is no place for a woman to be alone. As Rosa said, we shall be a family for as long as I can stay in the city. I won't talk politics. Our country is weary of politics and so am I."

Samuel Carleton nodded and looked toward Rosa. She stood and faced the table five paces away. She pushed her long hair away from her face. Her eyes were red and puffy.

"We shall be poor and have the hunger together," Rosa Montoya said.

Rosa took two steps toward the bed. She knelt, reached under the bed to her shoulder, and pulled out a small piece of wood.

The gringo and Francisco pushed their hard wooden chairs away from the table and stepped closer to Rosa who was standing by the bed. The woman cradled a narrow strip of fine-grained dark wood. To Carleton, it looked old and weathered like a small timber from some ancient sailing ship. Standing close to the brother and sister, the American counted nine roughly cut holes running the length of the scrap no bigger than the sole of his shoe. Candle wax encrusted the rim of each hole.

"Mamá's," Rosa whispered.

"I remember," Francisco said. Carleton breathed in the decay-like breath the brother exhaled. With his fingertips, Francisco's blackened nails touched the relic reverently and quickly. "All I really remember of Papá is that I never sat in his chair. Do it now for Papá and Mamá," he said, "even though sunset is hours away."

Rosa laid her precious stick of wood atop a cool corner of the iron stove. She closed the shutters across the window. Then she opened one of only two musty, peeling drawers in the old bureau beside the bed. Digging deeply, she found three small candles. Returning to the stove, she put a short white candle into the second and third holes of the wooden block. Kneeling, she opened the stove door and carefully waited for the third candle to catch. Carefully, she stood and protected the little flame with the palm of her free hand. She touched the two candles with the lighted candle and gently pressed the third candle into the scrap of wood.

Three little candles cast weak light in the small room. Beams of sunlight from the shutters fell brightly on the crude ornament. Samuel Carleton watched Rosa cover her eyes with her hands and mumble in a near whisper,

> Loaremos a muestro Dyo
> Loaremos a muestro Senyor
> Loaremos a muestro Rey
> Loaremos a muestro Salvador

Rosa wiped her eyes and looked up at her brother standing close.

"That's all I can remember from Mamá. I have to use it for everything."

"I'm sure our mother would be pleased," the brother said. He kissed his sister's temple glistening with sweat and he stepped away.

Rosa pushed the candle holder out of the stream of sunshine before she opened the shutters to daylight and a pleasant, soft breeze. She looked lovingly at her brother.

"Where will you live?"

Francisco studied his sister's beautiful, sad face.

"At the monastery. With the other priests."

"Other priests?" the American asked before he could conceal the surprise in his voice.

"Yes. God sent me here. In Spain, there have been priests for 400 years on our mother's side of the family."

"Go with God," Rosa whispered to her brother.

Francisco hugged his sister, exchanged courtesies with her gringo, and left. Even through the closed door, Carleton could hear the priest's sandals shuffling weakly across the hallway floor. Rosa sat on the edge of the bed and wept softly. Then the American heard the muffled voices of Francisco and María Teresa on the stairs.

"This island is killing my brother, too," Rosa said.

Her emphasis on "too" troubled the American.

Rosa stood at the muted double knock on the door. Keeping close to the woman when she entered, the girl looked younger than her years to the writer and Rosa's broader shoulders and weary face made the woman appear a little older than the age she claimed. To Samuel Carleton, the white Spanish woman and María's café con leche complexion were both beautiful in any light.

"I met your brother the priest," María said slowly enough for the American to follow her Spanish. "I told him that his church kept my parents and their parents in slavery for generations."

Carleton concentrated on the girl's Spanish. He knew that she was born into actual slavery, which had not ended on Cuban sugar plantations until 12 years ago.

"And what did he say, my brother?" Rosa looked coldly at the girl.

María put both of her hands upon her belly. Tears welled in her black eyes.

"Padre blessed my baby."

"Paco would do that. Did you tell him of your child's father?"

"No."

Rosa shrugged. She gently touched the girl's face.

"You know, *m'hija*, that my family never owned slaves. My brother loves his church. But he has always been a priest to the people."

Carleton followed the subdued Spanish. He knew that Rosa called María "Daughter."

"Yes," the pregnant girl said. "But Francisco's church goes with the land owners. Forgive me, Doña Rosa. You have kept the hunger from my door."

Rosa forced a smile, touched María's shoulder, and turned toward the writer seated at the table.

Carleton collected his pile of blank paper and raised his pen— a Havana luxury after months of writing field dispatches with pencils sharpened between his rotting teeth.

"Perdido," Rosa said. "You must spend today writing. María and I shall go downstairs so you can have quiet to help the words to come."

The three candles on the cold stove were gone before Rosa and María reached the bottom of the stairs.

Samuel Carleton lifted his dry pen and he studied it carefully. He wondered if it might be full of words. Laying the pen beside his inkwell, he separated his stack of paper into the written pile and the smaller, waiting pile. He reached into his pocket and retrieved a fragment of the sweaty physician's quinine pill and laid it crumbling upon the table. His spine burned and his faced flushed from a spasm of Cuban fever. He looked down at the quinine, thought of its precious relief, and lifted a blank sheet of paper to set it beside the inkwell. The quinine would quench his fever, but the correspondent needed to feel the sweat drip from his nose because that is what he felt that night after San Juan Hill. The shakes followed the hot flash of fever. He had to use both hands to aim his pen at the inkwell. He welcomed the wave of malaria which carried him and his pen from Rosa's table back to the beach between Santiago de Cuba and Guantánamo.

Back there now with his knees as sore as his spine, the last of evening twilight on July 1 smelled of mud, blood, death, and gunpowder. The 330-pound, General William "Pecos Bill" Shafter commanding Fifth Corps was paralyzed by gout and heat. At El Pozo Hill, the peace of a tropical night had descended on General Shafter's headquarters. The nearly full Moon was dazzling in the humid air. Wounded Americans were piled everywhere on the soggy ground at El Pozo. At Siboney, three hospital tents were erected end-to-end and the sweltering surgeons worked all night without their shirts. Only three ambulances had been brought ashore. No army field hospital was set up within two miles of the bloody, front line. Troops fought malaria with quinine purchased on the Cuban black market.

Friday night's brilliant Moon faded into an overcast dawn. Americans clinging to San Juan Heights had to keep their heads down. From their new positions closer to Santiago, Spanish troops maintained pockets of Mauser fire throughout the muggy day. In some places, the American and Spanish positions were only 600 yards apart. Mauser bullets struck Americans a mile away. The correspondent saw enough death that he could write that it came "with a kind of slow rhythm, leisurely taking a man now here, now there."

Saturday morning's humidity broke violently with torrential rain. The critical dirt roads between the Heights and El Pozo became a sea of mud. The San Juan and Aguadores Rivers began to rise dangerously. Lying in rows on the muddy ground at El Pozo, American wounded drank the warm rain as it swept across their faces.

At noon, General Henry Lawton's division straggled into El Pozo from El Caney. These American regulars had been ordered to take part in yesterday's San Juan assault after their predicted two-hour battle to capture the Spaniards' fortress El Viso. They arrived at the San Juan front 26 hours late, caked with mud and their own blood. The battered veterans from El Caney stumbled back toward El Pozo as the crumbling Spanish resistance permitted. One exhausted, black soldier from the 25th Infantry dragged himself down the dirt path past General Lawton and Major Creighton Webb. The corporal carried his own rifle and the heavy pack of a wounded man walking beside him. Under his other arm, the El Caney survivor also carried a shaggy, muddy dog. Major Webb stopped the infantryman and asked him, "Corporal, why are you carrying a dog after fighting and marching for two days?" The soldier thought about it and smiled, "The dog's tired, sir." Then the black corporal walked on to remain forever nameless in history.

Saturday's all-day rain dripped into the night. The American situation was precarious. The battered Spaniards were far from beaten. During the 36 hours since San Juan Hill fell, the Americans suffered another nine men killed and 125 wounded by Spanish snipers and a Spanish countercharge Saturday night.

By Sunday morning, July 3, the army field hospital at El Pozo looked like a slaughterhouse. The rain had turned piles of used bandages and dressings into oozing puddles of red. In three days, ten surgeons working around the clock had treated 800 casualties. Samuel Carleton had seen it all in Greece 18 months earlier. There he wrote that, "Through the door of the hospital could be seen a white-clothed surgeon, erect, serene, but swift-fingered. He was calm enough to be sinister and terrible in this scene of blood. This thing was a banquet for him." The correspondent saw nothing new here.

Santiago was starving. Early on the morning of July 5, the United States Navy shelled the harbor and triggered an exodus of 10,000 refugees that stretched for twenty miles. American soldiers shared their rations with the women and children. Only the Cuban prostitutes wore nice dresses. The Yanqui troops carried the old and sick on their backs. The surgeon of the Rough Riders ordered his men not to carry children for fear of catching yellow fever from them.

Samuel Carleton did not feel the hard wood chair at Rosa's table. He pulled the feverish words from his inkwell and drove them hard. Writing, Carleton shivered from fever when the remembered correspondent shivered and the pain shooting up his spine from yellow fever was the correspondent's own.

On Wednesday, July 6, the first case of yellow fever came. By July 9 yellow fever spread among the U. S. troops camped on the beach at Siboney. The next day, outbreaks put an end to Red Cross food relief for Cuban refugees. Within 24 hours, the Red Cross chief surgeon and three of his nurses were down with fever. One hundred cases were reported within three days. By July 22 some 5,000 American men were on the sick list. Four hundred more were added on the 24th and another 500 on the following day.

By July 31, so many men were dying each day that General Shafter put a stop to formal military burials. The daily volleys of rifle fire over the new graves and the blowing of "Taps" in the afternoon were bad for morale. "Taps," the last tattoo of American fighting men, tingled every nerve in the correspondent's war-numbed memory. Writing in Puerto Rico four months earlier, he had described "Taps" as "that extraordinary wail of mourning and song of rest and peace, the soldier's good-bye, a solemn heartbreaking song." So fifteen men were buried each new day in silence.

On the first of August, 689 new fever cases went down, of whom fifteen died. Within 24 hours, 75 per cent of the U. S. Army had malaria.

Although malaria from Cuban jungles thrived inside the correspondent's swollen liver, and yellow fever could ignite his backbone into charcoal-red heat, most of what Samuel Carleton wrote about disease was borrowed from reporters Richard Harding Davis, Harry Scovel, and Fifth Corps veterans. Carleton had recovered at the Chamberlain Hotel in Old Point Comfort, Virginia, after being evacuated with other yellow fever victims on July 8. There, he recorded the women in their summer dresses who looked like "a bank of flowers" to the correspondent with the malaria-yellowed eyes. The troops were unloaded in the street below. "Through this lane there passed a curious procession," he wrote. "Such a gang of dirty, ragged, emaciated, half-starved, bandaged cripples I had never seen. When that crowd began to pass the hotel the banks of flowers made a noise which could make one tremble. Perhaps it was a moan, perhaps it was a sob—the sound of women weeping."

He crawled back to Cuba three weeks later.

Navigating was slow all the way back from the fever-decimated Fifth Army Corps to Rosa's shanty home. His eyeballs still simmered with fever. Somewhere between the hospital tents at Siboney and Mary Horan's boarding house, a cool breeze rolled over the back of the correspondent's wet neck. Turning his head, he felt each bone in his neck scrape one against the other like dry sharp stones.

"Perdido?" Rosa said gently in the yellow light of Samuel Carleton's single oil lamp. Cool midnight air comforted the writer's thin face. The last breath of Friday felt like Indian Summer in New

Jersey. "Still you write of the war?"

"I know nothing about war, and of course, pretend nothing."

"But you speak of the war in Greece and you were at Santiago," Rosa said sleepily.

"I was a child who, in a fit of ignorance, had jumped into a vat of war."

When the writer sighed and laid down his pen, Rosa smiled at him from their bed to welcome him back.

"Did you write well?"

"I think so. I made copies of the few places that went well."

He carefully pulled one of his four precious sheets of sticky black, carbonic paper from between two sheets of new memories. Carefully, he used the carbonic paper to divide his old writing from the new before tying the cord around the entire manuscript.

"Did you take your quinine?"

"No," he said. "I can't travel on it where I need to go."

Rosa frowned and threw back the gray linen on his side of the bed.

"I think I wrote well tonight," Samuel Carleton said to Rosa's naked back as he climbed into bed with the lamp casting a shadow of her long neck and breasts on the dark wall. She said nothing when she rolled over toward the open window in the wall.

Carleton dimmed the lamp. He watched his Rosa sleeping on her side of their bed rented by the week. She gave him her back but that was enough.

THREE

Peace and its promise did not warm the air of Old Havana. Rosa Montoya wrapped her shoulders within a brightly colored shawl. Walking so close that his unsteady gait took him often into her side, Samuel Carleton wore his white linen suit, now as yellow as his eyeballs. He had driven fresh words across the blank paper well into the night, looking up only to watch Rosa sleep with her bare back toward his oil lamp on the table. His morning seizure of fever insulated him from Saturday's afternoon chill. Looking up, he saw small, puffy white clouds moving slowly across a navy blue sky. The clouds were coming together and their tops were rising. With the sun blindingly bright on the cloud tops, the bottoms of the clouds were flattening and turning gray. Though he could not yet smell it since Cuba was a month into the winter dry season,

Carleton knew that tropical showers would soon fall straight down beneath each cloud while between the clouds the earth below would remain dry as dust.

"You should have told me before yesterday that your brother was a priest and that your own son wore the uniform of Spain and fought against Francisco and us. You only told me that you took back your own family name after your husband died."

"We discussed all of that this morning. What difference would it have made to tell you about my brother, Perdido? I did not know that he still lived until I saw his face yesterday."

"No difference, Rosa. I just should have known."

"And I thought Alfonso was dead until three weeks ago. I had not heard from him for five months. An old friend told me that Alfonso was alive. But I did not believe her so I did not mention it. I did not want to burden you."

"But I burden you, Rosa." The American stopped walking. He reached out, took the woman's hand and squeezed it gently.

"You are no burden. With you, I am not alone."

Without releasing her hand, she pulled Samuel Carleton through the crowded square.

Word of the signing of the Treaty of Paris between the United States and Spain filled the streets with Cubans. The treaty would be sealed today in France. Hundreds of peasants from the countryside walked beside city-dwellers.

At the woman's side, Carleton wondered if the throngs of hungry-looking Cubans were inhaling the scents of La Habana Vieja just to see if freedom smelled differently than war and almost four centuries of Spanish rule. The American guessed that it did not. The people in the huge square near the harbor were subdued. Mostly barefoot, they shuffled more aimless than merry through the streets.

"There's Paco," Rosa said, pointing toward the Plaza del Catedral. Rosa and Carleton turned off a narrow street into sunshine streaming in glowing corridors between the looming clouds. They pressed through the quiet crowd and crossed the square. Francisco waved above the heads between himself and Rosa. Carleton followed her as she walked faster across the plaza.

In the broad plaza on the north side, the 150-year-old cathedral pointed toward purple sky between storm clouds coming together low overhead. Carleton studied the imposing stone structure as he walked. His writers' eye noticed that the three-story church looked remarkably like the Alamo in Texas with its climbing roof line peaking in the center. Two tall towers framed the cathedral. But strangely, when looking at the church from the front, the tower on the left was narrower than the bell tower on the right, perhaps to prevent the narrower tower from trespassing onto San Ignacio Street.

The American had a sense that he was invisible to the milling crowd. Some of these Habaneros pressing against each other were moving toward the open doors of the old Spanish church. Some men and boys wearing the baggy pants of rebel soldiers hobbled on rough-hewn crutches. Carleton saw proof of his conviction that, "It is an axiom of war that wounded men can never find straight sticks."

Rosa steered her way toward the left, western quarter of the plaza. Her brother leaned against one of the stone columns holding up the Palacio de los Marqueses de Aguas Claras. Francisco did not step into the sunshine until Rosa and Carleton were only a few paces distant. Brother and sister embraced. The American extended his hand, which Francisco took.

"Was there room for you at the church, Paco?"

"Of course, Rosita. The Spaniards killed or deported the priests sympathetic to independence, so they had plenty of empty beds."

"And food?"

"Much. But there's more, Rosita."

The three had to stand close together to keep the crowd from squeezing between them.

"More?" the woman asked her brother. The tall priest smiled and the skin at the corners of his sunken dark eyes creased deeply.

"There," Francisco said, pointing with his chin as sharp as a skeleton's and with his thin hand.

Rosa saw her brother's raised arm pointing down the western side of the plaza. To Carleton who watched silently, her gaze stopped at a young man in filthy white linen, the uniform of the peasantry pressing against them from all directions. The American saw her eyes widen and fill with tears.

"Alfonso!"

She broke free of the two men and ran toward the south side of the square. Francisco and Carleton followed her. Neither man had the lungs for running. When they reached the southernmost side of the plaza, they stopped beside Rosa and the young man she embraced. Mother and son separated when Francisco and the American arrived, panting hard.

Alfonso's face was thin and the sweat on his cheeks was blackened with dirt. Carleton carefully studied Alfonso in the cloud filtered sunlight. Alfonso could not be more than twenty years old. He might even be in his teens. This was a soldier's face, Carleton thought, a boy's face aged roughly and forever by combat, fear, hunger, and defeat. His clothing was different from the coarse blouse and loose trousers cinched with rope worn by rebel veterans in the square. Carleton could see that Alfonso's tattered shirt once had a collar which had been torn neatly away. Although the insurrectos wore blouses that they pulled over their heads, Alfonso's shirt had buttonholes and loose threads where buttons might once have hung. Only a piece of twine through a buttonhole on one side and a rip on the other side secured the shirt across his chest.

"This is Alfonso, my son," said Rosa as she wiped away tears. "Alfonso, this is my friend Samuel Carleton. He is an American."

"A gringo, Mother? You have taken up with our new masters?"

In the bustle of the square, Carleton required a moment to realize that mother and son were speaking English.

"I am not a colonialist," the American protested gently. "Just a writer. I have no politics."

"A writer?" the boy shrugged.

"The advantage of international complications," Carleton said cheerfully, "is the fact that it develops war correspondents."

The American stood speechless when Alfonso burst out laughing. To the writer's ears, the laugh sounded strained and full of contempt.

"So my mother now has a gringo companion who has no politics to match her brother who has no *cojones*."

"Alfonso!" the woman said firmly. "Show respect to your uncle."

Francisco laid his bony hand on his sister's shoulder.

"It is nothing, Rosita. The boy is just tired."

"I am not tired, Padre." Alfonso said the last word as if something very sour were on his tongue. "I fought for Spain while you did nothing but pray for your pathetic sheep in the jungle."

"The rebellion against Spain has won, Alfonso," Francisco said firmly. "Your Spanish friends will soon be on boats taking them back to their country."

"And those same boats, Uncle Paco, will be bringing more gringos to take over our country." Alfonso looked squarely at Carleton. Rosa's son raised his arm and gestured toward the American with the ghastly yellowed eyes. "They will all look like you in good time."

When the boy with no buttons raised his arm and the sleeve fell away, Carleton saw for the first time that his right forearm ended in a stump instead of a hand. Instantly, Alfonso followed the American's stare and he pulled his arm quickly back to his side. The tattered sleeve fell over the mutilated arm.

"Let's go home," Rosa said, sniffing hard.

"Home?" Alfonso asked.

"We're staying at Mary Horan's boarding house. She is a gringa from New York City who is always kind to our people. Your uncle is staying at the Iglesia del Espíritu Santo."

Alfonso squinted in the now gray afternoon. The sweat on his face glistened like rough, black diamonds.

"The oldest church on the island for my old uncle the padre. That makes perfect sense."

"Enough!" the woman said. A few peasants nearby turned toward her flash of anger. "We go home now."

Alfonso fell into step beside his mother. Francisco and the American walked five paces behind them. The priest walked behind his nephew and Carleton followed Rosa. As they walked, Alfonso's left hand—his only hand—reached inside his shirt. He pulled out a white and black bandanna, waved it over his shoulder toward his uncle, and wrapped it around his neck where the collar of his shirt should have been. Around his throat he placed a necklace of colored beads with sets of black beads alternating with sequences of white ones. Carleton glanced at Francisco by his side.

"That must be for my benefit," Francisco said, tilting his head slightly toward the American. "The scarf and bead colors are for a Santería *orisha*. African slaves brought their *orisha* gods with them centuries ago. Santería is everywhere in Cuba. White and black are the favorite colors of Oyá—the goddess of vengeance."

After an exhausting hour of pushing their way through crowded streets, the four arrived at the boarding house. The walk had taken all the wind from Carleton and Francisco. The American was coughing when they climbed the stairs to Rosa's room.

Alfonso lingered behind on the first floor. Looking over his shoulder from the stairs, Carleton saw Alfonso standing at María Teresa's closed door. The boy looked down at his ragged sandals and his only hand was a clenched fist. Without looking up, Alfonso tapped softly on the door. From Rosa's doorway the American heard María's sobs over his own panting breath. He pulled the door closed behind him.

A warm breeze blew through the open shutters. Carleton and Francisco sat at the small square table. Rosa busied herself at the stove.

"I shall make garlic soup," she said. "I have saved it for a special occasion."

Carleton was still trying to catch his breath which came with a wheezing rattle when he heard María's hissing voice on the stairs. He caught the Spanish he knew. "Cabrón." Bastard. "Cobarde." Coward. "Egoísta." Selfish. He did not hear Alfonso's voice until Rosa's son knocked on the door and announced himself. The girl followed him inside.

María Teresa's eyes were as red as Alfonso's sunbaked face. She sat on the bed and the young soldier took a place on a wooden cracker box against a wall of peeling whitewash.

Alfonso's tired eyes kept looking at the table covered with a thin cloth. Small boxes stuck out beyond the frayed edges. He tried to speak calmly but the back of his neck was redder than his face.

"They tell me the treaty will be signed this week," Alfonso said toward the American.

"Plans for truces are nice things," Carleton said.

"The Spanish leave and the gringos come," Alfonso said, shaking his head. "That is not much of a treaty." He looked at his uncle. "What side will you take in the war that comes, Padre?"

"No side, Alfonso. Nor should you."

"I killed many Yanquis at Santiago," the boy said with weary pride.

Rosa was mashing garlic gloves in hot oil at the stove. The pungent aroma overflowed the small room and out the open window across La Habana Viaja. She turned sharply and pointed her wooden spoon toward her son like a lethal weapon dripping olive oil and garlic vapors.

Looking at Rosa and her son, the American remembered young Henry Fleming saying that, "a man becomes another thing in a battle."

"Alfonso," Rosa fumed. "You will not speak of such things in my house."

"Your house?" The boy was furious, but his mother held him at spoonpoint and he did not rise from the corner. "This is no one's house. Father had a house. But Uncle Paco cost us that. And I know what Uncle and his kind have cost you. You even gave away my father's name."

"We shall have peace under this roof, Alfonso," the woman said through clenched teeth. "We are all wounded here. I will hear no more talk of killing."

The boy swallowed. Rosa returned to frying garlic beside a pot where thin chicken broth steamed. Alfonso was quiet for a long moment. He looked hard at the American coughing into his hand and at his uncle dressed in rags.

"You will stay with María Teresa?" the woman said to her son.

"No, Mother." He did not look at the younger woman. "I am staying at the officers' barracks. I'll be safe in Havana until the division leaves for Madrid. As you can see, I wear no military buttons or insignia any more."

"How can you leave me and María now?" the mother sniffed. "We didn't know for certain that you were alive until Paco told me yesterday that he had seen you."

Carleton tried to breathe in the garlic-laced, suddenly humid air, then closed his eyes to concentrate on his aching chest. The next voice he heard exploded from Alfonso.

"Mother, tell the gringo who cut off my hand."

The American opened his eyes. He saw Alfonso standing with his right arm raised so his sleeve could fall away from his stump. Francisco rose from his chair to stand between his nephew and his sister. The woman very gently nudged Francisco aside so she could look into her son's wild eyes before she answered. Her voice was so soft and so full of grief that the American could barely hear her above the sputtering of boiling oil.

"I did."

Rosa stepped back from her son whom she had crippled. She turned her wet eyes toward Carleton.

"You see, Perdido, how the revolution has come into my house? I have seen my husband murdered, my son wounded, and my brother beaten."

"Most wounded men conclude that the battle is over," Carleton said, looking at the boy.

"Not me and not my battle," Alfonso said without anger.

Old Havana disappeared quickly outside the open window in the remarkable speed of tropical sunset. After almost two years in south Florida and Cuba, the short morning and evening twilight still impressed the American. In New Jersey and New York, evening twilight came slowly and reluctantly compared to Cuba where the sun simply took aim at the western horizon and plunged into the sea with an eruption of red and orange. In morning twilight in the northland, the sun crept sleepily into a new day slowly enough for Samuel Carleton to shave, savor his morning coffee when he could afford coffee, and roll his first cigarette. But in south Florida and Cuba, the new sun seemed to jump out of the eastern sea.

"Light your candle, Rosita," Francisco said between his nephew and his sister.

When Alfonso reached with his surviving hand for the oil lamp on the table, his uncle stopped him with his all-bone fingers on the boy's forearm.

"Not that one," said the uncle.

Rosa looked into her son's angry empty eyes.

"I do this for your abuelos, Alfonso. My parents."

Kneeling, she found the hidden fragment of wood with its nine holes each bearing a halo of candle wax. Then she pulled four candles from the bureau with the small chipped mirror atop it.

When Alfonso faced his uncle and opened his mouth, Francisco shook his head and the priest's black eyes made the soldier shut his lips tightly without a sound.

Rosa placed three candles in the stick from right to left, closed the shutters, and lit the fourth little candle in the stove. When Rosa ignited the three candles from left to right, forced the master candle into the end hole, and covered her eyes before reciting her soft incantation, Alfonso raised his eyebrows creasing wind-burned furrows across his forehead. He looked at his uncle who raised a finger to his own lips. The boy waited silently for his mother to finish.

"What kind of Spanish is that?" Alfonso asked.

"My mother's," Rosa whispered. "And her mother's."

María Teresa crossed herself. Francisco watched her and smiled.

"I do not understand, Uncle," Alfonso said.

"Not everything needs to be understood."

"None of this is my world," Alfonso said, looking at the flickering candles and at his mother.

The soldier walked to the door, unlatched it, and turned around. Francisco touched his sister's face and walked toward his nephew's side. Clean shaven Alfonso and Francisco with gray stubble covering his emaciated jaw line walked together through the open door. To Samuel Carleton, it seemed that Rosa took a long deliberate step to hide the candles from the open door. She stepped away only when Francisco pulled the door closed. Then Rosa moved away from the stove but she did not open the shutters until the last candle gasped once and died in a long thin swirl of white smoke.

Francisco and Alfonso had not stayed for garlic soup.

The girl full of child lingered behind, close to Rosa who was now her mother, too.

Carleton stepped toward Rosa. He reached for her shaking shoulders but she stepped back from him. Tropical lightning flashed upon the clapboard wall from the open shutters.

"No, Perdido. Sit down and write." Rosa glanced out at the storm. "At least when you had your own army around you, it was like family, all of one heart."

When María Teresa stretched out on the bed, Rosa laid down beside her and she turned her head away from the American so she could look over the horizon of the girl's belly toward the window. Rain had stopped but cloud-to-cloud lightning flashed in the window.

At the table, Samuel Carleton pushed up the lamp's wick only enough to see his pile of blank paper. With head bowed, he closed his eyes and waited for the story to open wide enough for him to enter it in the dim yellow light and explosions of white on the wall opposite the window. He waited a long time, but when the flashing clouds slowly rolled eastward, so did he because the storm broke violently upon the dead and wounded on Saturday morning, the day after the Americans took San Juan Hill.

The correspondent trod the grim field and then the wet sand near the sea beside piles of amputated arms and legs between the surgeons' tents. This remnant of an army was family, and how strange that its black faces were his kin most of all. But the American Army was anything but family to its soldiers.

A distant clap of thunder in Old Havana startled Carleton in the yellow glow of his lamp. But another burst of white distant lightning on the little table thrust him back among men stinking of sweat and dried blood. He dipped his pen into the magic ink.

On July 15, the Americans burned the hamlet of Siboney to the ground to stop the spread of yellow fever.

The army's generals believed that blacks had a natural immunity against tropical disease. So suffering white troops were moved to higher ground away from the malarial low country and the four all-black regiments were moved to the sickly coast. Back home, the Secretary of War ordered more regiments of black "immunes" to Cuba for occupying Santiago once the Spaniards formally surrendered.

Saturday, July 16, the all-black 24th Infantry took up position at Siboney's field hospital to serve as nurses for the white malaria and yellow fever patients. The 24th volunteered for the risky duty after eight white regiments refused to help surgeon Colonel Charles Greenleaf. Within a month, the "immunes" suffered 167 cases of yellow fever, of whom 23 died. Of the 24th Infantry's 456 men, 432 had malaria or yellow fever by the war's end. Theodore Roosevelt's black manservant, Marshall, now retired from the black 9th Cavalry, was dropped by malaria, too. "A curious feature," TR would note, "was that the colored troops seemed to suffer as heavily as the white."

The correspondent first noticed the two separate worlds of the army, one white and one black, at the Tampa, Florida, staging area for the invasion of Cuba in June. The all-black 9th and 10th Cavalry regiments and the all-black 24th and 25th Infantry regiments camped in a segregated corner of Fifth Army Corps. Canvas saloons in camp and the camp whorehouse—which the officers ignored since morale was more important than morals—had signs proclaiming "Whites Only." Not a single Tampa public saloon or public store was open to them. They could fight and die for Old Glory, but they would have to do it dry. When the white 1st Brigade of 1st Division camped at Lakeland, Florida, in May and June, the troops were told that the county was "dry." But Private Charles Johnson Post of the all-white 71st New York Volunteer Infantry quickly learned what "dry" really meant: "Plenty of bourbon for the white man, but no gin for the nigger."

Keeping the four black regiments as far from Tampa as possible was just fine with Tampa's citizens. Posting armed black troops in town made the white townsfolk edgy. When black soldiers on military police duty arrested rowdy white soldiers on Tampa streets, citizens protested the racial outrage. On May 5, the editors of the Tampa *Morning Tribune* presumed to speak for everyone in the city: "The colored infantrymen stationed in Tampa and vicinity have made themselves very offensive to the people of the city. The men insist upon being treated as white men are treated."

In the Tampa countryside, some white boys from Ohio had terrorized a two-year-old black boy in front of his mother. When the 24th and 25th Colored Infantries heard about the incident, they took to the streets. Popping off their rifles into the air, they vandalized some of the whites-only stores and sacked a cathouse. The 2nd Georgia Volunteers went in to police the area. The white boys from the Old South fired on the black regulars and wounded 27.

When the nearly 17,000 Americans finally boarded 32 troop ships on June 8 bound for Cuba, the troop ship *Concho* became home to the all-black 25th Infantry regulars and the all-white 4th Infantry and some of the all-white 2nd Massachusetts Volunteers. In bunks four-beds-high below deck, the blacks were ordered to berth on the starboard side of the ship and the whites were confined to the port side. Mingling in between was officially discouraged. Even *Concho's* coffee kettles were segregated. Orders were issued that the white troops were to enjoy their coffee ration before the black troops of the 25th Infantry. Armed sentries were posted to enforce the racial segregation at the coffee bean barrel.

Only death was color blind on the Cuban beaches and in the jungles and on the mountainsides. Fifth Corps landed in rough surf at Daiquiri beach on June 22. The 153 landing boats unloaded 600 men every hour to wade ashore in rolling waves. Private John English from Chattanooga, Tennessee, and Corporal Edward Cobb from Richmond, Virginia, drowned between their landing boat and the beach. They were dragged under by their heavy flannel clothing. Samuel Carleton, war correspondent, watched as the two black soldiers from the 10th Cavalry struggled and died. White Captain William O'Neill dived into the pounding surf to help, but "Bucky" O'Neill was too late.

Commanding general William "Pecos Bill" Shafter loved his black regiments. Much of his army career of almost 30 years and a Congressional Medal of Honor had been spent commanding all-black regiments in war and peace.

A young white lieutenant now commanded a horseless troop of the black 10th Cavalry. John J. Pershing was proud that his black command had earned him the nickname Black Jack.

The correspondent knew how bravely the black units fought on San Juan Hill and nearby at Caney. The black 9th and 10th dismounted cavalries joined the Rough Riders in their suicidal assault on the San Juan Hill high ground. Captain John Bigelow, Jr., commanding D Troop, was wounded three times going up Kettle Hill. When white Major Theodore Wint was hit, black cavalrymen, Corporals Charles Parker and James Watkins from G Troop, risked their lives to drag the major to safety. When the 10th Cavalry reached the top of San Juan Hill, Sergeant George Berry capped his 30 years of military service by planting the regimental colors on the crest. Sergeant Berry also hauled up the hill the pennant of the all-white 3rd Cavalry when its color-bearer was wounded. "Dress on the colors, boys!" the black sergeant shouted above the melee of battle.

And when the malaria and yellow fever wasted veterans of Cuba returned home in August, the U. S. military remained the white man's army. Black troops left Cuba with 26 Certificates of Merit and 5 Congressional Medals of Honor. But the president from Canton, Ohio, declined to reward black heroes with commissions in the regular army. A few were awarded officers' commissions in temporary, volunteer units, but they were broken back to noncommissioned officer status when they returned to their regular army units. When the 10th Cavalry's Buffalo Soldiers mustered out, they were posted to camp near Huntsville, Alabama. The black soldiers were disarmed while white troops were allowed to keep their weapons. A local citizen offered a bounty on every black soldier Huntsville could murder. On October 10th, Private John R. Brooks and Corporal Daniel Garrett, both of H Troop, were killed. They were murdered by a black man hoping to earn the white man's reward.

So ended the war in Cuba. American combat casualties in Cuba numbered 369 soldiers, 10 sailors, and 6 Marines killed, not including the 268 dead in *Maine*. Another 1,445 were wounded. Seven hundred seventy-one men died from disease in Cuba. Training accidents and disease killed 425 men at the Chickamauga, Georgia, training camp, and 246 died in training in Florida.

Samuel Carleton watched his cramped hand. His eyes were glazed and blurry. Dipping the pen twice into the well of new words, he saw the hand scrawl, "When all has been said and done, the recent war was a most curious war," and then he laid down his pen. In his bones, the writer understood and accepted that his inkwell had suddenly run out of words.

For a moment he stood quietly on the old rusted pier at Daiquiri but he stood alone.

"Perdido?"

Looking over the water the correspondent heard a distant woman's voice, but it was not that of Cora, who was waiting faithfully for him.

"Samuel?"

The American blinked and looked up. His oil lamp flickered on a wisp of cloth wick nearly consumed by his blood- and sweat-soaked memories.

"You have finished?" Rosa asked sleepily from their bed.

Carleton squinted at her bed. He was all the way home now. María Teresa was gone and his side of the bed was empty.

"Rosa?"

"*Sí, Perdido. Soy yo.* It's me. Are you finished for the night?"

Samuel Carleton looked down at the 25 pages that his right hand had plumbed from the inkwell. And while he pondered the question, "Are you finished?," his Rosa waited in near darkness. The window was black. Even the lightning was exhausted.

"Yes, Rosita. I am finished. Finished for good."

Carefully, he pulled out three sheets of carbonic paper from his night's work. He laid his pages filled with the night's visions atop the stack of earlier memories. On that pile he laid the carbonic paper frayed and fragile. Then he put his last half-inch of blank sheets on top and tied all the paper with dirty twine.

"Rosa," he said in a shuddering wave of fever and panic, "my pen is dead."

The writer laid down his cold pipe and damped the lamp until the wick vanished in total darkness. He shuffled to the pot-bellied stove where a large, chipped basin of cool rusty water sat. He splashed water on his face and swished a mouthful before leaning over and spitting into a chamber pot reeking of ammonia on the floor. Washing his face and rinsing the stale tobacco from his mouth, he could not stop trembling. He knew that it was not only Cuban fever which shook him to his soul as he stripped and climbed into Rosa Montoya's bed in the humid darkness. The woman was asleep, breathing softly into his sweating face.

He lay on his back and looked up at the ceiling's peeling whitewash that was illuminated by starlight and an early December sliver of Moon. From La Havana Vieja beyond the open window, he heard a child cry far away and a dog barking closer. He thought of Cora and his dog Spongie in England, which he now called home. Cora Taylor had owned a Jacksonville whorehouse on the corner of Ashley and Hawk streets at the Hotel de Dream, named for its former owner, Ethel Dreme. Although never married, Carleton and Cora now called themselves husband and wife. Cora Taylor was really Cora Ethel Stewart, twice divorced and still legally married to British Army captain Donald Stewart. Too far from Cora to measure in miles, he smelled the departing storm and the cold embers in the stove and the sweat in his bed.

"It is finished," said a cold dry voice in his head. The voice would not stop and it was not his, and it repeated the three words till daybreak Sunday.

FOUR

"I WON'T HEAR OF IT," ROSA REPEATED WITH A VOICE LIKE SHARDS of broken glass. "One mass this morning and you are ready again to play at wearing God's armor. You were never a soldier, Paco, and there is barely enough left of you to be a priest. Your fever is worse than it was yesterday. I see it in your eyes."

Francisco and his sister paced the small room like boxers afraid to leave their corners. They kept the tablecloth between them. When their glaring eyes met, it was Francisco who kept looking away. Sitting on the edge of the bed, María Teresa watched them and she cradled her belly with her arms as if the hard warm swelling were already a nursing child.

"Rosita. I heard it from the abbot's own lips. Before they leave for Spain next month the Spaniards will surely kill our people they still hold as prisoners. I know of others in the country who will go with me. We can free them while there is still time, before the Spanish murder more of us."

"No. And I don't want you to say anything to Alfonso when he comes back with the American. You and my son will kill each other yet, or both of you will be the death of me." Rosa wiped her face with her apron.

"My fever isn't so bad. I haven't had the chills for a week now."

"That means nothing, Paco. The malaria and the yellow fever are in your blood. That is enough to strike you dead at any minute. You must stay in the city and rest."

Francisco stopped pacing long enough to smile across the clapboard room.

"You are still the nurse. You can no more give up your medical skills than I can give up the insurrectos still held prisoner in the west."

"I am not a nurse any more. And you, my brother, are not a soldier."

"Then I shall be their priest until they or I am dead."

Rosa turned her back to the tall, thin man. She bowed her head and raised both hands to her face. Francisco took one step toward her, leaving his safe corner. But he stopped when the door opened behind him. Alfonso came in with Samuel Carleton on his heels. They sucked in with them a blast of hot air from the hallway. Outside, Sunday, December 11, the warm noon air was heavy with humidity which smelled of sea, dead fish, and sewage.

"What is it, Mother?" the boy asked. He did not return María's cheerful smile.

"Nothing. Paco and I were just talking."

"We heard you shouting from the street and all the way up the stairs. Something about going into the country?"

"It's was nothing, Alfonso," Francisco answered for his sister.

Alfonso looked at his uncle. The American stepped between them before the priest could answer.

"We brought guarapo for everyone while you were in church," Carleton said. He reached into the cloth sack which hung heavily from his side. Its strap ran across his sunken chest and over his stooped shoulder. He pulled out a tall glass filled with crushed ice and sugarcane juice. "Five glasses and not one broken." He handed the first glass to Rosa.

Raising the drink to her lips, she closed her eyes.

"How did you ever? Ice?" she asked without opening her eyes.

The American handed a glass to Francisco, María Teresa, and Alfonso, and he kept the last for himself.

"I managed to hide a few dollars since coming to Havana. We found a street vendor not three blocks from here." Carleton smiled toward Alfonso. "My Yanqui money and Alfonso's Spanish can work miracles."

Francisco lowered the glass from his lips. Tiny particles of ice quickly turned to water on his week-old beard. He nodded and sipped again. Rosa pressed her cold glass against her face where her hair was matted to her perspiring forehead.

"A miracle indeed," Rosa sighed. "This island belongs to Madrid for another month. How did you ever get by outside, passing Yanqui money?" She spoke toward Carleton. But she did not open her eyes as the frosted glass moved between her mouth and her cheek. "The street children must have been all over you."

"No one bothered us," Alfonso said over his guarapo, now little more than ice dregs with the sugarcane sucked out. "It was like the gringo was invisible."

"No one seems to notice me here. It's a gift, I suppose," the American smiled. "I cannot help vanishing and disappearing and dissolving. It's my foremost trait."

Everyone finished the cool drinks as the heat blew in from the open window. Rosa returned to the stove and to yesterday's garlic soup.

"What is it, Uncle? We heard you speak of going west," the boy said squinty-eyed.

Francisco looked down at his nephew, whose old eyes glared hard from his young face.

"There are insurrectos being held in Viñales Valley. The abbot says their Spanish guards are likely to murder them before leaving for good. I have friends who can help them." He glanced toward Rosa's back. "Your mother does not think I should go."

"Where?" the American asked before the contempt in Alfonso's eyes could erupt from the boy's mouth.

"Pinar del Río Province," the priest said. "One hundred twenty miles southwest of La Habana. The abbot has contacts in the resistance. They don't think the prisoners will live another week."

A warm breath of Havana rustled the American's unkempt hair. Carleton felt a peculiar warmth rising in his wasted face and jaundiced eyes.

"How would you get there?" Carleton was leaning forward, resting his elbows on the boxes beneath the tablecloth.

"*A pie...* I'm sorry. On foot. There isn't much time."

Carleton reached across the table and pulled to his chest the pile of paper tied with string. He laid both hands on the stack as if silently blessing it. When he looked up at Francisco, the gringo's yellow eyes were narrow and bright.

"I could go with you."

Rosa turned around, ladle in hand. She opened her mouth, but the voice belonged to Alfonso, who laughed out loud close to the American.

"Two half-dead men in the country," the defeated boy sneered. "You wouldn't make it ten miles. And you, Yanqui, there could be real fighting out there. Were our Mauser bullets ever aimed at you in the east?" The boy's question was strangely civil, merely a question of fact.

"I thought they were all shooting at me." Carleton remembered not just Guantánamo Bay and Santiago, but Greece a year ago. "I thought every man in the other army was aiming at me in particular and only at me." He tried not to smile. And he tried not to feel in his heart what Henry Fleming felt 35 years ago: "In my first battle I thought the sky was falling down. I thought the world was coming to an end."

The American and the priest looked at each other. Francisco was little more than a skeleton useful for drying the rags which hung on him. Every time the Yanqui drew a breath, his chest rattled with a tubercular hiss. Rosa threw her wooden spoon to the floor.

"Alfonso is right, Paco. Look at the two of you. Two dead men, just like my son said." The woman looked coldly at the American. "And you, Perdido, have you lost your mind? The walk to the plaza yesterday was nearly too much for you."

"I have faced death by bullets, fire, water, and disease," the writer said firmly toward his Rosa. "But you are right about one thing," Carleton admitted to the woman. "The only man who has any business to engage in war is the soldier." Then he looked closely at Francisco and at the fire in his weary eyes. "One last campaign, Rosa. With Francisco."

When the priest took the few steps to the window and stood beside the American, tears rolled from Rosa's eyes.

"Alfonso will stay here with you and the girl, Rosita," her brother said from Samuel Carleton's side.

"No," the woman said. "I must go with you. If your insurrectos need a priest, they will also need a nurse. Señora Horan will help María when it is her time."

The boy at the table lowered his head.

"I'll stay at the barracks, Mother. Spanish officers in Viñales won't kill prisoners. When you, my uncle the priest, and the gringo turn around five miles from here, you'll know where to find me." He turned away from María's brimming eyes, which she wiped on her sleeve.

Rosa silently returned to the watery chicken broth on the little stove.

Lifting the stump where his right hand had been, the boy continued, "I hope you take better care of the rebels, if you get that far, than you did of your own son."

The woman turned from the stove.

"Had I not taken the hand when you were wounded two years ago, you would have lost the arm, maybe your life."

"Tell your gringo what you called my right hand when you cut it off."

"I don't remember," Rosa pleaded.

"*La mano para matar.* You can translate, Mother."

"The killing hand," the priest said for his trembling sister. Then Francisco laid both hands upon the woman's shoulders and pulled her into his chest. She lowered her face and wept into his ragged blouse. She lifted her head at the sound of heavy footsteps in the hallway. At a double knock on the door, she pushed away from her brother, wiped her face on her apron, and approached the door.

"Yes?"

"I'm Corporal Ruís. I'm here for Rosa Montoya."

Alfonso stood as his mother opened the door. He was at her side as the door swung fully open.

In the hallway, a young Spanish regular stood in dirty white linen. He wore a frayed straw hat as did all the regulars in the field. His black eyes quickly scanned the three men standing behind the woman. Then he stepped over the threshold without an invitation.

He carried a wooden box marked in Spanish, like the dozens of boxes under the tablecloth.

Before Rosa could say a word, Alfonso pushed past her and grabbed the elbows of the soldier. The box crashed to the floor, spilling shiny brass ammunition. Alfonso pushed the Spaniard back into the hall.

"I can wait my turn," the boy said respectfully with flammable rum breath. His face was as young as Alfonso's and the eyes were as old, hollow and empty.

Rosa moved to Alfonso's shoulder. Her eyes begged the stranger to leave. But it was too late.

The stranger was so thin and weak that he stumbled into the hallway under the weight of Alfonso's attack. When he went down on one knee, Alfonso punched him in the face. Blood ran quickly from his nose and the soldier on the floor crumbled, covering his face with his dirty hands. He whimpered with the voice of a tired boy.

"*¡Puta madre!*" the Spaniard shouted up at Alfonso breathing hard above him. "I'll wait my turn!"

Carleton worked to translate the shouting Spanish into English. But the words from the downed boy and from Rosa's son came too fast.

Alfonso stepped back and kicked the fallen regular so hard that Alfonso stumbled into the wall. The soldier doubled over in pain at the top of the stairwell. Alfonso kicked him again. The regular cried out and rolled backward down the steps. María sobbed as the boy fell. Dropping to her knees, she held her large belly as if taking Alfonso's kicks herself.

Francisco and the American pulled Alfonso back from the landing. Alfonso struggled just long enough for Carleton to start coughing and for the priest to begin shaking with malarial chills. Francisco fell back against the wall. Rosa pushed past them and ran down the stairs. At the bottom, she knelt beside the bleeding boy. His cheek bone was shattered from Alfonso's first blow and its jagged pink bone had torn through his thin face. Black teeth fell onto the floor from the bloody lips. The young soldier's body did not bleed so much as leak blood from his face and open mouth.

Rosa touched the young man's throat.

"He's dead," she called to the top of the stairs.

Above her, Alfonso was wiping his knuckles on his trousers. His sandals kicked the puddle of cartridges out of the doorway of his mother's one-room home. He looked down at his mother and the dead soldier. Then he turned to face his uncle, still panting and shaking against the wall.

"We must leave for the country before dark," Alfonso said with his hoarse voice trembling. "All of us," he added, glancing at María still kneeling. "The Spanish authorities will come for her to find me. They will hurt her. I'll get horses from the Spanish barracks."

At the bottom of the stairs, Rosa Montoya gently stroked the dead soldier's broken face since his own mother was three thousand miles away.

Carleton left Rosa cradling the most recently dead man he had seen in Cuba. He paced the room, glancing down at his manuscript each time he passed the table. Alfonso and his uncle had gone to find horses. Rosa found him there. He looked at her grieving face and at her bloody hands.

"What do you know of such things?" the woman hissed. She held up her red, wet hands. "What can you know of a boy dying in your own hands?"

To the American breathing hard and fast, the boy's death at his feet was so very close: a tiny battlefield of knotty wood and a small puddle of fresh blood and teeth on the floor. In Greece he had preferred his battlefields to be not quite so close nor quite so intimate. "From a distance," he had written but did not speak it, "it was like a game. There was no blood, no expression, no horror to be seen."

Rosa wiped her nose and gave the writer her back as she banked the last embers in the iron stove and closed the window's shutters.

Carleton looked down at his pile of paper. But did he know of death in his own hands? he asked himself. Once his pen had said of Henry Fleming that the boy "dreamed all his life of vague and bloody conflicts that had thrilled him with their sweep and fury."

What did Carleton really know, Rosa had demanded.

What did he know now—fourteen months after he had been a war correspondent in Greece and after six months in Cuba and a three-month war? He laid his hand upon his thick manuscript where the answer already had been committed to paper.

Samuel Carleton, newspaper reporter, had landed with United States Marines on the Cuban beach at Guantánamo last June 10. Military surgeon Dr. John Blair Gibbs had to dose Carleton with quinine for his recurring malaria. Spaniards opened fire from the high ground the next day. Toward dusk, a Mauser bullet plowed into Dr. Gibbs' head, a man's length away from Carleton now lying chin-high in the bloody sand which smelled of sea water and old fish. Twelve years earlier, Dr. Gibbs' father had died with Custer at Little Bighorn.

Carleton listened all night to the surgeon's gurgling death rattle beside him. "I thought this man would never die," his pen had remembered feverishly. "I wanted him to die," the reporter had remembered as the dreadful scene bled onto the paper at Rosa's tiny table. The sweating writer looked up at Rosa and he blinked blue-gray eyes. What did he know of death almost in his own hands?

"It's time," said the woman. "Alfonso and Paco are back with the horses."

FIVE

THE MOTHER, HER SON, THE GIRL, FRANCISCO AND THE AMERI-
CAN covered 35 miles on horseback since midday Sunday. Riding
at a walk for two hours before a thirty minute rest, dense tropical
foliage and open wild grassland marked the countryside at noon
Monday.

After ambling through patches of jungle and plains, they
stopped in a tangle of pale green lianas vines and giant ferns beside a small creek. Despite the Cuban dry season, water hyacinth
heavy with lavender blooms overran the stream. The horses nosed
aside the water's fetid surface and took long deep swallows of
brown water.

Careful to keep themselves and the animals hidden in the wall
of brown and green plantlife, without making a sound Francisco

raised his arm and pointed toward the close horizon. Half a mile away, ten men on foot in single file wore white linen and straw hats as they crossed open ground. Their silhouettes with the sun high and motionless marked them as Spanish regulars heading east to Havana. Their war officially ended two days earlier and they carried no weapons.

The five travelers under cover heard nothing from the distant Spaniards; only bird songs rang along the little creek a foot deep with calm, slimy green surface.

A flutter and hum of birds taking sudden flight startled Samuel Carleton who was sitting beside Rosa, his sweating wet head touching hers. Ten eyes squinted toward the ten Spaniards who now ran in all directions.

Dry air carried no sound of the dozen horses circling the terrified Spaniards and herding them like cattle into a tight group in a hazy, waist-high cloud of dust. Sunlight glistened on raised machetes slicing the air.

Hidden by ferns and vines, the family sat motionless with eyes wide and mouths open. Samuel Carlton could not look away from the quick slaughter. That "war is death" he knew well enough. He also had learned that, "A fight at close range is absorbing as a spectacle." At least his pen knew these things and he had to watch. Even the little drama of only 25 men doing war fed a full course meal to his notion of what his pen had called "war, the red animal—war the blood-swollen god."

Cuban horsemen hacked at the flaying Spanish arms and at hatless heads. Two Spaniards fell to their knees and raised their hands to the coldly blue sky. One horseman slashed off four arms at their elbows. Another severed both heads in a little geyser of bright spurting blood with one long, sweeping machete thrust like a scythe striking helpless, praying wheat.

María Teresa covered her eyes. Rosa's hand pressed her mouth so hard that the blood drained from her gray wet cheeks. Alfonso lowered his face until his chin touched his collarless shirt. Only Francisco's lips moved, trembling with whispered Latin. Samuel Carleton blinked at the priest and he squinted at the green mound of high grass and then up at the trees surrounding and protecting the family. He saw bright and shining and full-of-color Cuban tree snails hanging from the trees close to the ground. They hung suspended by nearly invisible webs of mucus. The reds and yellows looked like happy ornaments on a Christmas tree in the sudden silence from the field of tall grass splashed with blood as red as the tree snails.

When the mounted Cubans rode off fast and hard with their business quickly done, the American still heard nothing. Looking out at the green plain where ten men in straw hats were butchered into pieces, he saw only green grass with gray tops moving together like a chorus line in a light breeze. From half a mile away, Carleton saw no trace of ten dead men who had been homeward bound. The green waves dappled with high sun and emerald shadows absorbed the Spaniards—blood, bone, and sinew. They simply vanished until the red and blue land crabs found them and rejoiced.

Rosa's family rode in silence all day, following slowly the red sun's arc westward. Samuel Carleton kept looking at the bright clear sky and he remembered his pen saying that, "It requires sky to give a man courage." The priest swayed in his saddle at his nephew's side with Rosa, the American, and María side by side behind them.

By darkness Monday night with Havana 65 miles behind them, the family took shelter in a tobacco shed in fertile farmland untouched by war on the bank of the Los Portales River. The large vega stood two stories tall and its tobacco was long gone. The farmer who owned the land had argued with Alfonso against allowing the little company to camp for the night. Francisco wore a long friars' cassock which nearly touched his battered sandals. While the indignant campesino debated with the young soldier, Francisco pulled back the ragged brown hood which covered his head and face. He said nothing. By candlelight, the farmer studied Francisco, put his hands together at his breast, and bowed deeply. Then he walked into his hovel and closed the door.

The five weary riders huddled close to the single oil lamp on the floor of the tobacco drying shed. Through wide spaces between the weathered wooden slats on the sides of the vega, Carleton could see yellow light glowing weakly in the dry air at the open windows of the farmer's dilapidated home. His bohío was made from rough wood like the shed, but the peasant house had a thatch roof of palm while the tobacco barn's roof was tin.

"Lucky we have you, Uncle Paco," Alfonso said. His voice was too exhausted to be more than a whisper.

The priest sat on the earthen floor. His sister lay on a blanket with her head resting in her brother's coarse lap. He stroked her moist face. Rosa's eyes were closed and she slept easily. She wore a peasant costume of baggy linen trousers and a shirt tied at the waist with a length of braided hemp.

María huddled beside Rosa with too-large, men's trousers hiked up over her belly also covered with a too-long peasant shirt.

The American whittled a new pencil point and the top sheet of his pile of paper lay blank in his lap.

Carleton had left his one change of clothes behind at the boarding house to make room in his saddlebag for his paper tied with twine. The faces of the three sitting men were illuminated in shadows from their oil lamp damped low and by the light leaking down the hill from the house. Carleton had removed his precious package the moment the horses were unsaddled and tied to a fallen tree. Standing concealed among tropical trees close to the river, the animals were quiet. With his legs crossed and his once-white linen suit stained brown from the layer of tobacco leaf shreds beneath him, the American cradled the stack of writing paper in his lap just as the priest cradled their Rosa whom each of the three men shared in his own way.

"You cannot always make the words come, can you, Gringo?"

"Not always, Alfonso. But I have learned how to wait for them." Carleton pushed the paper pile a little tighter against his empty belly. When he coughed, the pile moved and caught wisps of the distant oil lamp. "I write what is in me."

Alfonso sat, too tired to keep his eyes open. But he could not let go of the American's soul.

Carleton looked away from Alfonso and down at the paper he could hardly see.

"The words will come when they are ripe. But maybe not tonight."

"Do you make up everything you write? You said you were *novelista*."

"Sometimes." Carleton thought for a moment. "Unless I am writing for the newspapers. That must be as real as I can make it."

"But are you real, Yanqui?"

The novelist turned war correspondent had to think again.

"The lives of some people are one long apology. Mine was once, but now I go through the world unexplained." Carleton looked into the boy's eyes. "A novelist must first invent himself."

"Mother says you write mostly at night."

"I work better at night. I am all alone in the world."

"*Pues*, well, you are alone now," Alfonso shrugged and closed his eyes.

The writer leaned sideways and rubbed hard on the dirt floor. He pushed aside what dried vegetation he could feel with his fingertips until he got down to raw earth. He removed a blue and

white, polkadot bandanna from his neck which he wore on horseback and he laid the rag on the ground. He placed the bound paper
squarely in the center of the cloth close to the single lamp. Between his fingers he twirled his wooden pencil. The need to write
clawed ruthlessly at his mind like a cat. The Cuba manuscript had
finished itself.

Weary to his bones and so tired that he hoped his soul would
keep up with him since he could drag it no further, Samuel Carleton still needed to feel his hand advance deliberately across blank
paper. So he allowed his pencil to return to the last good land he
knew and to Henry Fleming, boy and old man, whom he trusted
and who was only a ghost now because the storyteller had burned
him to death in a furious barn fire two years ago. The old man
incinerated after running through midnight flames to save two
suffocating colts. Seeing old Henry burn again, the writer shivered
when his own words ran like swift flame through his mind. "His
face ceased instantly to be a face; it became a mask, a gray thing,
with horror written about the mouth and eyes." But the drunk
Swede did not start that fire. Samuel Carleton ignited that barn
and Samuel Carleton drove old Henry into its red embers simply
by whispering something into his ear. The writer made Henry as
surely as fathers make children and Henry was his child and not
a single thought entered Henry's mind—boy or man—without
Samuel Carleton whispering it.

On the day he died, Henry walked on slow, bent, old man legs,
hand in hand with his little grandson Jimmy. Old Henry's son
George named his first boy for Si Conklin's son who was Henry's
brave tall friend until Confederate bullets killed him for wearing
federal blue at Chancellorsville. The next best thing George Gordon Meade Fleming could do for his father after giving old Henry
a grandson was to give the boy a good name to grow into.

As a newspaperman and as a novelist, Samuel Carleton knew

it was a sin to steal. But borrowing was another matter. He had borrowed from Richard Harding Davis in Greece nineteen months before this tobacco shed in the western Cuban wilderness. During the Greco-Turkish War, RHD covered the dreadful Second Battle of Velestinos. Determined to get as close as possible to the war, Davis was exposed to Turkish fire when he huddled for 13 hours in a front-line trench. War correspondent Carleton did not arrive until after the bitter battle, although the young war-lover had felt the earth shaking under his boots and had found his first real war to be as grand as anything he had imagined in his fiction.

"It was a beautiful sound—beautiful as I had ever dreamed." Carleton had written of the Turkish bombardment in Greece as if he had been under it with reporter Davis. "This is one point of view. Another might be taken from the men who died there."

In Cuba, he had borrowed a little from Harry Scovel and reporter Ed Marshall. At least he had paid Marshall back in full. On Friday, June 24, Carleton tagged along with the Rough Riders and the horseless 10th Cavalry to the ambush by Spaniards at a widening in the dirt road called Las Guásimas. The Americans held their ground, were badly bloodied, but drove the Spaniards back.

As the wounded were being carried out, Carleton found his colleague Edward Marshall resting in the shade. Marshall's spine was badly wounded and he asked Carleton to take his dispatches down to the press boat and to file them for him—after Carleton first filed his own, of course. Carleton cheerfully consented and personally ran the dispatch five miles to the New York *Journal* staff. Six weeks later, the New York *World*'s publisher Joe Pulitzer was still steaming that Carleton had dared to file dispatches from Las Guásimas for his *Journal* competitor, the crippled Ed Marshall. *World* business manager John Norris also taunted Carleton for filing so few of his own dispatches from Cuba. They fired Carleton who then went to work for William Randolph Hearst's *Journal*, which sent him back to cover the American invasion of Puerto Rico.

And when he had created Henry Feming, he borrowed a whole war from Century Magazine's series *Battles and Leaders of the Civil War*. He had borrowed so skillfully that real veterans of the federal army swore that they had once shared coffee and a chew with the author, Samuel Carleton, who was not born when Henry broke under battlefield terror which he remembered as a "red sickness."

Neither did Samuel Carleton smell the Battle of the Crater on the Petersburg line in Virginia. But survivors wrote about it for the Century and if the writer said that Henry was there, then Henry Fleming surely once offered General Grant a nip and a chew. And the newspaperman absorbed newspaper stories written by other reporters. These stuck to the sides of his brain like carcasses of crushed bugs until he needed them. That he smelled neither the crater nor the fire at the Pennsylvania coal mine did not matter. To a novelist, the line between the truth and fiction is as delicate as what another newspaperman turned Havana novelist would call "the dust on a butterfly's wings."

The exhausted writer retrieved the handful of still virgin paper. Laying his pencil on the paper yellow in the faint lamp light of the tobacco shed, Samuel Carleton and old dead Henry felt the story bloom and they waited for camp rumors to gestate into orders; orders that always came in their own good time and then descended through generations of children's children. When George Gordon Fleming heard the Petersburg stories at old Henry's knee, he no more doubted his father than he doubted the sun's rising come morning.

"But I have to go up there, Pa."

"You saw the telegraph. They're already dead most likely."

"Only been an hour. Some of them got to be alive in that hole."

"Listen, George, you're not the only boy in Fayette County

lucky enough to go to mining school. They have real mining engineers up at Dunbar. Your ma and me need you here. The corn's not ankle high and needs scouring. I can't do it myself any more."

"Grandmother in '63 didn't want you to go, either. But you went all the same."

Henry had to think about that one.

"Mothers see things different. Besides, ours was a war, not some coal mine."

The only son of Henry Fleming did not have to think at all.

"Those trapped miners have mothers and wives and children. I can help. And," the tall, muscular son had to smile, "you did your share of digging a mine at Petersburg."

"What about little Jimmy and your wife?"

"They have you and Ma. I'll be home as soon as we dig them out. Sooner if we can't. It won't be as bad as you had it—Bobby Lee tried to kill you."

"I suppose it won't be, son. What'll I tell your ma and your wife?"

"Tell our women what they tell us: 'The apples don't fall far from the tree.'"

The father shook his head. Then father and son smiled beside the small farm's hand-cranked water pump.

Samuel Carleton smiled, too, in the oil lamp's last drop of failing yellow light. He had crossed the mystic threshold of a new story and to feel old Henry's breath on his mind was as comforting as the smell of his mother's kitchen. For a moment he was home and Henry was family. The writer's worn pencil was suddenly only wood empty of words. But new words were only a few flakes of wood away by his penknife or his teeth. Confident of that fact with all his heart, the writer laid the pencil on the sweat- and sun-faded blue bandanna. All the unborn words were in that wooden stick. Whether young George lived or died the writer did not know. But the pencil knew, and writers know how to wait.

After an hour of going back to Henry's home in Fairchance, Pennsylvania, a sickly wheeze escaped from Samuel Carleton's mouth as he climbed to his feet. He extinguished the lamp. Everyone dozed around him. The American walked outside into the night beside the river.

Stars illuminated the water flowing slowly toward the sea. The air was comfortably warm. Starlight glistened on tiny eddies where clear water bathed rocks breaking the surface. Only the last wisp of a waning Moon hung above the trees. The American knelt beside the creek. He laid both hands just on top of the placid water. Cool water touched his palms, but the backs of his hands remained dry. Close to the surface he saw water lizards swimming and hunting for insects and frogs. The writer inhaled deeply and coughed deeply. Butterfly jasmine—*mariposa* to the locals—bloomed early and filled the night with sweet vapors. He recognized the flower from the war: Cuban insurrectos wore the white flower on their tattered clothes as a symbol of resistance. He squinted in the darkness to look for the thorny huiache, the "aroma bush," but he saw none. Carleton wondered if an early spring might come to cleanse the bloodied land of violence.

Spreading wide his fingers, he closed his eyes. He hoped that the water would cool the feverish blood in his hands and that the chilled red blood would relieve the fever burning his eyeballs. His eyes reminded him of teenage Henry's sense of heat and thirst in combat, which felt like "his eyeballs were about to crack like hot stones." But behind his moist eyelids he suddenly saw words that he could not stop because they were his own or the pen's at Rosa's table. He felt the water warming and he knew that if he dared to open his eyes the water would be red.

The American artillery barrage against San Juan Hill began at 8:00 o'clock in the morning on Friday, July 1. The American troops stumbled through thick jungle toward the Aguadores River flowing into the San Juan River. Seven thousand five hundred men converged on a 30-foot wide ford in the river opposite the hill. The fearless black Buffalo Soldiers cheerfully whistled "The Star-spangled Banner" in the bush. Spanish fire raked the Americans and the correspondent who followed them beside Harry Scovel.

The Spaniards would not have seen the approaching Yanquis were it not for a huge, hydrogen-filled observation balloon which followed the Americans, piloted by Lt. Colonel Joe Maxfield and Lt. Colonel George Derby of the U.S. Signal Corps. The correspondent saw the balloon as "a fat, wavering yellow thing; a bloated mass above the trees." The balloon drew Spanish fire into the Americans beneath it. The Americans were so badly mauled on the crooked dirt path to the river that they quickly named it Bloody Angle. Trying to cross the river, Americans were shredded by Mauser fire until the water ran red earning its new name, Bloody Brook. On an 800-foot long stretch of path one-man wide beside the Aguadores, 400 Americans were killed or wounded. A little curve in the red river's bank became Bloody Bend.

At Bloody Brook, the brass band of the black 10th Cavalry became nurses for the wounded, white and black. Bugler John Campbell carried 21 wounded men across the San Juan River under murderous Spanish fire. Private William Davis and bugler James Cooper pulled wounded men from the red water. Sergeant Edward Baker was awarded the Congressional Medal of Honor for pulling a drowning American from Bloody Brook. The black 9th and 10th Cavalries on foot lost 10 men killed and 92 wounded before the Americans crossed the river and took up attack positions at the base of Kettle Hill and San Juan Hill, and the correspondent saw it all and smelled it all six months ago. He remembered that river now as "a miserable huddle at Bloody Bend, a huddle of hurt men, dying men, dead men."

Kneeling now at the tiny river far in time and space from Bloody Brook, the writer regretted spilling so much blood which was not his upon those pages lying on the dirt floor of a tobacco shed. All the blood in Henry Fleming's war was made up and Carleton did not live with it. But the gray-faced wide-eyed bodies in blue flannel turned red as a Chicago slaughterhouse floor at Bloody Brook still haunted him where his soul lived and he gasped for breath in the darkness.

Carleton opened his eyes and he pulled his hands from the stream. By starlight he squinted at his cool wet fingers. He expected to see blood.

"You better come back, Gringo."

Samuel Carleton turned toward Alfonso standing behind him.

"Regulars have stopped at the house."

The American looked up the hill toward the little farm's bohío. Stooping to quench his fever in the water, he had not seen half a dozen shadowy figures in the faint light from the shanty's windows. He followed Alfonso back to the tobacco shed where Rosa and the girl sat tensely beside Francisco.

"The regulars," Alfonso whispered, "will want food. They're probably on their way to La Habana to board ships for Spain. They won't come down here."

Shuffling footsteps approached the tobacco vega. Rosa reached for her straw hat and tucked up her long brown hair. She rubbed her long fingers on the earthen floor and then wiped the dirt onto her face. María quickly did the same.

A lantern entered the shed first, followed by the soldier who carried it and five of his comrades.

Samuel Carleton rubbed his weary eyes at a sudden apparition out of a child's night terrors. One of the Spaniards had two heads.

A filthy man in threadbare rags carried half a man on his back. With gentle care, he swung the horror across his side so the hulk could sit like a tree stump on the floor. The thing had no legs and its spine touched the floor, held upright by its arms the way air roots anchor a Cuban banyan tree to the earth. A black beard obscured the face except for the eyes. Samuel Carleton could not look at the wet black eyes.

Alfonso stood while his family remained seated cross-legged on the floor.

"Long live our mother Spain," Alfonso said with his Cuban-accented Spanish. The six Spanish soldiers in the shed glared hard at Alfonso. The leader lowered his lantern to cast more light on the American, the priest, Rosa with her dirty face, and María Teresa. The man seemed to linger on Rosa. Then he looked at Alfonso.

Rosa's son dug into a pocket and pulled out five shiny buttons which he displayed in his only hand. The stranger glanced down at Alfonso's open, left palm.

"Look here," Alfonso said. "Spanish issue. I stood at Santiago."

The leader grunted, motioned to his comrades, and squatted on tobacco chaff. When the other soldiers sat on the hard earth, Alfonso joined them. With the lantern on the ground, Alfonso and six regulars faced the American, Francisco and the women. The leader of the strangers kept eyeing Rosa.

"Women?" the leader said with no trace of threat in his weary voice. Rosa lowered her face, trying to retreat into shadow.

"My mother," Alfonso said firmly. "And that one is heavy with child."

The regular nodded.

One of the regulars lifted a round bread and broke off chunks which he passed to the other soldiers. He did not share with Alfonso or his family.

"Yanqui?" the leader asked Alfonso, but he faced the American who worked his ears to follow the Spanish.

"He's just a newspaperman," Alfonso said with contempt. The

leader of the little squad of veterans bit into the bread and chewed hard.

"What are you doing with a priest?" the soldier mumbled around his stale ration. He looked toward Alfonso.

"My uncle. My mother's brother."

"Ah," the soldier chewed. "Your hand, you lost it under our flag?"

Alfonso raised his stump. Pride and lantern light illuminated his thin face.

"Cut off by Máximo Gómez himself. I was a Voluntario in La Habana this time last year."

"Wylerite," the regular said. He spat toward the ground where the lantern sat. "The boy was a Voluntario," he said to his friends. All six men looked at Alfonso and laughed like defeated men.

Alfonso's back straightened where he sat on the warm ground. The boy's eyes narrowed.

"General Gómez cut off my hand when we were captured in the jungle." He raised his stump and pointed it at the leader of the regulars. "This I gave gladly for the glory of Spain."

"But you are Cuban."

"My parents were born in Spain and came here as children. They met and married in Cuba. My heart is Spanish." Alfonso did not glance sideways toward Rosa.

The regulars all looked at Rosa.

"You are *peninsular*?" the leader asked.

"I am Cuban now," the woman said.

Francisco touched his terrified sister's cold and dirty hand.

"Our war is over, Padre," the leader said. "We will eat and then be on our way. We mean no harm to your women."

The American watched these regulars. He recognized their faces—they were all like his: emaciated from starvation and fever, with jaundiced eyes from malaria and the yellow jack. He took comfort that all of them were unarmed.

"Why do you hide here?" the leader asked the priest.

"We do not hide," Alfonso answered before his uncle could.

"I do not ask you, Voluntario," the soldier said. His yellow eyes flashed for an instant.

"We are going to the west," Francisco said. "My parish is there."

The regular nodded. He looked at the wasted gringo who clamped a cold, hand-rolled cigarette in his miserable teeth.

"And you?" the leader asked with sudden, halting English, pointing with a chunk of bread.

"I go to write about what I see."

The leader translated into Spanish.

"My name is Roberto," one of the soldiers said in Spanish without emotion. "Write about me."

When their leader translated, Carleton nodded.

"This will be your country when we go home to Spain."

"I think not," Carleton said very gently. "The American government only wants peace and freedom for the Cuban people. And I am nothing more than a writer."

"Writers are of no matter, Yanqui," the leader of the regulars said as he chewed the last bite of his bread. "But the gringos will try to do what Spain tried, and failed. Many Yanquis will die here. Our colonies belong to America now. We shall see how you like it. You will have to kill many Cubans as we did."

"I'm only a writer," Carleton sighed. He laid his hand upon the pile of paper at his side as if it were Exhibit A in his own defense.

"Then you can write about Roberto." The regular nodded toward the starving soldier at his elbow. "He is a brave soldier. He killed many Yanquis at Las Guásimas before the battle of Santiago. Were you there, Gringo?"

Carleton nodded and looked down at his lap. His hand still rested on his longhand manuscript. Carleton looked up into the leader's eyes which closely studied the American's face.

"But you killed no one, did you, Gringo?"

"No." He looked into the leader's eyes. "But I know what war is, señor."

"What is our war to you, Yanqui writer?"

"Heat, dust, rain, thirst, hunger, and blood."

The leader laughed with rancid breath into the gringo's face as he stood with a slight grunt from the effort. Then the other regulars stood. Roberto was so weak that the soldier beside him pulled him gently to his bare and bleeding feet. Another Spaniard hoisted from the carpet of tobacco stems the stump of the legless one who had not said a word. The soldier who heaved the half-man onto his back was not the regular who had carried it into the shed. When the thing was lifted, black water leaked from between the large knots tied at the root of each empty trouser leg. Still, the American could not look into its almost closed eyes.

"The Yanquis have taken our weapons," the leader said coldly. He glared hard at the American. "In another time, our meeting would have been different." The lantern light glistened in his black eyes surrounded by yellow. "Very different."

Alfonso glanced at his mother sitting beside his uncle. Then Rosa's son stood with the other regulars.

"Sit down, boy," the regulars' leader said. "Sit with you mother and the priest."

Alfonso remained standing. He raised his stump and the sleeve fell away. The leader of the regulars looked quickly at the wound and then down into the older woman's face.

"Many mothers have lost sons on this damnable island. At least most of your son came home to you, señora." The Spanish regular reached down and picked up his lantern. Then with a voice oddly casual, he turned toward Rosa's brother.

"You are Francisco, the rebel priest?"

Paco looked up with weary eyes and in the lantern light he looked like an old saint. The soldier shook his head and sighed deeply.

"Go in peace, my son," Francisco said.

Without another word, the soldier led his veterans into the darkness. An audible sigh blew from Rosa's lips when the last of them marched single-file into the night. Alfonso sat between Carleton and María Teresa. They were in darkness again. The American shivered when the departing Spaniards in the distant darkness made a chorus of cooing sounds like jungle doves. Rosa looked at Carleton's wide blue-gray eyes.

"I heard that sound at Las Guásimas before a Spanish ambush last June." Sweat beaded on Carleton's face as he remembered the dove-calls in the jungle, "soft, mellow, sweet, singing only of love." He remembered it as "the Spanish guerilla calling to his mate." And he remembered writing of the bird-calls, "I have never heard such a horrible sound as the beautiful cooing of the wood dove when I was certain that it came from the yellow throat of a guerilla." That was only half a year ago.

On Friday, June 24, only two days after landing in Cuba, 964 inexperienced Americans with the correspondent in tow walked into the jungle to find Spaniards even though their commanding officer had orders to wait until all U. S. troops were on shore at Daiquiri.

The correspondent strained his ears to catch the telltale cooing of the bird-calls which the Spanish mimicked to signal their sudden attacks out of the dense green nowhere. He silently cursed the boisterous blueclad targets in column all around him. Walking beside the mule carrying RHD whose sciatica was inflamed, the correspondent pulled out his pad. He labored to write while guiding his feet around fetid puddles from late night rain. With volunteer Rough Riders in brown shirts and blue regulars all around him, the correspondent jotted a newspaper dispatch: "They wound along this narrow winding path, babbling joyously, arguing, recounting and laughing, making more noise than a train going through a tunnel."

From camp at Siboney, two trails marked the course eastward to Santiago. Five hundred Rough Riders climbed the muddy slope of the Ridge Trail mountain path. One hundred forty-four troopers of the 1st Cavalry and 220 troopers of the all-black 10th Cavalry, all on foot, shuffled along the Valley Trail to the right of the volunteers.

The mountain paths crossed the main road three miles from the coast at a crossroads called Las Guásimas. Jungle visibility quickly shrank to twenty feet. The two American columns could not see each other on the parallel trails leading to the crossroads. At 5:40 in the morning, barely daylight, the cooing doves in the jungle started. Captain Allyn Capron, Jr., of L Troop from Muskogee, Oklahoma, took the point for the Rough Riders.

Twenty minutes later, the cooing bird-calls stopped and a wall of Mauser bullets washed through the palm trees and the impenetrable wall of jungle. And the correspondent was reminded again that his pen had been right: "Soldiering at its best is cruel, hard work."

Unseen Spaniards fired their deadly, smokeless-powder rifles 300 yards from the pinned-down Americans on the Ridge Trail. The Spanish line of 1,500 to 2,000 troops was 1,000 yards long. Their German-made Mausers caught the Rough Riders on their right flank.

Since Guantánamo with the Marines, the correspondent knew the Mauser well and respected it. "The Mauser is a fine weapon," he had written during his first week at Mary Horan's boarding house. With its five-cartridge magazine, its nearly half-ounce, 7 millimeter bullet could travel half a mile in one second. If the bullet hit a blade of grass, it would tumble and the tumbling bullet inflicted horrific wounds with a "frightful tearing effect."

Inside the correspondent's mind, the Spanish bullets defoliating the jungle were oddly familiar. He and Henry Fleming had heard it all before. "Bullets began to whistle among the branches and nip at the trees," young Henry remembered. "Twigs and leaves came sailing down. It was as if a thousand axes, wee and invisible, were being wielded." Always, the tumbling whining Mauser bullet made a sound inspiring to the correspondent. To him it sounded "as if one string of a most delicate musical instrument had been touched by the wind into a long faint note, or that overhead someone had swiftly swung a long, thin-lashed whip."

What the correspondent's pen remembered as a delicate musical instrument did real work in that jungle.

One Spanish volley killed Rough Rider Sergeant Hamilton Fish, grandson of President Grant's Secretary of State and the captain of Yale University's rowing team. New York *Journal* reporter Ed Marshall took a Mauser in the spine. How odd, the correspondent remembered, that the grass seemed to make everything clean. His dip pen remembered later that "when the wounded men dropped in the tall grass, they quite simply disappeared, as if they had sunk into water." But they did not disappear really.

The Rough Riders' K Troop was led by young Micah Jenkins. His father, Confederate General Micah Jenkins, had been killed in the Civil War. Within half an hour, Private Tom Isbell, a Cherokee Indian in L Troop, was wounded seven times. When Private Henry Haefner, 23, from Marissa, Illinois, fell gravely wounded, his buddies carried him to the shade of an old tree. Private Haefner of G Troop propped himself against the tree and shouted to Lt. Colonel Roosevelt to bring him a rifle and a canteen. TR obliged and the wounded boy kept fighting until he bled to death in the blazing sunshine. Roosevelt picked up another wounded man's rifle and led a countercharge.

After an hour of a two-front battle, the Spanish slowly pulled back. When Colonel Leonard Wood, the personal physician of the President of the United States, and Lt. Colonel Roosevelt moved forward, they had to step over the body of Rough Rider Hamilton Fish and of Captain Allyn Capron, Jr., who died in Cuba on his 24th birthday. "Don't mind me, boys," the dying Capron told his friends, "go on and fight!" Young Capron's father wore regular army blue a few miles to the east. As the volunteers advanced toward the withdrawing Spaniards, Richard Harding Davis forgot his crippling sciatica. RHD picked up a dead American's carbine and began firing at the Spaniards. After firing 20 rounds, Davis stopped soldiering and began acting as medic to the wounded. He knelt over the body of Hamilton Fish and found the dead cavalryman's pocketwatch. It was inscribed, "God Gives." When RHD stopped to comfort Private Telden Dawson, 22, of the Rough Riders' L Troop, Davis saw that Dawson had been mortally wounded by a bullet in his face. When Davis tried to give water to the dying boy, he could not: the soldier's teeth were too tightly clenched from pain.

Only two days before this fight, the correspondent had called the little war in Cuba "a grim and frightful field sport." There was no sport now as squadrons of vultures swept down from the purple sky.

When the firing stopped, 16 Americans lay dead in the jungle and 52 were wounded. Eight of the dead and 34 of the wounded were Rough Riders. The 1st and 10th Cavalries lost 8 killed and 18 wounded. Only ten Spanish bodies were found in the thick jungle where only the vultures moved freely.

The groaning wounded were dragged back to makeshift field hospitals on the beach at Siboney. Lying in the withering heat, the wounded sang "My Country 'Tis of Thee" to the ceilings of the canvas tents.

Samuel Carleton, remembering now, could not get that tune out of his head or the cooing of the wood doves that can kill.

"I want to go home," Rosa said weakly. "They could have killed us."

"They do not have the strength to kill anyone," Alfonso said. He turned his head toward the shadow of the American. "That is what defeat looks like, Gringo." The maimed boy faced his mother in the darkness. "We can't go back to La Habana. I killed a Spaniard. And I killed Cuban rebels in the war. I have no country, now. Not anywhere."

"That may be true," Francisco said to his nephew. "But we can still save the lives of our brothers in the country."

"That is your fantasy, Uncle, not mine," Alfonso said. He looked toward Carleton. "Even this won't be your fight, Gringo, will it? A woman and a sick priest are willing, but you are here only for the story. Is that not so?"

Even in the dark, the American could feel Alfonso's glare upon his face. The writer reached for his stack of paper and returned it to his lap.

"I will fight with Francisco," the American said firmly. He coughed. "Then I shall write."

"Another of your little war stories?"

"Hang all war stories," Carleton shrugged.

"My mother feeds you and warms your bed. My uncle takes you to another fight. And you make your words on old paper." Alfonso smiled without pity. "It is a good life, Gringo."

"I am simply a man struggling with a life that is no more than a mouthful of dust to him." Samuel Carleton could not look into the boy's angry eyes.

"More Spanish and Cuban blood will be ink to you," Alfonso said.

Carleton listened to four other souls breathing in and breathing out the warm Cuban night laced with the sweet aroma of dried tobacco. He spoke at last to the paper in his lap.

"To a writer, ink is blood."

With the war-weary Spanish regulars gone into the midnight darkness under bright stars and a thin, rounded edge of the Moon, Samuel Carleton put a match to the lamp on the vega's floor. When its wick caught, he damped it low. When his eyes adjusted, he saw Alfonso asleep beside but not touching María Teresa. Rosa lay wrapped in a saddle blanket close to the American and her brother lay on his back three paces from Rosa.

The writer took out his paper and chewed a new point on his pencil. The stick of wood tasted faintly like the scent of a mountain forest in June where the high country stops in eastern Fayette County where old Henry farmed. Sitting cross-legged and reaching as far as he could from where the half-Spaniard had leaked malaria's black water fever, Carleton picked up a handful of tobacco leaf shreds and tough stems. He soon chewed it as hard as old Henry's mules pulling a plow when the western Pennsylvania grass was full of new rain. It was warm in the tobacco shed's shadows and it was early summer warm at noon on June 16 in Pennsylvania and Samuel Carleton was finally there, eight years back in time.

George Fleming eased the two-horse team toward Charles Slone's dry goods store in Fairchance. Wrapping harness reins three times around the hitching post, he wiped his boots before he entered the general store.

"Esther," Henry's son smiled.

"George," said the girl behind the counter.

"Heard about Hill Farm?" he asked gravely.

"Nothing really new since the telegraph started at 10:30. Did they send for you, being schooled and all as a mine engineer?"

"No." He liked the girl who worked in her father's store when school was out. She was in her late teens, only a few years younger than the tall young man who seemed much older to her since he had married and had become a father.

"How's little Jimmy?" Esther Slone smiled.

"Full of himself as little boys will be."

"Wouldn't know much about that."

George knew that Esther had no brothers or sisters.

"Suppose not," he said. He had known the girl since they were both children. When old Henry took the buckboard and young George to town, they often saw the little girl run across the street from rooms above her parents' store to Doc Bill Patterson's home. Always she had a book under her arm. She would cross to Doc's and run out five minutes later with a different book. The town physician allowed the little girl to read through his floor-to-ceiling library of popular books, one book at a time.

"I'll need a blanket, two or three days of coffee, and the heaviest pair of work gloves you have, please."

"You'll need more than that if you're going up to Dunbar," a woman's voice said behind him. He recognized the strange Eastern European accent of Esther's mother.

George turned to see a small head perched atop a pile of blankets in the older woman's arms.

"You take these up to Hill Farm. Let's hope you have need for them."

"Thank you, Mrs. Slone. But I can't pay for but one."

"We can settle up when you come home with whatever you don't use." This thickly accented voice belonged to Esther's father, a stern-faced man whom old Henry respected greatly. Charles Slone's voice still made George feel like a small boy.

"Yes, sir," George said. "Thank you."

Charles took the pile of wool blankets from his wife and walked outside. Esther picked up one of several boxes of overalls new and used. She followed her father into Monday's noontime sunshine.

"Ladies Aid Society," the girl called over her shoulder. "We knew someone would be going up to Dunbar. I said it would be you, George Gordon."

"That's what she said," Mrs. Slone smiled behind him. George held the door open for the girl's mother carrying another box.

Charles took the box from his daughter and pushed it into the wagon. He and George loaded ten boxes of food and clothing.

In front of the store beside the railroad's telegraph pole, Esther kissed her mother, gathered her skirt, and climbed into the wagon's front seat.

"Esther. Where are you going?" George asked impatiently.

"With you, of course. I can help with the children up there. I'm going to be a school teacher, you know."

"Yes, I know. But ...".

"Then let's go. The accident was almost two hours ago." Esther tried not to smile.

George looked at her grim father.

"The girl has made up her mind," Charles said. "You take the main road and stay well clear of the back roads and them shiners along Neal's Run, you hear?"

"We'll take the main road, sir."

"I know you will," the gravel voice said.

George took the reins from the hitching post, climbed to the seat beside the girl, and said, "Come now," as he flicked the long reins. The wagon creaked northeast out of tiny Fairchance.

Out of earshot of Esther's parents who still stood outside, George spoke to Esther without looking at her.

"You didn't kiss your father good-bye."

"No."

Her dry tone of voice turned the young man's head toward her.

"When father was a boy in Russia, my grandfather always kissed him good-bye before walking to the next village. Then one time my grandfather never came home—murdered beside the road probably, for being different. So my father never kisses me before I go away."

"I'm sorry, Esther."

"Me, too. But I love my father and I know he loves me." She looked straight ahead between the two horses. "The railroad man at the telegraph office said there were 60 miners underground when the explosion happened. Do you really think anyone's alive down there?"

"We'll see."

"You know Dunbar is fifteen miles by the main road but only twelve if we stay closer to the mountains."

Old Henry's son looked carefully at the girl beside his right elbow.

"Yes."

Between the peace of the green mountain road and the soothing sound of small streams running clear and cool down the mountain inside his head, Samuel Carleton's pencil grew too heavy to push further into the trees full of new leaves. So he smothered the oil lamp three hours before sunrise and curled up beside Rosa smelling of horse sweat on her bed of tobacco dust.

SIX

GREEN FARMLAND AT DAWN GLOWED LIKE THE AMERICAN IMAG-
INED Ireland to shine in misty first light. Rich fields climbed shal-
lowly toward the Sierra del Rosario mountains. Tuesday morning
fog hung like God's warm breath on tall palm trees at the crease
in the hazy horizon where the plain touched the mountains. The
cork palms of Cuba grow only in this valley. The horses shuffled
cracked unshod feet, resting with their riders ten minutes every
hour.

Riding further into the valley, they saw few farmers. Their
only company was the momentary burst of cheerful color from
trogon feathers against green trees. Rosa called the bright birds
"tocororos."

Carleton swayed in the pain-making saddle and he chewed

bitter strips of mahogany bark, which Francisco had given him to sooth his lungs. His only relief was climbing down to lead the horses by hand across the north-south railroad track north of the hamlet of Calab.

Beyond the wooden shanties, the riders returned to the sheltering cover of groves of trees and thick brush. They stayed in the shadowed canopy of green leaves and palm fronds when they approached a small hut only one hundred yards away. They were so close to the thatch roof hovel that they could see where summer rain had washed away a layer of mud wall exposing bright yellow veins of straw within the clay bricks.

The five riders stopped in the shade of a guasimilla grove when four mounted Spanish guerillas rode through green tobacco fields toward the tiny peasant house. Alfonso led his family and the gringo behind the tall trees with gray bark and dismounted when the too close irregulars climbed down from their horses whose ribs could be counted from the nearby trees. Carleton jumped back, nearly falling, when his hand on a branch touched a harmless, 7-inch long "bird-eating spider" whose hairy, repulsive body resembled a tarantula. Alfonso grinned widely and silently.

A woman's scream penetrated the trees when the Spaniards dragged her, a man, and a small boy into the late morning sunshine. The Spaniards forced the man and boy to kneel in the red soil. A tall, pale-faced guerilla put a pistol into the kneeling man's mouth and the back of his head exploded. When the boy cried out, another Spaniard kicked him. The boy fell sideways, felt the same hot revolver touch his left ear, and he moved no more.

In the trees beyond the small cohiba field, Rosa held María Teresa tightly with the girl's belly between them. The three men held the rope bridles of the horses. Their hands and Alfonso's right forearm covered the horses' muzzles to keep them quiet as they nervously pawed the soft earth.

In half a minute, the Spaniards stripped naked the surviving woman, leaving bleeding tracks from their fingernails on her body. Her bare maternal breasts hung brown and flat to her elbows.

Francisco gasped and looked away. Carleton looked up between the branches. The climbing sun reminded him of Guantánamo where his pen remembered that "the sky was bare and blue and hurt like brass."

The Spaniards threw the sudden widow onto the rippling folds of her naked belly. One of them sat on her back while another unsinched his horse, heaved off its saddle, and tossed the saddle beside the woman kicking and screaming. Two men grabbed her arms and white-soled bare feet. They dropped her face down on the saddle with her naked buttocks now raised a foot off the ground.

Time stopped for the American listening to the woman screaming and kicking. It felt strangely like his battles where "seconds, minutes were quaint little things, tangible as toys, and there were billions of them, all alike." The naked woman cried to a distant God.

Dropping their baggy trousers in turn, the four irregulars took the woman six times. One held both of her arms and one sat upon each of her legs. After the second man took her face down in the red soil, she never made a sound which could be heard in the trees. There, the two women held each other tightly, wept softly, and never looked up. Holding three of their horses with their three good hands, Alfonso and Francisco looked only into their animals' black, anxious eyes.

Samuel Carleton held two horses. He gripped a pair of reins in one hand and with the other he stroked the whiskered nose of each horse in ten-second turns to keep them quiet. None of the horses made a sound. The American looked into the deepset horse eyes and when the woman stopped screaming and the only sound was the Spaniards laughing, the correspondent suddenly remembered the eyes of warhorses amid shot and shell, "eyes deep as wells, serene, mournful, generous eyes, lit heartbreakingly with something that was akin to a philosophy, a religion of self-sacrifice." When the woman stopped screaming, he looked away from the horse eyes and saw near the tiny house a thick almácigo tree 40 feet high, thick and majestic. The copper-colored trunk glowed in the sunshine like a shiny new bronze penny.

Only the American looked toward the clay hut. But all he saw was the stark red sun reflecting off the blue wings and yellow bellies of a flock of American warblers wintering in Cuba and flying low over the naked woman who now lay with a bullet in her forehead beside the dead man and dead boy, flat in the dirt at her own doorstep. When the Spaniards were satisfied, they swung the wet saddle onto their one bareback horse, mounted, and rode slowly away.

"We must bury them," Francisco said after the Spanish irregulars were out of sight.

"No, Uncle," said the boy with a trace of real grief in his voice.

"Why not?" Samuel Carleton asked, looking up at the towering guasimillas full of their December blossoms brightly pink. So beautiful, he thought.

"As Uncle has said, and I have heard him say it, 'Let the dead bury the dead.' We cannot waste daylight."

"Paco," Rosa begged with tears rolling down her face. "At least we can ride to the Sierra de los Órganos and hide in the caves there until all of the Spaniards are gone from Cuba next month."

Rosa looked desperately at the American.

"There are many caves there," she said. "We can hide there and you can write all you want for as long as you want."

Samuel Carleton shook his head, No.

"Francisco wants to fight Spaniards. And no good story about fighting Spaniards can be written in a cave."

"For the love of God, Perdido," Rosa wept.

"God wasted no love here," Alfonso said without looking toward the hut where three bodies lay in puddles of blood and brains.

A ten-foot, 100-pound Cuban boa snake suddenly crunched through dead leaves on the ground. The horses pulled on their reins and Alfonso felt the American shudder.

"Only a majá," Alfonso said to the American. "Harmless to you, Gringo."

Mounting their skittish horses, the five riders left the massacre behind them and rode all day.

After two and a half days and most of two nights on horseback for almost 115 miles, by dusk the American was in too much pain to ride and was almost too weak to walk. His skin and bone hips could no longer sit a horse so he trudged on foot at the left flank of the horse carrying Rosa. Carleton had swung his right arm over Rosa's animal's withers and he gripped the front of the Spanish cavalry saddle. His aching arm carried most of his weight and he stumbled beside the bony, swaybacked mount for the next five miles toward a town. Rosa weaved from side to side as she rode head-down, eyes-closed. Carleton could feel her warm thigh against his arm as her thirsty horse carried one and dragged the other. Alfonso rode in the lead. The priest's horse stumbled onward, following the tail of Rosa's horse which swished in its face. The reins of the American's riderless horse were wrapped around Francisco's saddle horn.

Warm winter wind blowing dryly through Viñales Valley lifted dust around the horses' hooves. Oddly rounded, almost vertical hills gave the valley's distant ridges a tropical appearance. Each strange mogote hill ended abruptly in a plateau of densely green vegetation. The party found the banks of the Rio Guamá river, which cut the village of Pinar del Río in two.

Two miles from town, the air carried the scent of evening bread in clay ovens. Farmers walked behind gray oxen with ringed noses. The campesinos paid little attention to the four swaying bodies on horseback and the man in the filthy, once-white linen suit who stumbled beside them. The farmers worked their fields between the cork palms they called corchos.

Carleton did not look up from the earth between his boots until a tiny creature flew into his face and tickled his nose. He swatted what felt like a moth which spread its brightly colored wings and continued into the bright sky. The butterfly bat is the smallest bat on the planet. The American's yellow eyes watched the bat soar toward the nearest limestone mogote.

Suddenly, the arid breeze carried the cooing of doves. Carleton nearly collapsed when he let go of Rosa's saddle and his numb arm thumped against his side. His brow creased as he strained to listen to the birds. His wheezing breath came faster and louder. In the lead, Alfonso reined his horse to a stumbling stop. The boy turned around and looked down into the American's face.

"These birds have no bullets, Gringo," Alfonso said with a cold smile.

Carleton blinked up at the one-handed rider whose teeth shone in his darkly tanned face. The American on foot saw Rosa raise her head and open her sleepy eyes.

"What is it, Alfonso?" she sighed.

Her son glanced down at the Yanqui and then over his shoulder toward his mother.

"Nothing. Your gringo frightened himself again." Alfonso looked forward and raised his left hand over his horse's drooping, mulelike ears. "There. Pinar del Río, as you requested, Uncle."

Francisco nodded toward his nephew.

Samuel Carleton squinted down the hillside toward the hamlet of Pinar del Río, a tiny blister of shanties in the middle of Vi-

ñales Valley where round, green mountains marked the valley's
distant perimeter. The Sierra de los Órganos touched the sky in
the northwest and the Sierra del Rosario blotted out the distant
ocean to the southeast.

Alfonso's sandals kicked the sides of his horse, which stepped
into a slow walk. Rosa waited. Behind her, the American gathered
his reins secured to Francisco's saddle. Carleton grunted when he
heaved his frail body into the saddle for the short ride into town.
The saddle was sticky where his saddle sores had wept through
his trousers.

The riders followed the brown water of the Rio Guamá into
the center of the village. Men and women with trailing, dirty-
faced children raised dust on the dirt streets. Rosa pulled her
straw hat down over her ears. Her long hair was a tangled knot of
sweat and grit inside. Alfonso doffed his straw hat when the riders
rode past the one freshly painted shack on their side of the river.
He saluted the posada where whores leaned out the windows to
watch the strangers pass. The pregnant girl looked away from the
shabby public house. The priest, hidden by the hood of his cassock, did not look to the left or to the right of the American's horse
that walked ahead of his. The *putas* shouted obscene greetings as
the priest passed and his nephew waved with the arm which still
had fingers.

Francisco said nothing until they approached a ramshackle
hovel at the far end of the village.

"Here," he called weakly to Alfonso.

All five riders pulled their mounts up to the peasant who stood
quietly outside. The man reached out and took Francisco's reins.
The priest slid down from the saddle into the old man's open arms.

"Manuel," Francisco said. His dry throat made only a whisper.
"I prayed that you would still be here."

"Where would I go?" the wind-burned face smiled broadly.

Rosa climbed down on stiff legs and helped María to the ground. The American and Alfonso dismounted.

"You must rest, Paco," Rosa said.

Manuel studied the face of the priest and led him into the shack with Rosa's help, followed by Alfonso, María, and Carleton carrying his saddlebag.

Tuesday's last, red daylight streamed from gaping holes in the thatch roof and through open seams in the walls. The single window had no glass and dust blew in from the street.

A knee-high, scruffy dog ran into the doorway and sniffed the strangers.

"Pecos," the old man smiled nearly toothlessly. The American knelt to rub the animal's ears. Manuel did not protest that his dog was drawn to the Yanqui's side as if by gravity.

"I adore dogs," Carleton smiled warmly toward Pecos.

"My house is your house, Padre," Manuel said to Francisco. A wave of sadness darkened Manuel's black eyes when Francisco sat down at a little table in the center of the dirt floor. Francisco's bones creaked like old timbers. His fevered eyes were sunk deep into his skull. He looked up at Manuel from under his bony brow. There was little meat between bone and skin anywhere on Francisco's weathered face. He licked his cracked lips to speak.

"I heard there is a Spanish camp for Cuban prisoners thirty or forty miles west of here between the mountains, beside the Río Cuyaguateje. Will you guide us?"

The farmer glanced fretfully at the older woman. Rosa removed her straw hat and her hair fell over her shoulders. She sat on a wooden box beside the open door. Carleton saw a small wooden figure resembling a child who held a stick at the doorway on the dirt floor. It stood in a small stone bowl filled with black-eyed peas. The American blinked at its bright eyes made of polished cowrie shells. The haunting seashell eyes did not blink back. Near the doorway Alfonso stood between the American and María. Manuel took the other chair at the little table. He looked across the knarled surface into priest's diseased eyes.

"Padre, our war is over. The treaty should be signed by now. The Spanish are leaving. There is no one left at the old camp in the valley." Manuel blinked and looked down at his thick, hard, farmers' hands which he folded. "You have done your duty. You can do no more now." He said "now" like a whispered benediction over a freshly turned grave.

"I told my brother that," Rosa said before Francisco could answer. She reached forward and laid her hand upon her brother's shoulder. "The jungle will kill him. Tell him, Manuel."

The farmer sat with his mouth open as sunlight streamed in to illuminate the large black spaces between his teeth. December light carved hard angles and shadows across his leather face. Like the priest, the world had aged him too much for Carleton to guess his years by calendar. The Cuban peasant stood slowly. For the first time, he removed his straw hat and held it at his heart.

"Are you Rosa Delgado?"

"Yes," the woman nodded. "Rosa Montoya."

"I did not recognize you from the prison camp, señora. Forgive an old man's failing memory." He bowed deeply, as if to royalty. When the woman smiled, Manuel took his seat. His gaze froze on Francisco's eyes.

"Manolo," Francisco said. He leaned forward, reached across the table, and put his hand upon the farmer's wrist. "If there are Cuban prisoners there, I must go to them. These Spaniards include irregulars and deserters who cannot be trusted to behave like Christian soldiers. One last fight, old friend. Then all of us can rest when peace comes with the Americans."

"But, Padre, we will need supplies and ammunition. I am a poor man. The Spaniards took everything."

Francisco sat back in his chair. Carleton saw the sudden grief in the old farmer's eyes. The American reached into his pocket and pulled out a gold pocketwatch and chain.

"My father's," Carleton said. He handed the heirloom to Manuel. "For ¡Cuba Libre!"

Manuel took the watch and studied it. He collected the dangling chain and put the gift inside his shirt against his skin. He looked past the priest toward Carleton. The afternoon sun made the American's eyes glow yellow like cats' eyes. Manuel cocked his head toward Francisco.

"I shall lead you, Padre. But there is nothing out there."

Instead of words, Francisco lowered his face until his chin touched his chest. His sigh blew dust from the table.

"Well," Alfonso said behind his seated uncle. "The old will lead the sick. I'm going outside."

As the boy stepped across the threshold, María Teresa called from behind him, "Only tend to the horses."

Alfonso waved over his shoulder. Rosa watched her son through the open window—a square hole in the clapboard wall. She watched him until he disappeared into the setting red sun which glowed on the gravel path which ended at the brightly painted hovel where loud women leaned from the windows.

Carleton eased into the corner of the cramped shanty. He wedged his aching back into the angle where two walls met at a seam so ragged that it failed to keep out the warm breeze. He slowly slid downward until he sat cross-legged in the corner like a scolded schoolboy. Pecos followed Carleton and spread his mangy body across the stranger's ankles. In a moment, the dog was snoring.

Something in the distant sounds of laughter from the whorehouse entered the writer's trail-numbed brain. The sound put down the tiniest roots like wild violets on a forest floor.

As he pulled out his pipe and lit a bowl of dry chewing tobacco, Carleton listened to the vague laughter of desperate men. The
writer laid his hand atop the saddlebag full of his memories and
he waited for the violets to bloom within his mind. When cheerful
hard boys' faces arrived in his head on a wave of sudden chills, he
pulled out his paper and licked the nub of a well chewed pencil.

Six months ago at the bawdy Tampa Bay Hotel, the American
Army's officers lounged within clouds of cigar smoke at the hotel's
Oriental Annex saloon. Twenty-five thousand troops camped far
from the hotel's luxuries in a tent city waiting to ship out for Cuba.
In the thick Florida humidity and wilting heat of the first week in
June, young soldiers far from home laughed manfully over rot-gut
whiskey at the suttler's tent under its sign, "Noah's Ark." The ban-
ner outside the canvass whorehouse proclaimed "Restaurant."

Outside in the night, the merry Spanish voices from the distant posada mingled with memories of Tampa. The writer closed
his eyes and listened. With Pecos asleep beside his bare feet, he
wondered how many of those Fifth Corps boys still alive in his fevered head were now dead from battle or from yellow fever. When
he sighed at the page under his pencil, the little dog cocked an ear
toward his new friend, who needed desperately the peace of green
mountains and tall trees that dropped their leaves on silent white
snow where rivers run without turning red.

Pinar del Río's night breeze warm and thick moved the dense
green canopy of ancient maple trees along a dirt road no wider
than George Fleming's wagon. Slanting shafts of white sun alter-
nated between long minutes of shadow robbing the Pennsylvania woods of their early afternoon colors. Bird songs and squirrel
chirps broke the steady rhythm of the two small draft horses puffing their way along the path.

"What made you go to mining school?" Esther asked. Her
brown eyes sparkled a little when she faced George so he kept his

face toward his team.

"Pa's stories, I suppose."

"Your people have worked the land for generations around Fairchance. No miners among them that I heard of."

"I know. But Pa dug a mine shaft once in the war. That made me interested in the science of it."

"Everyone knows your father was a war hero. But a miner? Never heard that one in my parents' store and I've known your folks as long as I've known you."

George did not look sideways. He could feel her looking at him in a sudden burst of sunshine between the tree tops.

"Well, Pa joined up in early '63. They moved him from the Fayette County regiment to the 304th New York before Chancellorsville. But after they got tore up real bad there by the Johnnies, Pa was transferred into the 48th Pennsylvania, which was mainly miners from Schuylkill County out east. They followed General Grant for two solid months in the spring of '64, smacking into Bobby Lee hard all the way to the doorstep of Richmond in the Petersburg trenches. The lines didn't move an inch for the next ten months. Pa lived in his dog tent or in a hole in the ground all summer just trading fire between us and the Rebs. Pa says the lines were so close that at night the boys would come out of their trenches and holes on both sides to meet in the middle to swap Yankee coffee for Rebel tobacco like a friendly camp meeting. That's where Pa learned to take a chew now and again."

"That's pretty," Esther said as the path widened and moved away from a grove of huge hickories toward the railroad tracks. In full daylight, beads of sweat ran down their faces.

Across two miles of flat sunny country, George encouraged the horses to pick up their pace toward Dunbar. They were almost half way there, having skirted Uniontown through the forest. Uniontown had a real bank which Fairchance did not have. Once

every week, Charles Slone went up to Uniontown to do his bank-
ing without kissing his only child before he headed north.

The horses worked themselves into a lather in the bright sunshine so George steered them back toward the cool green shade of
the mountains more to the east of the main road beside its double-
track spur of the Pennsylvania Railroad.

A warm breath of mountain air blew Esther's hair away from
her face and Samuel Carleton felt the same breeze on the back
of his sweating neck. It shattered the magic spell of following his
pencil through the thick trees old enough to have known Indian
moccasins on their young roots when they were saplings.

SEVEN

The warm, soft darkness of Tuesday night lay lightly upon Pinar del Río. The sky was clear and wide and there was no Moon. A dome of stars twinkled in the dry air above Rosa Montoya who sat outside the hovel of Manuel the old rebel. Her hair fell down her back. She balanced on a three-legged milking stool that had not been set beneath a cow since the Spanish Army years ago had confiscated the island's animals for beef. Illuminated by lanterns from a dozen shanties, the night air carried the sounds of laughing women in the posada at the far end of town. When a comfortable breeze carried the happy voices of men, Samuel Carleton lifted his face from a tree-covered Pennsylvania road and he recognized Alfonso's voice in the distance. Rosa listened to Manuel and Francisco through the open door and the window hacked in the wall behind her. On the dirt floor against the wall, María Teresa cradled her huge belly where she lay on her back upon a mattress stuffed with corn husks.

Carleton had perched an oil lantern on the window ledge so he could write. Its light glistened on the top of Rosa's head on the far side. As the priest and Manuel spoke Spanish in a whisper, the American sat on the floor by the doorway and he waited for his story to call him back. Pecos rested his head on Carleton's crossed ankles and perked his ears toward the sound of his master's voice at the table. The songs of insects in the cozy night and the muted Spanish at the table five paces away all blended into one warm and soothing buzz. It felt like a June afternoon in Pennsylvania woods. The American asked no questions of the writers' muse who sometimes comes without condition and who sometimes does not come no matter the seduction.

Samuel Carleton's pencil found the wagon where he had left it. Long drooping branches of bur oaks hid the wagon road. Instead of wide occasional corridors of sunlight, the path felt like evening although it was only 3:00 in the afternoon.

Impatient to get to Dunbar where the miners had been trapped nearby for nearly six hours, George had to rest the animals. He pulled up beside a stream clear and smooth as glass gurgling down a mountainside. He dropped the reins and the horses lapped vigorously. Climbing down from the seat, he carried a tin cup to the water, filled it, and handed it up to Esther. She drank and leaned over to return the empty cup to George who knelt, refilled it, and stood to pour it down his dry throat. In the gloom of the dense canopy of leaves, the sweat on his neck glistened gray when he tilted his head back. The girl watched the rise and fall of his Adam's apple.

"Well," he said as he took a seat beside her.

"Well," said Esther. "You were telling me about your father

digging a mine in Virginia."

"It was a mine shaft. All they got out of it was dirt and sore backs. The purpose was not to take out anything of value but to put something in the hole—explosives. They dug the shaft right under the Confederates to blow the Johnnies up."

George pulled hard on the reins to drive the team back from the creek toward the hidden wagon path. Pulling and twisting on the hard seat, he felt a sudden jab of pain in his back. But George Gordon did not own the spasm running up his spine.

Samuel Carleton dropped his pencil, blinked his eyes to return to the thatch-roof hovel, and he rubbed his sore back with both hands. He leaned away from the too hard corner beside the doorway. He looked up at the two men still sitting at the table. They spoke in hushed voices and the American could not follow their Spanish.

"The gringo is dying," Manuel said softly. He glanced down at the writer who did not raise his hollow face, eyes closed, as he massaged his spine with both hands. "I know the look, Padre." In a short story finished ten months before he sat in the corner of a hovel at Pinar del Río, Carleton had created the character called Swede and he had written that "In his eyes was the dying-swan look." Manuel recognized that look in the gringo's pale eyes.

Francisco nodded in the light of a lamp atop the table. The sigh from his soul left his frail body through his nostrils. The priest had removed his heavy cassock and he sat in campesino trousers and blouse which were too small for his long body. Manuel had given Francisco the clothing of his brother, two years dead in a jungle skirmish against Spaniards who had left his body to feed the vultures and the blue land crabs.

"Your sister has changed since I last saw her in the camp." Manuel spoke so softly that Francisco leaned forward to hear.

"Yes, Manolo, she has suffered much: her husband killed because of me; her son wounded again and given up for dead at Santiago last July."

"She was among the concentrados in our camp for my six months there." Manuel nodded gravely. "How long did the two of you stay in the camp after my escape?"

"They released both of us from that camp about a year ago. We were much trouble, I suppose." The priest smiled. "We had been there eighteen months. I don't think they wanted me to die on them. When I wouldn't leave without my sister, they sent both of us out."

Manuel refilled Francisco's cup, a jícara—the fist-size seed pod of the güira tree—and his own with warm white rum. Then he looked toward the open window where the Yanqui leaned over the paper in his lap.

"Señor Carleton, it would please you more rum?" Manuel had to pause and think between each English word. "I learned the English from selling my cohiba—tobacco—to the Yanquis for fifty years. And I lived in your New York City for a year with Martí, ten years ago."

"No más, gracias. I still have some." Carleton never looked up.

The old Cuban reached down and lifted a threadbare sack from the floor. Opening the sack, he leaned toward the writer.

"Take this, señor. It is *quina-quina*. Aguedita tree leaves for the fever. How do you say it, 'quinine'?"

The American reached for a pinch of dried oval leaves, put all but one of them in his pocket with the last crumbs of quinine pills, and he kept one out to chew slowly.

"Thank you, Don Manuel," the American said. He rested his writing hand, sat back into his corner, and closed his tired yellow eyes.

Manuel nodded and smiled toothlessly, then lowered his voice to a whisper toward Francisco. "The Spaniards killed the woman's husband? But you are *peninsulares.*"

"Yes. Rosa and I are Spanish-born. But I went with the people. Her husband never did. Rosa had to go with her husband. But in the end—at the very end—he did not give me up when the Spaniards came for me. So they killed him and they took Rosa. It did not matter that her son followed General Wyler and joined his Voluntarios to pillage the countryside. The Spaniards caught me and threw me and Rosa into the camp."

Manuel nodded thoughtfully. Lantern light shone wetly on his angular face with its white stubbled beard. He sipped his rum and lowered the seedpod cup to the table. He did not raise his eyes when he spoke after a long moment.

"Your sister spent much time on her back for you, Padre." The farmer's black eyes squinted down at his cup as if he were in physical pain. He waited for the priest to answer. María Teresa turned her dirty face from the wall toward Manuel.

"She brought us black beans and rice from the officers' kitchen," the priest said. "Without my Rosita, twenty men would have starved to death. God will have a special blessing for her."

"*¡Ojalá!,*" Manuel whispered as he crossed himself. "May it be so."

"Tomorrow we leave for the country." Francisco spoke firmly.

Samuel Carleton opened his eyes and looked up when the priest's unintelligible words made Rosa rise outside. When the writer leaned toward the window sill, he saw her stand and walk slowly into the darkness. The light on the ledge caught her white hands and the white soles of her bare feet as she walked along a pebbly path toward the dirt street. Carleton turned to watch the two men at the table who had not stopped talking.

Manuel looked squarely into the priest's face.

"Padre, you cannot trust anyone in this revolution. The hunger turns men's hearts to stone. Because I love you, I beg you not to go further. Please."

Samuel Carleton looked up at Manuel, whose Spanish sounded like a prayer.

The priest glanced over his shoulder and looked down at the wooden figure with seashell eyes on the floor at one side of the open doorway. Carleton watched from the other side of the hole in the clapboard wall.

"You follow Santería in your old age, my friend?" Francisco asked gently.

"Elegua guards my door against Spaniards and evil, Padre. It does no harm," the old man smiled.

Francisco turned his wasted face back toward Manuel. "I leave tomorrow with the sun," the priest said.

"Tomorrow," Manuel said with a peculiar sadness in his voice.

For an hour, the priest slept with his bearded face nestled in his arms folded on the table. Manuel at the table silently watched him sleep and moved only to reach for the bottle.

Carleton rested his pencil atop the new words which had surged out of his fingertips. He looked closely at the two men at the table who sat in silence with their jícaras between them. When the warm night breeze blew through the doorway which had neither hinges nor a door, he picked up his pencil. The dirt floor beneath his sore spine felt hard as a buckboard seat.

"So your father learned to chew tobacco and spit and dig mines in the war?"

"And more, I suppose," George smiled and gave the horses a flick of the reins across their wet backs. "Petersburg was 20 miles south of the Rebel capital. The federals came up with a plan to dig a mine shaft from General Burnside's position all the way to the Rebel line, plant explosives underground, and blow a hole in the Rebel works. Pa says the whole 48th regiment—400 men—started digging the shaft. He was one of the few boys who had never been inside a mine."

George felt the girl shiver at the thought. He drove the weary team harder to ignore the feeling of Esther's shoulder touching his. The girl rode with her hands on her knees. Her skirt touched her shoes. George glanced at her beautiful hands with their long fine fingers like a surgeon or a musician.

"Pa dug into that Virginia hillside for a whole month. The Johnnies had lookouts and snipers in the trees on their high ground. So the federals worked at night. To keep the Rebs from knowing what the Yankees were up to, they carried away tons of earth by daylight in cracker barrels reinforced with hickory and iron hoops from army pork barrels."

"Pork barrels?"

"That's what Pa and the boys lived on for three years. 'Fat back' and hard crackers called hardtack which they called worm castles 'cause of all the bugs in them."

"Oh."

"They finished the mine on July 23. It went 511 feet into the hillside. General Meade approved four tons of gunpowder for the underground magazine."

"Your Pa and the others carried 8,000 pounds of gunpowder into a mine?"

"Yes." George looked sideways at Esther, whose eyes glistened in the first burst of sunlight to penetrate the forest canopy in an hour. "My father and the others were like that when they were my age. Most were even younger."

"Did they blow up the Rebels?"

"Yes, at dawn on July 30. Blew a crater in the Rebel line 30 feet deep, 60 feet wide, and 170 feet long. Then Burnside sent Pa and four whole divisions up to the crater and the hole in the Rebel fortifications."

"Did we win, George?"

"Not that day. The Rebs drove us out by the afternoon. Pa said we lost 3,800 men. It was a real slaughter."

"And a slaughter made you become a mine engineer?"

"Not exactly." George smiled straight ahead.

"What then?"

"Trying to be as good a man as Pa." He swallowed hard. "I suppose." He drove the team to pick up their pie-plate size hooves. "Come now," he shouted to the horses working heads down, uphill.

By 5:00 o'clock the wagon approached the one-horse hamlet of Ferguson. Thirteen hundred feet above sea level, the mountains on their right side looked too steep and green to climb even on foot. So when three filthy, bearded men with shotguns slid down the hillside ten feet in front of the wagon, George pulled his long reins hard to stop the horses.

Esther Slone screamed.

A woman's scream shattered the stillness. For a blurry instant, Samuel Carleton did not know if the scream was in his pencil or in his ears. He recognized the second scream.

The writer stood as Rosa's voice scoured a deep trench through his mind. Manuel was standing beside the table by the time Francisco could command each of his bones to move in unison to propel his weary body from the hard chair. All three men stood in the doorway and squinted into the thickly black Cuban midnight. They ignored the girl on the dirt floor who rolled over heavily and pulled herself up by her hands climbing the table legs.

Through distant shadows illuminated by stars and lantern light streaming from hovels beside the road, Rosa Montoya ran toward the rebel's shack. Three shadows were running behind her.

Rosa stumbled toward the shanty. She tripped and fell headlong into Carleton. Not until he knelt to hold her shaking body did he realize that she was naked from the waist up. He could feel her arms folded tightly across her breasts. As her brother and Manuel looked into the dark street, Carleton peeled off his filthy, sweat-crusted shirt and draped it gently over her bare shoulders. Three young men breathing hard stopped running twenty paces in front of the open doorway where lantern light gilded the gravel path in flickering yellow. One of the panting men held Rosa's shirt.

"We want the *criolla*," another of the men shouted in Castilian Spanish. Carleton could not make out his words, but he recognized the lisping accent of Spain. "We go home to Spain next week," the Spaniard explained with remarkable courtesy, "so we need the *criolla* now."

"She is not *criolla*," Francisco said. His peasant clothing bore no signs of the priesthood nor of his war against these Spaniards. "She is not Cuban-born Spanish. She is Toledo-born—and she is my sister. Go back to the whorehouse where you belong."

The three men stood side by side calmly facing the priest, the bare-chested American, and Manuel. The strangers wore the tattered fatigues of conscripted Spanish regulars. Only the Spaniard who spoke had removed his straw hat in strained courtesy.

"Sister or no, we have had our share of Cuban *putas*. Now, we want a white one. Then we leave for home." Lantern light glistened on the soldier's perfect, white teeth. He kept his smile after he was suddenly airborne, rising toward the star filled sky.

Behind Manuel, María Teresa screamed.

Alfonso had thrown his whole body into the backs of the three Spaniards. The two quiet ones crumbled to the dirt path. One fell hard and lay motionless with his head cocked oddly to one side. The second rocked on his back while holding one of his legs cradled in his belly. The third regular soared half a body length into the peaceful nighttime air before slamming down on the warm ground. He lay stunned for an instant before he struggled to his feet. He steadied himself while Alfonso stood.

The unsteady Spaniard pulled an old, black-powder pistol

from his belt, eared back the hammer, and aimed the cap and ball revolver at Alfonso who threw himself at the armed Spaniard a second time. The instant Alfonso made contact, the weapon discharged. Its lead ball spun into the night toward Carleton. The American felt a tiny shockwave touch his cheek as the bullet's wake blew past his ear before the ball melted in the side of the window sill just behind his head. When Carleton ducked out of the bullet's path, the round was already imbedded in the clapboard siding.

Alfonso clawed the Spanish regular with his left hand and they rolled on the ground together. They cursed in Spanish and gouged at each other's eyes. Francisco steadied the woman wrapped in the American's shirt and shoved her toward María who stood terrified in the shanty doorway. Manuel and Carleton rushed to Alfonso. As they grabbed the Spaniard who had fired the shot, one of the two soldiers who had not moved since hitting the ground climbed to his feet. He pulled Carleton to the ground. Manuel stepped over Alfonso and reached for the arms of the man wrestling the American. When they rolled so the Yanqui was on top, Manuel began kicking at the head of the man on the ground. Barefoot, the Cuban stomped the Spaniard with the side of his instep until the man's eyeballs rolled back into his head and his arms dropped away from the American's neck. Samuel Carleton rolled off and lay gasping for wind.

Manuel took two quick steps toward Alfonso whose one good hand pounded the Spaniard's head. Blood ran from the soldier's ears. Manuel grabbed the boy's waist and pulled him off the regular's limp body. The Spanish soldier's face was shattered and distorted from Alfonso's good fist and from the terrible blows by the bone-hard stump of his right forearm. Starlight illuminated a smooth, broken face no older than Alfonso's. Manuel touched the Spaniard's throat and then stood beside the breathless Alfonso.

"At least you did not kill him, boy." Manuel glanced at the two other bloodied regulars who lay close to Carleton who had not yet risen from the ground. "Their friends will come for them soon." The rebel reached down and lifted Rosa's peasant shirt from the hand of one of the unconscious men. He tossed the shirt to the younger woman who held Rosa in her arms. "Stay inside."

The girl steadied Rosa and guided her toward the shack. Rosa clutched tightly at Carleton's shirt around her shoulders.

Alfonso stood and breathed hard. When he kicked the side of one of the motionless regulars, Manuel spun him with his hands.

"Enough for one night." Manuel looked hard into Alfonso's bloodied face. "Those men wear Spanish buttons just like you did. Go inside. We shall have trouble plenty now. I must find a horse so we can leave quickly."

Alfonso glared at Manuel and then pushed past him toward the one-room house. He paused when he reached Carleton. The American stood between Alfonso and the dirt-floor hovel. But he stood bent over and his hands rested on each knee. His breath came fast and deep with a sickening, rasping sound as he exhaled. Like old Henry so long ago, "the flesh over his heart seemed very thin." Carleton did not look up but he saw Alfonso's sandals close beside him. So he turned his face sideways to look into the wild, bloodied face of Rosa Montoya's son.

"Words on paper do not sting like fists and bullets, do they, Gringo?"

Alfonso staggered inside, leaving the American hunched over and breathless. Under brilliant stars, Manuel picked up the feet of each Spaniard and dragged the bodies one at a time 25 yards into a dense stand of algarrobo trees whose leaves had closed for the night. Two of the bodies moaned as their backs carved a shallow path in the rock-strewn dirt street. The last soldier had made no sound since Alfonso had dropped him and his head wobbled from side to side while Manuel pulled and grunted. Manuel mumbled something about feeding the land crabs. Coughing blood onto his own knees, the shirtless gringo could neither hear nor understand. In half an hour he was back in his hard saddle, riding into darkness.

EIGHT

THREE HOURS BEFORE DAYBREAK, SAMUEL CARLETON BESIDE Rosa felt Francisco gently awaken the woman. Brother and sister stepped quietly on bare feet into the Tuesday night darkness of their camp in Viñales Valley.

Carleton slept until Rosa returned warm and sleepy.

"Where did you go," he whispered.

"Paco and I had to find the new Moon," she said. "It requires two witnesses. We did it for our mother when we were children."

"What?" the American said no louder than a breath.

"Sleep, Perdido," she said but the writer did not hear her. He was weary to the bone and slept heavily without dreams for another hour.

Before daybreak Wednesday, Manuel led the way further into

the green valley. They had walked their horses on loose reins out of Pinar del Río. No one had come down the lane to search for the three missing soldiers, not even the *putas* who had taken their Spanish money by the hour.

The horses, now six, were skin and bone, barefoot and sway-backed. Down the flanks of the old Cuban's horse, hungry flies on raw pink flesh formed the perfect outline of a plow harness. The animals dragged their cracked hooves westward across the green grass of the great plain, which was surrounded by smoothly green mountains. Pecos yelped cheerfully at their heels. By noon the riders were well into the valley's heart, 25 miles west of Pinar del Río.

Horses and riders sweated freely in the warm December air. The animals walked with their heads close to the ground, with the Sierra de los Órganos mountains on the western horizon and the green Sierra de Viñales range toward the north. Carleton rode with his chin touching his breast and he moved only his eyes from side to side to study the land close to the trail.

Rich red soil was plowed by mules, horses, or oxen too thin for Spaniards to eat and fields in second plantings were brilliantly green with sugar cane, tobacco, and rice. Tall encina oaks dotted the landscape. Flamboyan trees held their buds tightly, awaiting their March bloom. The American squinted at the strange limestone hills coming closer with each weary step of the horses. These mogotes reminded the writer of a scene from a picture book about Hawaii. He made a mental note on the back of his eyelids that "the land was very empty; one could easily imagine that Cuba was a simple vast solitude."

When the large, white tropical sun hovered motionless in the southern sky at noon, Manuel pulled his mount to a stop. Dropping the reins, he allowed his horse to drink from a small clean creek that cut through the valley. The other riders pulled rein beside him and the horses drank together. Manuel spoke to the priest, dismounted, and the others followed. When Alfonso walked away, Carleton coughed around his cigarette butt as he helped María down.

"This stream leads to Los Portales River," Francisco translated for Carleton and turned from the American toward Manuel. "We shall find the prisoners near there."

Manuel shrugged and sat down hard on the soft earth. He kept his reins in his hand. He leaned full backward until he lay looking up at soft white clouds riding easily in the perfectly blue sky. The rebel lay with a belly palm tree eclipsing the sun and a cool shadow crossing his face. While Manuel rested, the others knelt beside their horses and drank from the creek. Everyone but Alfonso cupped hands to drink. On his knees, the boy lowered his whole bruised face into the cool water, drinking like the horses lapping on either side of him.

The American tied his mount's reins to a young palm and sat near Manuel. Pecos rolled into a furry ball beside the old man and went quickly to sleep. Carleton found the sight of the old Cuban rebel to be disquieting. With the barrigona palm shielding his face, the grizzled Cuban on his back looked with his up-turned face at the fine sky. Samuel Carleton suddenly felt that he was again in the company of freshly dead men on a battlefield. Watching Manuel, Carleton could not turn his gaze away. He had imagined once a war-dead man before he had seen his first real, war-killed boy. The words parading through his mind had already been used, so they could not be used again: "The wind raised the tawny beard. It moved as if a hand were stroking it. He vaguely desired to walk around and around the body and stare." Now sitting cross-legged, the American felt a passing shudder of malarial chills. The momentary seizure broke the spell of the haunting picture of Manuel, dead.

Still wearing campesino garb, Francisco sat beside Manuel.

Rosa stood briefly, looked carefully at her brother and the Yanqui, and then sat beside Carleton. She touched his knee with her hand. Looking up, she watched her son sit on the sunny side of Manuel's shade tree. The one-handed boy leaned his head against the tree trunk, closed his eyes, and seemed to savor the heat of the sun on his tanned cheeks and two blackening eyes. Last night's bruises under his eyes glistened purple and raw. María Teresa reclined beneath her belly close to Alfonso. No words passed between them.

Carleton saw something hovering at the corner of his eye. He looked toward the creek and saw a brilliantly yellow sulphur butterfly fluttering near the horses. That it was out of season for butterflies did not bother the creature. The writer squinted and watched the sulphur closely. He raised his arm toward it as if expecting it to perch on his finger like some trained parakeet. It did not. It turned on the soft breeze until the American could see its full wingspan. Carleton's yellow eyes smiled at the broad yellow wings.

Rosa Montoya squeezed Carleton's knee when she saw the momentary light extinguish in his eyes as he lowered his face to rest. He gently touched her face before folding his hands in his lap, closing his eyes, and lowering his chin to his chest. As the American nodded off, Rosa glanced across the sparse grass which separated her from Francisco.

The six travelers slept for a full hour with warm sunshine soothing their trail-worn bodies. Rosa's head found the American's dust crusted lap and she dozed with his hand shielding her eyes as the sun moved across her face.

A sudden stab at his spine by yellow fever nudged Carleton from the edge of full sleep. When he opened his eyes he did not look down at the woman. He could feel her soft face in the cup of his hand. He kept looking toward his horse and the saddlebag tied to his battered cavalry saddle. The worn leather sack had four square corners matching the bound paper within. Comforted by his work safely at hand, he closed his eyes and waited for the next wave of pain and chills.

The nickering of the horses and their hooves pawing at the ground awoke Alfonso first and Manuel last.

Carleton pushed sleeping Rosa up into a sitting position so he could stand. Alfonso and Francisco were already standing.

Five thin men in linen rags and straw hats approached on foot. Each carried a sidearm tucked behind his rope belt. They stopped beside the horses at the creek bank and stroked their thin, mouse colored necks with admiration.

"These are fine horses, boy," one of the strangers said to Alfonso. "We shall borrow them."

Alfonso reached with his left hand into his pocket. The eyes of the strangers watched him closely.

"Look here," Alfonso said. He opened his hand filled with brass buttons. "I am an officer."

"We were officers, too," a second Spaniard said through a scraggly beard. One of his eyes was covered with a crude patch made from the sole of a boot. "We took leave of Spain when our country abandoned us to the Yanquis at Santiago." He looked quickly at Carleton. There was no trace of violence in the man's Spanish. "We shall take your horses now, boy. We shall leave the women since one is too old and the other is already full, caguama," he laughed with his single eye creased and twinkling. He executed a too-deep bow toward Rosa. "At your feet, señora," he said as courtly as a filthy, hungry deserter could. María Teresa held her belly, feeling like the fat turtle the Spaniard had called her in Cuban Spanish.

"You can't take the horses from me," Alfonso protested. He raised his stump of a right arm. "General Calixto García himself cut off this hand."

"You are lucky, boy," the one-eyed man smiled. "At least the old rebel did not cut off your feet." With a wink of his good eye, he threw his leg over one of the horses and gathered the reins. The four other deserters followed. The last man picked up the rope reins of the sixth riderless animal.

"Please," the American said in halting Spanish. "My bag." He stepped toward his mount.

The man in the saddle pushed the American away with his bare foot.

"There is nothing of value in the bag. I beg you."

Something in Carleton's voice made the rider lean backward, untie the saddlebag and look inside. He laughed out loud when he pulled out the stack of singed paper. He studied it for an instant, looked at his leader, and then tossed the paper toward Carleton's feet.

"*Para el culo*," the rider laughed.

As the five riders reined their horses back toward the path which ends at Pinar del Río, Samuel Carleton picked up his little paper bundle bound by dirty string. Rosa touched his shoulder and then his stubbled cheek. The softness in her beautiful eyes became stone when she turned to face her brother.

"Now, Paco, we walk home. We are finished." Rosa looked so hard into the priest's sun-burned face that he blinked and turned away.

Francisco looked at Manuel, whose eyes were still half asleep under mid-afternoon sunshine.

"We walk to the camp, Manuel." Francisco waited for the rebel's nod.

Manuel looked exhausted. Bone-deep sadness welled up into his black eyes.

"Padre, it is finished as the woman says. Already we are two full days on foot from my village. We must start back now."

"No."

"Paco," Rosa pleaded.

"No. You go with Manuel. I go that way." The priest pointed toward the west. Without another word, he gathered his straw hat and carried it toward the western mountains.

"What does it mean," the American asked Alfonso, *"para el culo"*?

"To wipe your ass," the boy grinned broadly.

They stood beside the creek and watched Francisco make his way down a narrow path which crossed the great valley. Alfonso looked into his mother's eyes, said nothing, and followed his uncle. María waddled barefoot behind him. Manuel mumbled in Spanish.

"Now you are happy, Perdido?" Rosa said through clenched perfect teeth.

"Happy?" he asked with no happiness to be felt anywhere in his cells and none to be seen between the valley's blue horizons. "About what, Rosa?"

"You encouraged Paco to come here so you could feed your little bloody stories. But you bring no food for him, for us, or even for yourself. Now my brother walks under the hot sun with nothing in his belly except fever. He fights for a country you do not love and for people you do not respect."

"Francisco made his own decision."

The woman sweated heavily but her brown eyes were narrow and cold as ice.

"He would not have come alone. He will die out here. Look at him."

"Without me, your brother would still be here, walking toward the prison camp he believes is out there."

"No, Perdido."

"Rosa," Carleton pleaded. "War is a spirit. War provides for those that it loves. It provides sometimes death and sometimes a singular and incredible safety."

"Sometimes, you talk like still you are writing your little war book."

When the American and the woman walked westward with the sun painfully in their faces, Rosa had to steady the writer's body with her own.

By dusk Wednesday, Rosa no longer had the strength to support Carleton so she walked beside Francisco. The priest in peasant clothing kept the lead as they walked deeper into Viñales Valley. Now Manuel bore half of the writer's weight as they stumbled arm-in-arm along a narrow trail. The path had been beaten down to hard mud and gravel by farmers and their oxen. The Spaniards brought the oxen to Cuba centuries ago, calling them "*zebus*." The American thought they were so thin that the tics could get a square meal off them only by bleeding each other. The two men lingered one hundred yards behind Alfonso and María Teresa, who walked sullenly behind Rosa and Francisco. The defeated soldier had said nothing since losing their horses to his own rough kind.

With nightfall, Rosa and Francisco rested shoulder to shoulder on soft moist grass beside the trail while they waited for the others to catch up. A chilly breeze blew across the valley floor and picked up speed as narrow breaches in the towering mogotes compressed the night air into a biting wind.

"We can make a fire here," Manuel said casually. He was still breathing hard after dropping Samuel Carleton's weight close to Rosa. "We are in my country now. We do not have to hide here. Before we started, I sent word ahead that we were coming."

With half-open eyes, the American watched the rebel build a fire with twigs, dry grass, and Spanish matches. When the fire crackled hot and comfortable, the six exhausted marchers huddled close to it. Still living wood from nearby brambles sent white smoke into a clear dark sky. Stars twinkled undiminished by a sliver of a new Moon.

"They took our food with the horses," Alfonso complained.

Manuel looked across his fire toward the boy's hard and dirty face. The purple skin under Alfonso's eyes had blackened and fire light glistened on his badly bruised cheek. The old rebel's eyes focused intently upon the boy.

"One night of hunger will do you good," Manuel smiled.

Alfonso grunted his disgust and he stood. When María struggled to her feet, the boy pushed her back gently and he wandered alone into the darkness.

"Alfonso," Rosa called from beside Francisco. Her son did not answer.

"The boy will be all right," Manuel said. "Bring us back a fat *jutía*," he shouted toward Alfonso's back.

"Hutia?" Carleton asked.

"Delicious, big sweet rats," the old man grinned.

Francisco put his arm around his sister's shoulders. She was cold even with the fire burning brightly and she tucked her hands under her armpits to keep them warm. When Samuel Carleton started to kneel beside Rosa, she looked away, so the American inched closer to the fire and María Teresa sat close beside him. Perspiration ran down his face, not from the ordeal of walking ten miles but from a wave of fever.

The smoke from Manuel's blazing fire of dead and live wood swirled deep into Samuel Carleton's mind. María Teresa lay beside him on his right and ragamuffin Pecos slept soundly against his left thigh. With smoke burning his yellow eyes, he pulled out his dwindling pile of blank paper and he chewed a new point on a fresh pencil. He blinked to clear the sting of smoke from his eyes so he could focus upon the menacing void of an empty sheet of paper. His dry eyeballs were hot with fever and smoke, but the blurry-eyed pain pulled him where he needed to go.

"I can smell the mine smoke, now," George said.

Esther said nothing. Her wide eyes saw only three dirty men in bib overalls and they carried shotguns aimed up at her sweating face.

"What you children doing on our mountain?" Only one eye was open with the other squinting over his raised weapon. Each of the other two, much younger men had only one eye open.

"Going up to Hill Farm to help get the trapped miners out of the pit that blew up this morning."

"You ain't Hochstetlers?" the squinty man asked, three steps in front of his bearded associates. "This here is Miller country where strangers ain't welcome."

"They're moonshiners," Esther said breathlessly, grabbing George by his right arm with both hands. "Like my father said."

"My name's Fleming," George said firmly. "We don't carry any guns, just supplies for the men trapped up at Hill Farm Coke."

"And your girl there?" asked the gunman doing the talking.

"She's not my girl." George did not glance sideways. "We're from down in Fairchance. Her people are Charles Slone."

"The peddler kike at Golden's mercantile store on East Church Street?" He looked up at Esther.

"That's my father," Esther said. She was angry now. She released George's arm and glared at the man who stood close to the horses.

"Look in the back for yourself," George said. "We're taking blankets and supplies to the mine. I'm a mining engineer."

The man in front lowered his weapon. Both of his pale eyes were open like beacons inside his wild beard and long greasy hair. He used his shotgun to point toward the rear of the wagon. One of the other men walked toward the back. He did not lower his shotgun and kept his gray eye and bearded cheek on its rough wooden stock as he shuffled barefoot around the prisoners. At the back of the wagon, he used his blued shotgun barrel to lift blankets and roll around cans of food.

"T'ain't nothin' but groceries back here."

"Leave the wagon alone, Harley," the man said, lowering his shotgun until its stock caught his armpit and the barrel pointed down at the brown clay path. "Her Pa gives our girls new shoes every September for school when they can go and he don't take a dime. Let them be, boy."

"But, Pa, blankets and coffee and food for the taking."

"Step over here now," said the man beside the horses. The one called Harley did as he was told.

"Tell your pa," the older man said, "that Millers pay their way when we have it."

"My father knows that," Esther said as if it were true.

"Yes'm," the older man slurred since his tongue touched only gums.

"You children be careful now. There's Hochstetler and Pritts folk out here even though this mountain is our'n. Go on now."

George pointed his team toward a fork in the path which led north toward Hill Farm after the road crossed a double railroad track. Looking over his shoulder, he saw the three men absorbed by a stand of massive-trunked white walnut trees. He let out a long breath.

"You did well, Esther."

"Both of us have strong-willed fathers," she said with their shoulders touching as they left the forest behind them. They crossed the railroad's rusty tracks north of Ferguson and just south of Pechin and Dunbar.

In the riptide of relief which follows terror, the girl accepted that she could want this strong young man but could never have him; this, as old Henry's son knew suddenly that he could have this strange young girl but did not need to.

"I can smell the fire real strong now from the mine," George said with an oddly thick, dry throat.

"Me, too."

Less than a mile south of Hill Farm, the early evening smelled of the smokey sweet scent of burning soft coal which brings up warm memories of hearth and home safe and cozy when fresh white snow is dusted black with chimney soot. But this Monday evening, June 16, it smelled like death.

"It's been eight hours," Esther said gently.

"Yes," George said as his weary team plodded heavy-footed uphill past arch-topped brick coke ovens growing out of a steep hillside. The Dunbar Furnace Company's ovens glowed blood red beside the dirt road which ended at the Hill Farm Mine and Coke Works and its deadly hole in the Pennsylvania hills.

When the smoke in his eyes smelled of thick burning branches of a ceibon tree toppled from a nearby mogote instead of a suffocating coal fire and explosive gas, Samuel Carleton blinked and looked up. His mind traveled slowly back across eight years to Pecos sleeping warm against his leg.

Alfonso had been gone for nearly two hours.

Manuel stood first when ten mounted men came slowly out of the darkness. The American's wide eyes glowed yellow when his feverish mind registered men with machetes in their rope belts. Two of them carried Spanish-issue Mauser rifles.

"These are mine," Manuel said in the fire light. When the two lead riders dismounted, Manuel greeted them in a three-way bear hug.

"We have food, Manolo," one of them said. He tossed a sack to Manuel.

Eight other men in peasant rags dismounted and stayed close to their thin, tic-covered horses. The two leading riders sat beside the fire at each arm of Manuel. To Samuel Carleton, they looked like all Cuban rebels: "brown bodies sticking out of a collection of rags." He kept this thought between himself and the pen that had written it.

"So this is Father Francisco?" one of the Cubans asked. The priest nodded and the stranger studied him closely. "I remember you from the camps, Padre. You look older now." The priest smiled wearily. "And Señora Montoya, I remember you, too." The Cuban cavalryman did not smile. "You brought us beans and clean water so we would not die from hunger." The woman looked down and said nothing.

"These are the last and the best of my men," Manuel said to the priest. "I have ridden with them for twenty years. They are proud insurrectos and good soldiers." Manuel watched the priest's eyes narrow and his face harden beside the fading fire. "We killed only armed Spanish soldiers, Padre." When Manuel looked at the veteran rebel by his side, the new man smiled with a face full of teeth as brown as his face. He caressed the long blade in his belt.

"Yes," Francisco said, turning toward the rebel at the side of Manuel. "We are looking for a camp of insurrectos still held by the Spanish in this province. I was told in La Habana that it was in the valley. Do you know of such a place?"

"Yes, Padre. Not more than fifteen miles from here. Maybe fifty Cuban prisoners and a dozen Spaniards. But those Spaniards have more guns and rice than honor. Our people are sick and very weak."

"I told you they were there," Francisco said, looking first at Rosa and then at Manuel.

"We will attack them, now that you are back to lead us," the rebel leader said to Manuel.

Manuel looked down at the fire and nodded.

"Did you see anyone on the trail?" Rosa spoke for the first time to the strangers. "My son left us hours ago."

"Your son?" one of the rebels asked. "We saw no one for the last three hours, since sunset, señora."

"Tomorrow the prison compound." Francisco pulled his arm from his sister's shoulders. He spoke to Manuel whose ten sweaty comrades listened intently. "We shall approach the camp, demand its surrender, and attack if the regulars refuse to release their Cuban prisoners."

"Demand surrender?" one of the insurrectos asked respectfully.

"Of course," the priest said. "Perhaps they do not know that the armistice was signed in Paris four days ago."

"It was signed by the Spaniards and the Yanquis?" the rebel asked beside Manuel.

"Yes," Francisco answered. "December 10."

"In France?" the unnamed rebel repeated with a chuckle. "Some Spaniards in Cuba have not heard of this treaty in France. We shall have to educate them."

A murmur rose from the eight rebels tending the ten horses at the edge of the darkness where the comforting fire lost its power to push back the Cuban night.

Carleton struggled to navigate the dangerous footing between delirium and consciousness. He shivered. When he tried to speak, only air puffed past his lips. The tattered men on either side of Manuel watched Carleton's face closely while fire light glistened on his sweating white forehead and in the yellow of his eyes. Francisco's voice sounded far away to the American.

"We cannot wait for the Spaniards to leave for La Habana," said the priest's distant voice. "They might not know the treaty has been signed. They might not believe it if they were told by General Toral himself. This may be our last chance to fight for our own people and our own country—before the Americans take over everything." The priest looked at Carleton's thin wet face when he spoke in English. "Your people do not much care for our people."

"Not since San Juan Hill at Santiago." Carleton looked uncomfortable. "I have to tell you that the Cubans took no real part in that dangerous assault." He looked at Francisco's narrowed eyes. "It was the Americans alone who stormed those positions. And it was American blood that was poured out in the green fields."

"We fought Spaniards 400 years before you came to save us, Gringo."

"I'm sorry, Manuel. I only know how the Americans feel about their Cuban comrades on a battlefield," he looked squarely at Manuel. "An American could do the fighting while the Cuban back of the firing line stole his blanket roll and his coat, and maybe his hat."

"It's time we ate and rested," Manuel said without cheer.

Manuel reached into his new sack of provisions. Carleton waited for his legs to steady under him and then walked into the darkness. He kept his distance from the new rebels busy building another fire to cook their own field rations.

Within a dense stand of belly palms, the American stood near the well-trod trail. In the calm dry air, he could smell his own ammonia striking the dry earth. One hand kept his balance against a thin palm. His other hand buttoned his trousers.

His heart skipped a beat when he heard the brush crackling ten yards away. He squinted in the darkness. A round shadow pushed into the brambles. Carleton recognized María's quick breath and her faint groan as she squatted in dark brambles which exhaled a faintly tropical sweetness into the night air.

Samuel Carleton felt suddenly faint. He gripped tightly the sapling no thicker than his own leg. He swayed against the tree when he heard the girl's water flowing fast and hard upon the ground. But inside his fever tormented mind, the distant shadow was no longer María Teresa and her unborn child.

Behind his closed eyes in the dark wilderness, he thought of Maggie who "blossomed in a mud puddle," a street urchin created by his pen five years ago. When no publisher would buy the story he printed it himself, calling the author Johnston Smith instead of his real name. He pawned his share of his dead mother's estate to his brother for $1,000 to raise the money for printing the story. The little book was a flop. The writer had given Maggie a sordid life and he had denied her a peaceful death surrounded by friends who loved her. Listening to the girl straining in the dark, Samuel Carleton heard Maggie's imaginary voice grieving for her bitter world where "souls did not insist upon being able to smile."

"Maggie?" Carleton whispered.

He heard a voice inside his head which sounded familiar. He shuddered to recognize his dead father's voice, the preacher's voice—the voice of the man who hated all novels for being "trashy literature" and "nauseous descriptions of lawless passion" and his father hated novelists. The dead father had urged "total abstinence from novel reading henceforth and forever." His living son, Maggie's creator, could not shake the voice roaring through his brain. "Under the trees of her dream-gardens," said his father's dead voice, "there had always walked a lover."

The writer embracing a tree remembered Pete who had taken Maggie with lies of love. When Pete abandoned Maggie full of his child, she slipped quietly into the river where the lights from a factory sparkled yellow on the killing stream.

"Maggie," the frail man whimpered. A wave of guilt and pain swept through him. How could he hate Pete so? He made Pete. It was Carleton's own pen which sometimes writes without him which forced Pete on top of Maggie. But it was the writer who killed her, not Pete.

Hot tears ran down Carleton's sunken face. He could hardly open his eyes.

"Maggie!" he cried as he staggered toward María Teresa standing now. "Forgive me. I meant no harm."

María Teresa shrieked. Cradling her belly with both arms, she ran in the darkness toward the distant camp fire.

As Samuel Carleton opened his eyes and wiped his face on his filthy sleeve, he heard footsteps behind him as he looked up through the trees toward cold stars. Like a sailor squinting through his brass sextant toward a hole in the clouds, he tried to conjure where he might be in time and space and dense green thickets. A chill crept up Carleton's back and his spinal pain made him suck in his shoulders and he leaned forward. He felt a firm hand upon his shoulder. He saw Manuel.

"You are sick with the fever," the Cuban said. "It is getting worse."

Carleton nodded. "Yes," he coughed. "With these fevers comes a great listlessness so that men are almost content to die, if death requires no exertion." He looked into the old man's face illuminated faintly by the stars bright overhead. "What is to become of me, Manuel?"

The Cuban looked carefully into the American's sweating face.

"Let us see," Manuel said with careful English. Digging into his pockets, he pulled out a clenched fist. He knelt on the dry tinder of dead leaves. Reaching up, he pulled the American down beside him. Manuel looked up and pointed to a single ceiba tree nearly six-feet thick. Its small white blossoms looked like the stars overhead.

"The tree is sacred," the Cuban said.

With his eyes fully adjusted to the nighttime star glow, Carleton watched the Cuban open his fist and put down seashells like the eyes of the idol at his doorpost.

Manuel laid out eighteen small cowrie shells. They had been filed flat on one side and each sat with its open cleft pointing toward the thousand stars overhead. The Cuban took two of the shells and set them apart from the others.

"These two are the *edele*," Manuel said. Beside the group of sixteen shells, he laid a small black stone and a shred of egg shell, upon which he laid a tiny bone.

Manuel reached for Carleton's sweating hands. He put the fragment of egg shell into one hand and the black stone into the other. Carleton breathed hard and squinted at his open palms. Then Manuel took the tokens from the American's hands. Cupping them in both of his hard brown hands, Manuel shook them and then made two fists under the writer's chin.

"Pick one hand," the Cuban said.

Carleton tapped the Cuban's left hand and the black stone fell to the earth within the circle of sixteen shells, whose open mouths gaped toward the flickering stars.

The old man's face hardened. He picked up his shells and grimly drove them into the deep pocket of his baggy trousers. When he stood, Carleton placed both hands on the ground and pushed himself upward to stand facing Manuel.

"What did you see?" Carleton asked.

The old rebel handed the American a small clay flask with a cork stopper.

"Aguardiente," Manuel said. "New rum. It will give you strength."

"But what did you see?"

"Nothing, Gringo. Today, the *ordun* do not speak to me. It happens."

Carleton took a gulp of the liquid from the flask. It went down his throat like fire. He shivered and gasped on the powerful alcohol made from Cuban sugar cane.

"Is this for the fever?" Carleton asked, handing the pottery jug to Manuel.

"It is not for fever, Gringo." There was a strange tone in the rebel's voice. "Why does the woman call you Perdido, 'the lost one'?"

"Rosa thinks it fits me." Carleton tried to smile. Only a cough rattled from his jaundiced yellow face.

"The writing on your papers, this helps you not be lost?"

"Once it did," the American sighed in the darkness.

"When the sun comes up tomorrow, Perdido, it might not matter." Manuel grinned when he took a deep swig of the strong drink. He wiped his mouth with the back of his unwashed hand.

Samuel Carleton stood as straight as his spinal pain would allow. He licked his lips which tasted of sweat and fermented sugar cane. His watery eyes looked into the old man's face and he took the flask from the Cuban's hard hand. The writer believed much but knew little. What he did know was this: All that a writer believes or knows or accepts on faith does no work in the world until it is cast in ink on paper. Then it becomes scripture even if no one reads it.

"I must write tonight if we are to fight Spaniards tomorrow."

"See, Gringo? The medicine already it works."

After another swallow, Carleton and Manuel walked toward where the others waited. The Cuban squinted in the darkness and paused with his bare foot just above the ground. He bent over and picked up a five-foot long snake, black and white. Gripping its body well behind the head, the snake spread its cobralike hood and hissed. Manuel pushed the animal toward Carleton's wide eyes. The American stumbled backward, his flight arrested by a tree trunk.

"Only a jubito magdalena," Manuel said, laughing, as he tossed the racer snake into the bush.

The two leaders of Manuel's men and Francisco, Rosa and María Teresa roasted round sizzling lumps of meat on sticks over three good fires. Manuel joined them. The rest of Manuel's skin-

and-bone cavalry did the same ten paces away. To Samuel Carleton, the night smelled better than Delmonico's at the corner of Fifth Avenue and 26th Street where Richard Harding Davis had his own table in New York City. Carleton studied the steaming gutted corpses of fat, ten-pound hutias. Smouldering black twigs protruded from their tiny rat mouths. When Rosa pointed one of them at the American, he realized that she held one in each hand. Carleton took the cool end of the stick, put the meat under his nose and inhaled deeply. As he sat on the ground, he had to wipe a trickle of drool from the corner of his mouth warm with rum. He licked his lips and his eyes closed as he blew on the hot meat till he could take a bite. Carleton heard Manuel's voice close to the crackling fire.

"Now, Perdido, you know what is the hunger."

Samuel Carleton did not answer. His mouth was too full of Cuban wild rat.

Half an hour later, Rosa slept rolled in her musty blanket beside the priest. María on her back rubbed her belly making circles on the high hard mound beneath her blanket. Francisco, Rosa and the girl lying in a row reminded the writer of sardines in a can. Manuel bedded down with his men.

The American picked up his writing paper and tried to read by firelight. Malaria and raw rum had turned his eyeballs into milk glass. With Pecos soundly sleeping against his leg, he rolled a cigarette around ash-dry crumbs of Green Turtle chewing tobacco. With a burning twig, he put fire to his cigarette and smoke smelling like licorice wafted through his nicotine stained fingers. Well after midnight, Samuel Carleton put pencil to paper by fading fire light. Words flowed from the full pencil and from his full warm stomach beside the pleasant smell of red embers.

The pleasant hearth-scent of burning coal was everywhere. At 7:00 o'clock, with only three hours remaining of daylight from the smoke-grayed sun in the west, George Fleming drove his tired heavy-legged horses past two dozen soot-covered shanties which lined the hills close to Hill Farm a mile west of Dunbar. Being born in coal country, he and Esther were not surprised by the hundreds of hunger-aged faces which pressed against a line of grim policemen guarding the coke works and mine. George and Esther knew that any rumble of the ground beneath the shoeless feet of mining towns would empty neighboring villages like a communal fire bell. That fretful quake from Earth's belly nine hours ago would have drained from Hill Farm, Ferguson, Mahaney and Pechin's tiny islands of company-owned squalor and from the real town of Dunbar every coal miner's wife, mother, child, and widow-by-coal-mine.

And here they were, all pressing tearfully against a police cordon ordered by Dunbar Furnace Company's starched-collared owners in Philadelphia. Without a word between them, George and Esther suddenly felt sinfully overfed. But they were beyond hungry and were covered with sweat and trail dust.

Toward the rear of the crowd were a few men too hobbled by mining accidents or from sucking coal dust for a lifetime to be on any mine's payroll. Up front, as close as smoke billowing from the mine allowed, were strong working miners. George gently eased the wagon through the people toward the miners.

"I'm a mining engineer," George shouted.

"What you say?" a huge man in coal-dust-black bibs shouted back. The miner shoved through the police line.

"I said I'm a mine engineer from Fairchance. We brought supplies for the families and we have blankets for the men going in and anyone rescued."

"Come over here, boy," the big man gestured, pointing away from the women cursing the guards who locked arms at an outbuilding close to the Hill Farm Mine entrance.

Away from the press of people, George and Esther could hear the tall miner.

"What you got that we ain't?"

"I'm a mine engineer," George repeated.

"And we brought blankets, clothes, and food," Esther said beside George.

"You brought your woman up here?" the miner frowned.

"I'm from Fairchance Ladies Aid," Esther shouted before George could deny her again.

"Come on down, boy." He looked hard at the girl. "Can you drive yonder to the womenfolk?"

"I most certainly can."

For an instant from where he stood beside the miner, George saw Charles Slone's face flash in the girl's narrowed brown eyes already red from the smoke in the evening air.

"Then off you go," said the miner to Esther. She gathered the reins and steered the team toward the loud conclave of women and the sickly old men. She had never seen so many people gathered on one plot of sloppy black mud. As George watched her drive his team as well as he could handle the broad animals, his anxious face smiled.

"Mine engineer, you say?"

"Yes. Name's George Fleming."

"Never heard of you."

"I farm near Fairchance. The mines call me when they need me."

"Don't do regular mining full time?" The long thin face frowned, covered with sweat flowing black.

"Not any more. But I'm an engineer all the same—and my father mined once."

"Been into a pit, boy?"

"Yes. At school, and off and on in the last two years. And the name is George."

They studied each other's faces for a long moment.

"Glad for any help, then," the coal blackened face said grimly. "The main rescue party is digging over there." He pointed in the first evening twilight to the apex of the police line this side of the Dunbar blast furnace. The sea of people expanded from there. "We Dunbar men are going into the Hill Farm Mine through the Mahaney Pit north of here. Fire and water are blocking us from Hill Farm just past the main shaft entrance. Did get an air shaft dug, but it flooded. So we're going in from Mahaney. Had to run over the owners' police to get in." The miner smiled for the first time. "You game, mister mining engineer—George?"

"My pa had worse odds, I suppose."

"Should have brought him instead of a skirt."

"How many men are trapped?"

"Thirty-one. Twenty-six escaped after the flood before the first explosion. The mine flooded when a six-inch air shaft full of water got nicked. When the fire damp ignited, it trapped the rest. The men are 800 feet down and nearly a mile in from the Hill Farm main entrance by the coke ovens."

"Which way?"

"Follow me. We have a hundred men already digging at Mahaney. My name is Scovel."

I know a Harry Scovel, Samuel Carleton thought as he drifted at the feathered edge of his story pouring out whole from his pencil.

Old Henry's son and Scovel the miner walked across the Mount Pleasant spur of the Pittsburgh and Connellsville Railroad, which serviced the complex of mines southwest of Dunbar. With the sun low and orange above the western hills, they arrived at a grim company of dozens of men black-faced with coal dust outside a blacker hole in a steep hillside. As they had done for nearly twelve hours, a line of filthy, sweat-soaked men marched single-file into the Mahaney Pit on one side while on the opposite side of the hole a line of identical figures shuffled out. The only color was the bloody fingers of the diggers walking into the cool night. The only voices were the company police shouting at the men going into the pit, begging them to stop.

All Samuel Carleton heard clearly was Pecos snoring close to his ear when the writer laid back only for a moment on hard, warm Cuban soil two hours before sunrise.

NINE

DISTANT LAUGHTER—DRUNKEN LAUGHTER—RANG THROUGH THE towering mogotes at dawn. The new Thursday sky was clean and clear and to Carleton as blue as deep-water ocean.

Five dark-faced rebels on horseback rode single file. Five rebels walked, having lost their mounts to Manuel and his friends. They followed the two women, the priest, and the coughing American. And all of them followed Manuel, who rode ten horse lengths ahead. Manuel rode with his back ramrod straight where he sank into his pathetic animal's deep swayback. In the pale light of tropical dawn, Carleton thought that the old man's long faint shadow upon the dirt path might have been Caesar's leading his legions, or at least the Quixote.

The muffled laughter grew in volume until the little band of liberators could distinguish individual voices shouting in Spanish. All the ears except the American ears heard Cuban accents instead of *castellano* Spanish. Then the warm morning wind shifted into their faces. All night, the Yanqui had wheezed on the stench of malnourished horses and filthy rebels. Now the scent in Carleton's flared nostrils was neither warrior sweat nor mid-winter Caribbean foliage—the smell was the gagsome, suffocating rot of unburied human flesh.

Manuel raised his hand and the riders behind him reined their mounts to a halt. Just ahead, rising between the living cork palms, a wall of pointed palm trunks lashed together with rope and barbed wire marked a large stockade in the middle of a well trampled clearing. Several of the horses whinnied and chomped hard on their rope bits when the valley floor swirled to life at the base of the stockade. A black wall of vultures, their heads as red feathered as the new sun, surged into the morning sky. From twenty yards away, Carleton could clearly see human bodies with purple wounds lying where the birds had been. Dead arms with gnarled blackened fingers pointed toward the sky in a ghastly salutation to the new day which made some of the rebels on horseback shiver. Rosa covered her mouth with her hand. Beside her, María leaned over her swollen belly and vomited upon her horse's infected tic wounds.

The American blinked at the pile of dead. He remembered putting into old Henry's head a boy's view of his first battle dead. "It seemed that the dead men must have fallen from some great height to get into such positions. They looked to be dropped out upon the ground from the sky." He and his pen had made that before Carleton had ever seen a real battlefield or a pile of dead men beside a stockade wall. How could he have known, he wondered.

"Who goes there?" a voice shouted in Spanish from the stockade wall.

Rosa stood in her rope stirrups.

"Alfonso!" Rosa shouted. Tears exploded from her exhausted brown eyes.

"Come into the clearing," Alfonso yelled. His words were too slurred for Carleton to make out his Spanish.

Manuel led them into the sunshine.

Midmorning sun low in the southeastern sky shone brightly upon Alfonso's red face. He leaned over the pointed parapet and looked down upon Manuel and the riders behind him.

"You saved my life, Uncle," Alfonso called. Then he looked over his shoulder and shouted toward the stockade.

Sharpened palm trunks swung on hemp hinges toward Manuel whose horse tossed his head and stepped backward. When part of the front wall opened, Alfonso walked into the sunny clearing. Four insurrectos in peasant dress came out with him. He ignored Manuel and walked directly to Francisco who steadied his mount beside Rosa's horse.

"You saved my life, Uncle. Had they found my brass buttons in my pockets, they would have killed me, too." Alfonso glanced toward the bodies of decomposing Spaniards piled in a heap beside the prison walls. "But I told them the great Father Francisco Montoya was my devoted uncle." The boy smiled a drunken smile and gestured toward the mounted man for the benefit of the four rebels on foot beside him. "I told you he was my uncle." Alfonso looked up at the priest in peasant rags. "Tell them."

"I am Francisco. And the boy is my nephew."

Carleton listened to low murmurings of slurred Spanish.

The rebels reached up and touched Francisco's horse. With the same hand, they made crosses upon their thin chests. Not one of them actually touched the priest as if he were too holy a relic of the church for that, a splinter from the True Cross. One of the Cubans shouted back toward the camp. Twenty more rebels staggered into the clearing. With a flurry of Spanish, each touched Francisco's nervous horse. The priest struggled to keep the horse in formation close to Rosa and behind Manuel.

"Who is in command here?" Manuel demanded toward Alfonso.

"Maybe the Spanish rum is in charge now," Alfonso said, laughing hard.

"Are all the Spaniards dead?" Manuel looked from side to side, over his horse's head as the animal tried to spin away from too many men pressing in beside him.

"No," Alfonso answered. "We kept a few for hostages in case more regulars came. But most of them," Alfonso pointed with his half-empty sleeve toward the corpses. "Most have been released from their duty to the Queen Regent of Spain. All of you are welcome inside."

With little more than a sour grunt and nod of his leathery head, Manuel pressed his legs against the sides of his restless horse. The animal jumped forward and Manuel led the way into the compound. An honor guard of drunken Cubans stumbled on either side of the priest. They had shouldered their way between Francisco and his sister until Francisco rode surrounded by thin dark Cubans and Rosa walked her horse beside the American. Carleton thought that these Cubans would have covered Francisco's path with palm branches were they not too drunk. Without a word, Alfonso reached for María Teresa's reins and he led her animal into the stockade.

Inside the camp, the newcomers dismounted and tied their rope reins to hitching posts outside an open hut with thatch roof. Under the roof of mildewed palm fronds, dozens of rebels milled around stew pots suspended above fires smoldering on the earthen floor. The rebel band that had followed Manuel stayed close to him, wary of so many filthy insurrectos armed with Mauser rifles.

"This was once the officers' mess," Alfonso said in drunken Spanish, pointing to the hut open on all sides to the warm December 15 breeze. "And those were once the officers."

Samuel Carleton followed the boy's remaining hand, which gestured in the direction of an open-air pen where a dozen men in ragged white linen and straw hats sat in wet mud. They were walled in by coils of rusty barbed wire held in place by rotting wooden stakes. Two Spaniards stood urinating into a trench dug at a corner of their pen. Black urine drained from one of them. Another Spanish prisoner stood apart. Carleton watched him frantically pacing and mumbling to himself in an animated conversation with only noxious air and clouds of mosquitos.

"*Como los chanchos,*" Alfonso laughed.

Carleton looked toward Rosa at his side.

"Like pigs," she squinted in the bright sunshine.

By noon, Manuel and his men, the priest and the two women, and the lone gringo were fed well with Spanish beans and rice at the former officers' mess. Alfonso sat beside María without looking at her. The Cuban prisoners of war had overrun their captors in a brave, suicidal uprising four days earlier after a Spanish courier had brought official word of the signing of the Treaty of Paris and the promise by the Yanqui government to finance the return voyage of the Spanish Army to Spain. Many Cubans had died in the camp's open center, but two dozen Spaniards were torn apart by the rebels' bare hands. In his slow and careful English, Manuel told the wet red story through mouthfuls of rice to Carleton, who sat beside him on a cracker box.

"*Muy* angry, *muy* hungry," Manuel said gravely as if the massacre of mostly disabled Spaniards had to be explained. To the American, Manuel admitted that the Spanish guards were rejects or maimed survivors from active service who were too weak from yellow fever or battle wounds to man the trenches in the east at

Santiago de Cuba. "War makes the animal," the rebel said. "There is no teacher like the hunger." The weary American nodded.

"Look at them," Manuel said softly. With his gray and white stubbled chin, he nodded toward the priest surrounded by emaciated Cubans.

"Is Francisco loved like this everywhere?" Carleton asked.

"Probably. Many of these men know him from concentrado camps where the good priest was a prisoner." Manuel pointed with his wooden bowl toward Rosa Montoya, who stood outside the circle of admiring pilgrim-soldiers. "The priest saved many lives in many camps by standing between our people and the Spaniards. That much is true. But it was the woman who paid for their food. It was the woman who gave herself for the bullets we used to kill Spaniards." Manuel looked closely into the American's pale face and yellow eyes. "Father Francisco saved their miserable souls, but Rosa Montoya filled their empty bellies and their rifles which killed Spaniards."

"Rosa bought bullets? I don't understand."

Manuel shook his head with impatience at Carleton's ignorance.

"Our guns were fed by the *putas* of La Habana, Gringo. This you did not know? And good clean women like Rosa sold themselves for Mauser cartridges at the price of 100 cartridges for a private soldier, 200 for sergeants, and 1,000 rounds for giving their bodies to a Spanish officer." Manuel lovingly touched the weapon which leaned against his leg. "Rosa might have put cartridges in this rifle."

Samuel Carleton could not speak.

"Tell me, Gringo, you have a woman and children in your country?"

"No children. And no wife; not really. Do you have family?"

"I have a wife and two sons," the Cuban said without a smile.

"Where are they now?"

"The real war against those Spaniards," Manuel gestured with his face toward the prisoners' pen, "it began twenty years ago in what we call the Ten Years War. Then it comes the cholera that killed 5,000. The cholera took my woman quickly."

"I'm sorry, Manuel. Your sons?"

"My sons. My firstborn fought with Martí. I told you I spent time in the *Nueva York* with him. Martí was soldier and poet. '*Cultivo una rosa blanca.*' He planted white roses. And revolution. It was 19 of May, it makes three years now that he was killed fighting at Dos Ríos. My son fell with him."

The Cuban looked Carleton in the eye.

"I'm sorry."

"My youngest son died beside General Maceo at Punta Brava. It makes exactly two years."

The American could not say "I'm sorry" a third time.

"Gringo, you know García and Gómez. But have you heard of Antonio Maceo and José Martí?"

"No," Carleton swallowed hard.

"*Claro que no,*" Manuel nodded. "Of course not."

Ten rebels left Francisco's side and walked directly toward Manuel and Carleton. They stopped, looked down at Manuel who did not stand, and pointed toward the American with the yellow eyeballs. Carleton could smell their alcohol breath as they spoke rapidly in Spanish. The American was uncomfortable at the sudden laugh that erupted from the old rebel.

"The priest told them that the gringo was a hero at Santiago," Manuel chuckled. Rice fell through the spaces between his remaining black teeth. Rice and beans were piling into the Cuban's lap as he translated. "They think you charged San Juan Heights almost by yourself." Manuel licked his lips and wiped the rice from his chin. "Did you do that—Perdido?"

The living skeletons standing too close looked at Samuel Carleton. Manuel waited.

Carleton looked at Manuel but not at the Cubans. In his heart he felt the slow procession of his own words written after seeing a friend and boyhood classmate wounded on a Cuban mountainside. "The apparition of Reuben McNab, the schoolmate lying there in the mud with a hole through his lung, awed me into stutterings, set me trembling with a sense of terrible intimacy with this war."

"I was there," Carleton said softly, with his head bowed.

"You knew el Señor Roosevelt?"

"Yes."

"He is your friend?"

"I liked his dog. The dog's name was Cuba."

Manuel grinned and spoke in fast Spanish.

The American did not know what Manuel said to the men surrounding them, but in an instant the Cubans were pressing against Carleton and were patting him hard on his back and shoulders. He felt Manuel stand, heard him drop his bowl to the ground, and watched him walk away. Inside the sudden reeking press of rebels who had torn the Spanish wounded limb from limb, Carleton could hear Manuel laughing.

The day passed quickly for the American. It was a good afternoon. When he finally broke away from his Cuban worshipers, he found Rosa sitting alone on a blanket spread on the ground near the officers' mess. He sat and reached for his manuscript and he began to write. As the afternoon sun crossed the sky, Carleton's well chewed pencil drove words across the pages slowly and carefully. Whenever a new rebel would approach with straw hat held in both hands, lower his head respectfully, and gently touch the American's bony shoulder, the pencil moved faster upon the dirty paper.

With his pipe burning well, Samuel Carleton entered quickly the world of his story. The stench of the stockade, the reeking sweat and breath following close to the Cubans touching him, and the bloody sewer of the Spanish prisoners' pen propelled him into the mysterious ether where a writer's stories grow like mushrooms in fertile darkness. So he entered easily the dark hole in a Pennsylvania mountainside. He walked carefully at the side of George Gordon and Scovel the miner. In the netherworld of Mahaney Pit, only the burning gauze in the Davy lamps or the simple, tin oil lamps on the miners' soft hats illuminated them. Samuel Carleton kept looking over his shoulder. He watched the shaft entrance shrinking and then disappearing in its softly pink glow of evening twilight.

The men moving steadily in opposite directions on each side of the horizontal shaft no longer had faces. They were only a steady silent procession of light beams.

Under the ceiling timbers passing overhead, George counted his paces into the mine. Always he performed this ritual when he entered Earth.

"We ain't strangers to accidents like this here," Scovel said over his shoulder.

"I suppose not," George said, counting his steps in his mind.

"Forty-two Fayette County men have been taken by these mines in the last eight years. The Leisenring mine killed 23 good men seven years ago. I knew some of them."

The oil lamp on George's forehead nodded and he silently counted 255 steps. From there on, each new step put him two feet further into the cold wet ground than his father had gone into the Petersburg shaft. In every mine, he hoped that each successive stride beyond 255 paces proved him better and braver than old Henry by 24 inches. And every time he passed 510 feet underground, still he knew that he would never be the true and good man that was his father.

"Only found two bodies going in at the main Hill Farm entrance. Could only identify them poor souls by what weren't burned of their clothes."

"What about the others?"

"Trapped behind a cave-in where the roof timbers burned."

George's boots were now 500 paces into the dark shaft.

After half an hour, Mahaney Pit ended at a wall of coal seven feet high and ten feet wide. Twenty-five men hacked at the end of the shaft with picks, shovels, and bare bleeding hands. George looked sideways and upward, the lamp on his soft hat illuminating the blackened, glistening face of Scovel, half a head taller.

"What you got better than digging with all our hearts, mister mining engineer?" Scovel asked with respectful hope in his weary voice.

"Nothing, I suppose."

The tall miner's light nodded and he handed George a heavy shovel.

"Well then," said Scovel.

Heaving the shovel into the wall of black oily rock, George took a twenty-pound bite out of the ground beneath Robert E. Lee's Army of Northern Virginia, which was already beaten but would not accept it.

Scovel watched George fight the mountain. The young man bent his back almost horizontal and he threw all his weight into the shovel's handle as if he wanted to hurt the cruel mountain.

"You don't dig like no college boy," Scovel said behind the glowing Davy lamp strapped to his crushed wool hat.

"Suppose not," George puffed without looking up from the small dim circle of light under his coal-dust-black wet face. When he saw the tall miner's pickax flaying at the mountain close to his shovel, George felt a twinge of surprise and just a little guilt that he was thinking not of his wife and son but of Charles Slone's daughter 800 feet above him in cool, fresh, clean, high-country air. Her father had to love her, he thought. But he could not kiss her good-bye on her forehead.

Esther drove the wide-shouldered, foot sore team chomping impatiently on their foam covered bits into the assembly of families. A red sun settled upon blue, distant flatlands in the west under clear amber sky. A light wind blew eastward toward Pechin and Dunbar the black dense clouds of smouldering coal and billowing white clouds of steam from boiling, underground water. The eye-burning, breath-choking smoke from the open mouth of the Hill Farm Mine entrance forced hundreds of people a quarter mile back from the belching hole in the hillside. Twelve hours of waiting, praying and grieving had burned away the crowd's early panic and rage as the flames 800 feet below them turned to charcoal the living flesh of their husbands, fathers, sons and brothers, who did not escape the first flood. Only waves of weeping swept the red-eyed congregation of hope-drained mourners. When each towering ball of black smoke rolled out of the ground, the families exhaled one collective groan starting and stopping with such precision that Esther imagined that some unseen conductor had raised and lowered his baton with one terrible sweep through the sootful air.

She stopped the wagon beside a row of a dozen wagons large and small. All their horses or mules had been unhitched and led to livery paddocks in Pechin.

"May I take your team, miss? They look pretty well used up."

Esther looked down at a kind, middle-aged face. Deep creases in his thin face with its two-day beard looked like ruts in the backwoods path to Fairchance. His large hands on her team's harness tack were badly gnarled with swollen crooked fingers from a lifetime of hard iron tools and cold wet mines. A hacking cough from his sunken chest and rounded shoulders was the badge of his trade.

"No, thank you. I have supplies from the Ladies Aid in Fairchance to unload. Then I have to get back up to Mahaney with these blankets for anyone they can bring out."

The frail man nodded.

"There are boxes of clothing, canned goods, coffee, and trinkets for the children."

"That's very kind, miss. I'll get some boys to help unload."

The man secured her reins to the wheel spokes of the closest wagon before he shuffled head down into the crowd. The sun was gone, taking the red sky with it. A thin crescent of the last night of this waning Moon faded in and out of the Hill Farm Mine's volcanic plume of oily smoke. Brief holes in the eastern sky revealed the Moon's pale yellow sliver over the mountains.

Esther felt the wagon shift. Turning on the hard wood seat she saw the crippled man and four teenaged boys lifting boxes from the wagon. They did not touch two piles of blankets. When a group of small children dragged their mothers toward the wagon, Esther climbed down. As the children and their haggard young mothers came closer, Esther felt unseemingly clean.

In the darkness well lighted by hundreds of hand lanterns, she stepped toward the full boxes on the ground beside her wagon.

"Everyone please take whatever you need. Please. There's food and clothes from the people of Fairchance."

She knelt down on one knee and reached into a deep box. She pulled out a handful of bows of brightly colored ribbons. Tiny girls without shoes took them eagerly in small hands with dirty fingernails. Their brothers without smiles reached for whistles and wooden pencils.

Esther stood and felt the gaze of the mothers, most of whom were her age but with eyes much older.

"Please, the food and clothes," she said with a smile she worked to hold.

No one stepped forward.

"Miss?" said the familiar voice.

She turned toward the bent-over man. He spoke softly and close to her ear, and she could smell chewing tobacco and an empty belly.

"The women won't take charity in front of you."

"This isn't charity," Esther said softly.

"We know that. But still," he smiled without teeth.

"I understand. I better be on my way up to Mahaney anyway."

Esther climbed to the seat. The man untied the reins and handed them up to her.

"Tell the ladies of Fairchance we're very grateful."

"I will. We wish we could do more."

"You remembered us. That's enough." He stepped back. His weary red eyes narrowed. "Do you have a man in the Mahaney Pit?"

"Yes," Esther said as she pulled her team around to point them north.

Slowly the women opened a path for the wagon to pass. As the sea of lanterns closed behind her and around the dozen boxes on the ground, Esther did not feel the ground shake at 10:00 o'clock. But she heard a loud moan from hundreds of dry throats. An instant later, a red fireball erupted from the ground at the main Hill Farm shaft half a mile away.

Esther slapped the reins hard across her laboring horses, which tried to rear up at the rolling thunder but did not have sufficient leg after the climb toward Dunbar.

"Come now," she shouted above the keening wail surrounding her as darkness returned with the speed of a heavy curtain falling.

Esther felt tears running down her sweating face. Since her father had told her as a child that only little girls cried, she had never shed a tear and was proud of it. Now in the darkness she wished she could see her own face in a mirror to learn if this tear stained face was really hers.

"Come now."

In the sudden darkness after the underground explosion, Samuel Carleton looked up blinking at the ferocious red sun low in the Cuban sky. Feeling Esther Slone's terror as she drove her team hard toward Mahaney Pit and feeling the P and C Railroad tracks clattering painfully up his spine, Carleton squinted as he searched for Rosa. The oily scent of burning coal deep in the ground slowly became black beans and rice stewing in iron pots over a dozen little fires.

A few Cubans by ones and twos bowed deeply to Rosa and whispered, "*Mil gracias, señora.*" A thousand thank-yous.

Fifteen pages went from the blank stack to the written pile by the time the sun touched the southwestern rim of the stockade wall. Carleton only put the pencil down to cool when Alfonso approached.

Alfonso carried three bowls of steaming beans. He held them close to his muddy shirt with the stump of his mutilated arm and his good hand. Carefully, he handed a bowl first to his mother and then to the writer. He pulled a bottle of rum from inside his shirt and set it carefully on the ground close to Rosa. Only when he reached up for his ration did Carleton realize that his writing hand was stiff and sore. He smiled. When Rosa passed her bowl to María, Alfonso shuffled away and returned with beans and rice for his mother. Then he sat.

Rosa thanked her son as she sat cross-legged close to María and the writer. Rosa translated Alfonso's cheerful chatter. The boy was now drunk only to the point of mellow. The morning's loud, lewd drunk had worn off. He took a swig from the bottle and handed it to his mother. She shook her head and passed it untasted to Carleton, who took only a mouthful and worked it to swallow slowly. He blinked when it made his eyes water.

"Alfonso says that he personally saved five of the Spanish prisoners over there. They were Spanish Voluntarios and one regular Spanish officer." Rosa paused to think in English. "The officer is, how is it said, 'touched' in his head."

"Voluntarios?" Carleton asked through his tasty dinner. He could feel that the rum had made his tongue just a little too big for his mouth. Having watched the whole 71st New York Infantry collapse in panic at Bloody Brook at the foot of San Juan Heights, he tried not to think about the babbling arm-waving Spaniard in the pen nor about the battlemade exhaustion of mind and soul which the American Army called cannon fever.

Alfonso spoke merrily. He was becoming too drunk again to use his passable English so his mother translated without emotion.

"In La Habana last January, after Governor-General Valeriano Wyler was replaced by Ramón Blanco, Spaniards and Cubans loyal to Wyler formed a group called Voluntarios. They burned newspaper offices and started riots."

Alfonso's eyes twinkled merrily with the low sun directly in his face. He spoke with intense pride and animation. As a second swallow of warm rum crept into the folds of the American's brain, his mind began to wander and he lost track of Rosa's soft voice. But he turned to face her when his buzzing ears tripped over Alfonso's repeated mention of the word "Maine."

"The ship, *Maine*?" Carleton slurred. Alfonso stopped talking and waited for his mother's translation to catch up.

"Yes, Perdido. Alfonso says that it was these Voluntarios who blew up your country's ship in the harbor of La Habana last February."

When Alfonso poked his stump into his mother's knee to

make her hurry, Rosa gently kicked her son with her bare muddy foot. Alfonso chuckled and lifted the bottle.

"He says they only wanted to make the Yanqui ship go home. It was an accident that it blew up and killed so many innocent boys."

"Then the Spanish government in Havana did not sink her?" Carleton forced his mind to focus in the twilight. He blinked hard to stay alert.

"No. Not according to my son."

Carleton looked at Alfonso who nodded and smiled broadly. He raised his stump and the American could imagine a clenched fist at the end.

By full darkness Thursday night, a perfect star-filled sky brought peace to the prison camp at the western end of Viñales Valley. In the officers' hut, rebels sat in quiet stupors induced by Spanish rum. The least drunk rebels stood slumped against rough-hewn railings on makeshift guard towers. Some navigated the dangerously narrow catwalk, which ran the length of the palm-tree stockade. When one of the Cubans stumbled from the parapet and fell, the moist soft ground broke no bones. He hit the earth with a muted thud and was probably asleep when he landed. The Spanish prisoners did not sleep but lay half-awake in the cool night air, stirring only to shuffle to the trench latrine, black and stinking from bloody dysentery.

Manuel slept sitting on a cracker box. His back was braced against the stockade wall. His ten followers slept on flea infested blankets at this feet like loyal, well fed puppies. Samuel Carleton sat awake with Pecos sleeping tightly against his leg. Ten paces from the writer, Rosa slept between blankets near her brother. The priest's head rested upon his saddle with the leather worn down to its wooden tree. Next to Rosa, María rested fitfully beneath a Spanish Army blanket.

Although little rain falls during Cuba's winter dry season, the trees and ground sweated out water vapor all night. The humidity and lingering heat made the air thick and damp. Samuel Carleton listened to Pecos panting against his side as if the warm ground and the stockade's stink had sucked all the oxygen from the moist night air. Reaching for his last sheets of blank paper, the writer's freshly whittled pencil trembled. His tubercular lungs could not breathe. When he gasped for air sitting alone beside his oil lamp, Pecos raised his ragged head. With his left hand over his sore chest and with his heart pounding in his face, Samuel Carleton laid his pencil on the empty sheet of paper. That he could not breathe one gulp of clean cool air was perfect because George Gordon Meade Fleming could not breathe either as he crawled on his hands and knees.

When Hill Farm pit exploded a mile away, Mahaney Mine shuddered for ten harrowing seconds. Dunbar Furnace miners who had climbed over company police to extend the Mahaney shaft into the burning Hill Farm Mine stumbled and fell. Davy lamps on hats and handheld lanterns failed in the tangled mass of two dozen men. A few cap lamps cast faint yellow beams from the rocky ground to the ceiling where thick timbers rained down dust like a blizzard of black snow where the beams held up the quivering mountain of coal.

George lost his footing with the first quake and he fell to his knees so fast that his face struck the wood handle of his shovel. He could not see or feel how many teeth he was spitting out but he could taste the iron of his blood flowing from his mouth, down his neck, and onto his hands that kept his shattered face off the ground.

With the second quake rumbling uphill, the wall of coal collapsed where George fell. Invisible rocks and coal rolled over him, covered him, and subsided only after he was nothing but a man-size bulge in a ruptured coal seam two feet deep. Choking on coal dust and unable to breathe, all he could do was dream.

Out of the sudden breathless darkness, George saw a man in blue approaching him through charred stumps of a burned-out forest. The man came closer and the coal black sky opened to sunshine. In full daylight now and cool spring air, he watched the blue-clad figure walking toward him and moving left or right around blackened tree stumps. The figure only paused to kick away gray balls poking out of the well turned earth. Looking around where he lay, George saw human skulls rising from the soil as on Resurrection Day. He shuddered. Then he remembered. Rain this May had washed away the shallow graves of Rebels and Yankees who had fallen at Chancellorsville exactly one year earlier.

The blue man drew closer, kicking the skulls of heroes from his path through the Virginia jungle of trees and knotted brambles known as The Wilderness. Here, during the first week of May, General Grant had fought Robert E. Lee for the first time and their running battle for two blood-soaked months ended at Petersburg.

The man in federal blue stopped and looked down at George and George looked up and saw a teenage boy's face which was his face and not his face.

George Gordon looked up into the face of old Henry as a boy in blood-spattered Yankee blue.

"Pa?" George gagged on coal dust.

"You still alive, boy?"

George blinked up at a yellow beam of light shining into his eyes. He lay on his back in near darkness.

"Thought you was gone for sure, mister mining engineer." White teeth in a broad smile glistened in forehead lamps looking down at him and criss-crossing the tall miner where he knelt beside George. The miner Scovel was still lifting rocks away from George's aching body.

"You'll live," Scovel nodded. "But I don't know what that you might lose your right hand, I'm afeared."

Struggling to collect his wits, George raised his right arm in the strange twilight of a dozen beams of oil lamps. When his sleeve fell away, he saw that his throbbing right hand was a raw bleeding stump. He could not see his thumb or his fingers beside it. Above his wrist a filthy shoelace was tied tightly. A coal-black handkerchief held together the broken jagged bones.

"That's all we had to stop the bleeding after we dug you out."

"Thanks," George mumbled. When his head moved, he felt that he was propped up in another miner's lap. Lowering his hand, he felt ice water through the searing pain in his crushed forearm.

"Water's coming in from the last explosion down south, already a foot deep in spots. We're done here. Can you walk?"

"Don't know."

The tall miner and another man lifted George to his feet. His legs buckled before he took a step.

"We got you," a new voice said. George saw only small lamps without faces under them. Scovel and the other miner pulled him from the shallow water and wrapped his arms around their shoulders. When the tall miner grabbed George's right forearm, he knew pain which he could not have imagined.

"Water's rising, George. We have a mile to go."

"Okay," George whispered. Desperately, he wished that he was carrying the regimental colors toward the enemy's yawning guns. He wished that the bloody makeshift bandage circled his head instead of what remained of his right hand. "Okay."

After the third deep rumble in the mountain and the momentary straining of the roof timbers which still held, Mahaney Pit was quiet except for the heavy breathing and the splashing of legs through black water knee high and rising slowly. The mountain above, below, and on both sides of George was as quiet as a ship already sunk with her men below decks not knowing it yet. The

sudden silence of the mountain horrified him and Samuel Carleton beside him sloshing toward daylight.

The American writing by oil lamp marveled at the quiet.
Putting down his pencil and lifting his rum bottle to his lips, he
listened hard to the night sounds. He heard only nighttime humidity dripping like soft rain and the rustling of the startlingly
blue land crabs feasting on the rotting Spaniards on the far side of
the stockade wall. He heard the living Spaniards moaning in pain
when they squatted in the darkness over the bloody latrine. Compared to the prisoners, the clicking of hundreds of crab claws was
strangely tranquil and the warm rum flowing over hot beans and
rice made the writer's pencil too heavy to drive across the paper
toward the distant entrance of the dark mine.

Carleton fell sideways in his sleep and the Cuban earth gently
welcomed his body, more bones than flesh.

An hour later, the American sat bolt upright. In the darkness,
he heard wood doves cooing, a sound buried in the cemetery of his
mind along with the young American soldiers killed and wounded
at Las Guásimas after the bird-calls made by Spanish guerillas.
Then the tropical stillness of the prison camp exploded with rifle
fire.

Carleton's malaria swollen liver and his yellow fever ravaged
spine protested painfully when he staggered to his feet. A dazed
rebel from Manuel's band nearly knocked the writer off his feet
when the Cuban ran from the former officers' hut into the darkness.

Manuel awoke with his rifle in hand. Within seconds of the
first volley, two dozen Cubans had climbed the inside walls of
the stockade. They were aiming blindly and firing their captured
Mauser rifles and pistols into the darkness where distant muzzle
flashes were bursting white outside the compound.

Francisco and Alfonso rushed toward Rosa and the girl at Carleton's side. The men pushed the women into a pigsty, whose occupants had long since been sacrificed to *¡Cuba Libre!*

Inside the shed, the girl crumbled into a thick pile of old pig dung softened by the night's thick humidity. María Teresa moaned and gripped her belly. When Rosa knelt beside her, Rosa felt the hot wetness of María's trousers and looked up at her son.

"María's time has come," Rosa shouted above the outside gunfire to her son, her brother, and Carleton.

"You are a nurse," Alfonso said coldly.

"I am a mother," Rosa answered.

Francisco pulled Alfonso from the three-sided manger into the tiny nighttime battle. The American followed. Crouching as they ran into the darkness, the priest and his nephew stopped breathlessly to wait for Carleton to reach them.

"Spanish regulars?" the American asked Francisco.

"Spanish and a few Cuban Voluntarios," Alfonso answered for his uncle. "They have come to liberate the Spanish prisoners."

For the first time since gunfire had awakened him, the American realized that all but one of the prisoners in the pen were silent. He understood when muzzle flashes inside the pen illuminated the darkness and he saw Cubans close to the prisoners.

"They're shooting unarmed men," Carleton shouted over the melee.

"*No es nada,*" Alfonso said hoarsely. It is nothing.

Before Carleton could speak again, wooden fragments stung his ear. A bullet had struck the hut behind them. All three men slouched and moved carefully across the compound where Cuban rebels were running, screaming, and firing like mad men toward the top of the parapet. A few fading fires on the ground revealed shadows scaling the walls from the outside. The American, the priest, and Alfonso moved through the darkness like blind men with their hands and one stump stretched out ahead of them.

They reached the storage hut and took cover behind sacks of rice. They watched as the stockade's tall gate opened and half a dozen mounted men firing revolvers rode hard into the prison camp and fell quickly in the hail of bullets.

In ten minutes, the firing slowed. Whimpering from the wounded and María Teresa's screams from the pigpen filled the night.

The American and the priest stepped carefully over the bodies. Rebels stoked the camp fires two hours before daybreak. Fresh fires illuminated two dozen dead and wounded rebels and seven Spaniards lying on the ground. Manuel examined them. Carleton knelt down for a closer look.

"A .44 caliber revolver," the American said dryly, "can make a hole large enough for little boys to shoot marbles through."

Manuel said nothing. The musical crack of the Mausers and the dry popping of revolvers subsided except for an isolated round fired from outside the compound.

Newly kindled fires in the dirt drove the darkness toward the night sky. Carleton staggered toward the stockade wall where he waited for sweating Cubans to bring down the last of their wounded and dead. Then the thin American climbed the ladder to the catwalk well splintered by heavy Mauser bullets.

From the narrow parapet, Samuel Carleton looked down into the stockade. He saw Manuel pointing up at him, with Alfonso and the priest breathing hard beside him. Reaching into his pocket, Carleton pulled out his tobacco pouch and a ragged square of cigarette paper. He rolled one, licked it sealed, and put a match to his face.

With western stars overhead fading opposite the pink dawn in the east, the American paced the catwalk ahead of the little cloud of tobacco smoke following him. He did not flinch when a few bullets threw palm splinters into the thick air close to his face.

Vaguely, as in a half-dream before waking, Carleton stepped outside of his crowded and feverish mind. Up there on that stockade wall warm and dark and stained with old and new blood, he saw or he imagined or he dreamed that he was watching a thin man on the slope of San Juan Hill last July. That man in long white duster calmly paced the hillside while Mauser bullets thudded into the bloodied Cuban earth at his feet. Around that lone figure whose malaria swollen liver bullets could not touch, there crouched brave American soldiers and audacious newspapermen. Twice they pulled the standing man to the ground. Now on a prison camp wall in another jungle, Samuel Carleton wondered if he recognized that other lone figure from five months ago. He could not be sure.

After a final long draw on his cigarette and a deep cough, Carleton climbed down from his wall and walked to Manuel, Alfonso, and Francisco.

Four Voluntarios were still alive. Cubans dragged them to the stockade wall close to one of the fires beside the thin wall of the former pigpen closed on three sides. The Cubans laid them roughly down. Faint, not quite red, first light of Friday glistened on four contorted faces wet with blood and sweat. All four were boys no older than Alfonso. After Manuel promised the priest that the survivors would not be executed, the rebel had to pry Francisco's fingers from his arm.

"I promise, Padre," Manuel repeated.

In the fire light brighter than the wisp of dawn in the east, one of the prisoners who could open his eyes looked toward the pile of dead Spanish prisoners near the latrine. No one moved where the newly dead were heaped like garbage.

Rosa came out of her pigpen and stood between her brother and the American. She hugged them both—the priest first. She looked around and saw Alfonso hobbling nearby between the blazing fires. Blood trickled from a rip in his baggy trousers. The boy was smiling broadly.

"Are you hurt?" the mother asked breathlessly.

"A scratch," Alfonso said. He looked down at one Spaniard panting with his eyes closed. Alfonso squinted at the wounded boy. "Pedro?"

The teenager against the wall opened one eye. Dry blood glued the other shut.

"It's me, Alfonso Delgado." Alfonso did not move closer to the wounded man and did not touch him.

The boy on the ground tried to focus his open eye on his captors. Another Spaniard next to him opened his eyes and winced in pain. He spoke first.

"Alfonso? The priest's nephew?"

"Alfonso Delgado. I was a Voluntario in La Habana last winter."

The prisoner looked hard at Alfonso in the fire light. He smiled with fresh bright blood on his teeth. He spit toward Alfonso's bare feet.

"You are nobody," the prisoner said in Spanish through clenched teeth. "I remember you. General Wyler sent you home to your mama." The man looked down at his wounds. Frothy pink blood oozed from his lung-shot chest and thick, dark blood leaked from both legs. "You refused to do soldiers' business." He chuckled a gruesome laugh and closed his eyes.

Rosa stepped close to her son.

"What does he mean, Alfonso?" Rosa stood in the rum vapors of her son's fast, warm breath.

"He lies even at the hour of his death. Pig!" Alfonso kicked the Spaniard in the hip. The wounded man groaned. Francisco pushed his nephew away and knelt beside the four men.

"No harm will come to you, my son," Francisco said. He looked up at Manuel.

"Alfonso," Rosa demanded, "what did he mean?"

The youngest prisoner, still a boy, opened his one eye again and spoke for the first time.

"He means that Alfonso would not follow orders and kill civilians who killed Spaniards." He smiled up at Alfonso. "Now you hide behind a woman. You were *bijirita* then and you are *bijirita* now."

Samuel Carleton was trying to follow the gasping Spanish. He looked at Manuel. The rebel smiled and grabbed his own groin.

"*Bijirita* means *nada* down here, Gringo." Manuel laughed and released his grip on his own trousers.

Rosa looked into her son's face. Alfonso's eyes glistened with rage. When Rosa touched his shoulders, Alfonso pushed her away. He raised his stump toward her face. When he spoke, his voice cracked.

"You cut off my hand for nothing, Mother."

Rosa blinked her red eyes.

"Your child comes soon," the mother said.

"Someone's child," said her son.

"You shame me and you shame the good name of your dead father." Rosa spoke through perfect and clenched teeth.

"But at least I kept my father's name, Mother." He glared in fury. "You abandoned his name when you abandoned his bed."

The woman's dirty hand moved swiftly toward her son's red face. But she stopped it before slapping her only child's mouth.

"What do you know of our marriage bed?" She was whispering and hissing furiously, her eyes full of tears and anger. "Your father inherited slaves from his father—men, women, and children. Especially women. He took the women when he wanted because he owned them. And when I saw the puss in the chamber pot, I left his bed for good so I would not get the whores' sickness, too."

Rosa Montoya bit her lip so hard that it bled, a red trickle cutting through the dirt on her chin.

Alfonso walked away. His mother's face streaked with fresh tears and old sweat turned toward the girl's cries in the shed. Mother and son walked in opposite directions when Rosa returned to María Teresa naked in the darkness of her labor.

"Doña Rosa," María whimpered. "You lied to me about owning slaves? I heard you. Why?"

Rosa swallowed and looked down with brimming eyes at the girl.

"Shame."

The underside of a few wispy clouds in the east turned from faint orange to red as the sun approached the delicate soft edge of morning. Samuel Carleton followed Alfonso as far as the officers' mess nearly dark in twilight. He sat again in the imprint of his own frayed and filthy pants. He leaned against an empty pork barrel. As he reached for his thin stack of blank paper hungry for new words, Pecos waddled toward him at a slow shaggy trot. The writer held out his writing hand by which he lived and Pecos licked it before rolling against the American's thigh. The dog closed his black eyes and breathed slowly and peacefully. Carleton smiled at Pecos and words flowed from the sleeping dog's face into the writer's mind to be used later, if he lived. "Down in the mystic, hidden fields of his little dog-soul bloomed flowers of love and fidelity and perfect faith."

Samuel Carleton looked toward the stockade's eastern wall. The sun was still well below it. But the warm sleeping dog and the certainty of blooming sunrise filled the American with a wave of hope. Digging his penknife from his pocket, he sharpened his pencil and laid his whole manuscript in his lap as his paper desk. The red sky felt like the color of hope for men wading a black river 800 feet underground. Since only the writing hand knows how a story ends, the writer put pencil to paper and prayed for the best precisely as Esther Slone prayed, close to a line of grim Dunbar Furnace police guards who pushed a crowd of exhausted miners and fearful women away from a black hole in the side of the mountain at Mahaney.

At least the Mahaney shaft did not belch smoke and poison gas like Hill Farm. Word had already percolated up to Mahaney that the 13-hour rescue effort at Hill Farm officially ended at 10:30 with the last explosion. The 25-year lifetime of Hill Farm Mine and Coke Works was over and no more lives would be risked digging for dead men. Thirty-one Fayette County miners were declared buried where they burned or drowned. Among the newly dead were five fathers and their own sons and two miners who were brothers. The youngest dead miner was 17 years old.

Esther stood in the glow of lanterns lighting gray dry faces that were all cried out. Expectant murmurs surrounded her and when a Mahaney Pit rescuer stumbled into the sooty night air, a wife or mother screamed and the thick-armed guards quietly stepped aside.

No one spoke to the girl as if they sensed that she was from outside. Drying her face with the palms of her hands, Esther reached into her wagon and lifted a pile of clean blankets. Elbowing her way to the front of the women and children huddled in the comfortable nighttime breeze, she laid the blankets at the muddy boots of the guard closest to the waiting families.

"For the men coming out," she said.

"Fine," the coke works policeman said. "Now step back, please."

Esther stepped away as two more men walked out of the mountain. Each was soaking wet up to his waist. The group raised a familiar groan at the evidence of another flood beneath their feet, most without shoes. Two women, one very old and one very young, rushed to the two men. As they passed through the police cordon, each stooped without looking at Esther and picked up a blanket soon thrown over weary blackened shoulders. Esther stepped backward into the mass of anxious families.

Men emerged into the soft glow of oil lamps for tearful re-unions and a new blanket. Some dragged a shovel or pick so Dun-bar Furnace would not dock their seventeen cents per hour wages for equipment lost or abandoned in the shaft. And still George Fleming remained in the hole.

Half a mile from the entrance, George could not feel the ground beneath his boots. A dip in the shaft floor formed a black oily lake ten paces long and waist deep. The tall miner under his right wounded arm and a short Polish miner speaking little Eng-lish under his left arm lifted him through the high water. George stumbled when he felt the uneven floor where the black river was only above his knees and still rising.

"How far?" George asked over his right shoulder. The tall min-er's head lamp beam shone on two men limping ahead of them.

"Two thousand feet maybe. You ever been in a tight like this in a mine?"

"No."

"This'n makes five for me. I lost my pa at Reed's Works nine years ago." The tall miner's light followed two ceiling timbers. "Shaft seems to be holding good enough."

Above the sloshing legs George heard the ceiling and wall tim-bers groaning like some old sailing ship under full sail.

When the shaft floor became a slight incline, George felt the weight of the freezing cold river move slowly down his legs to his knees then to his aching calves then to his ankles. Feeling his feet pump water over the tops of his boots, he knew they had climbed to dry ground. The floor leveled out and the men picked up their pace. But they did not run. Several men leaned heavily on others. Ahead of George, the tall miner's lamp briefly revealed two miners carrying a third man whose legs ended above his knees. Black water drained from the severed pantlegs of the bib overalls on the miner with no feet and no shins.

George tried walking to take some of his weight from the strong shoulders on each side of him. He looked up when someone laughed out loud.

Two hundred yards ahead, George saw a square hole which opened into dim yellow light.

"Looky there, boy. That be home. Now's the real scary part."

"How's that?" George asked.

"This here mountain has to give us ten more minutes. And she has a cold hard heart."

By now George could smell smoke. His heart quickened but he sensed that the smoke did not come from behind him. He felt light-headed and nauseated. At least there was no pain in his right hand and arm. They were numb. He glanced to his right and was relieved to see his unfeeling arm still behind the tall miner's neck. Forcing his eyes to stay open, he watched the tunnel entrance grow. He heard women shouting one or two voices at a time.

The blankets were gone when the legless miner was carried out of Mahaney Pit's black mouth. Esther watched half a dozen women fall upon the two and a half men who shuffled from the hole into the lantern light. Lamps swinging in cramped hands made the eerie glow move from side to side, ebbing and flowing like a gentle tide. When the weak night wind shifted on her moist face, Esther looked up. High clouds of black smoke blowing north from Hill Farm made stars wink on and off like beacons. Moonlight glowed in a hole in the high black clouds of coal soot. She squinted up at the Moon's round, bright left rim. The old waning Moon's right side was gone in its eternal cycle as true and mysterious as the rhythm of Esther's own new body.

The sudden cries of two women drew her face back to the

mine. A short miner and a tall one dragged a third who left toe tracks which disappeared behind them into the pit. Rushed by their shrieking women and small children, the two men carefully laid down their burden.

Esther recognized George Gordon on the ground. Commanding her legs to walk calmly, she crossed the police line and dropped to her knees beside George lying face up with his eyes closed. She saw his bandaged stump and the shoelace tourniquet above his right wrist.

She touched the coal-dust-black face while she willed her eyes to remain dry. Proud that no tears rolled down her face, she felt her heart driving all her blood into her cheeks.

"George Gordon?"

The young man opened his eyelids. He blinked in the yellow glow.

"Esther? Are we out?"

"Yes. Are you hurt badly?"

"Just my hand." He tried to raise the wreckage of his right arm, but it was too far away.

"Doc Patterson will fix it when we get home."

George nodded. Esther felt a strong hand upon her shoulder. Looking up, she saw the tall miner standing with his other arm around a woman whose belly bulged with a fetal Pennsylvania coal miner.

"The boy did good down below. Is he your'n?"

Esther looked down at George. His eyes were closed but he might be awake. So she only nodded.

"You two can't go home in the middle of the night. You can stay with us and leave for Fairchance tomorrow."

Esther nodded again.

"Did they get anyone out at Hill Farm?"

"No," Esther said.

"How many lost?"

"Thirty-one."

The tall miner shook his head slowly. The Davy lamp on his black soft hat still glowed.

"Our wagon is over there," Esther said on her knees.

The man reached down and pulled George to his wobbly legs. He put George's good arm around the miner's neck again. Esther took the broken side. The miner's woman put her arm around Esther as they led George to Esther's wagon.

Laying George in the empty bay, the two women climbed in and sat on each side of him. The miner took the wood seat and gathered the reins. Esther noticed that one of his boots flapped loosely on his large foot. The boot had no shoelace. Behind them, cries from women and children greeted the last men to leave Mahaney Pit.

Before the miner on the hard seat could collect the team of horses, a young woman and soaking wet miner approached the wagon.

This miner was African black and his fragile-looking woman had hollow cheeks, thin arms, and a coffee-colored face. Her full round belly protruded like the woman facing Esther in the back of old Henry's wagon.

The woman standing in the mud leaned over her unborn child, reached into the wagon, and covered George with her man's clean, new blanket. Then she stepped back, put her arm around her man, and both of them walked into the night which smelled like a thousand chimneys over coal hearths. The woman who gave the blanket to warm George never said a word.

As the tall miner steered the wagon to his company-owned hovel, Hill Farm pit ahead of them glowed orange from underground fires. Families were dispersing from Hill Farm to disappear into the midnight darkness and lonesome grieving.

Crossing the Pittsburgh and Connellsville tracks, George moaned as the wagon lurched. Samuel Carleton could not take his eyes off the red glow of the Hill Farm tomb even as the railroad iron sent white pain up his spine. Passing the Hill Farm Mine, the writer felt heat upon his face. Looking up from Esther's half-closed brown eyes, he saw a Cuban sun peek over the southeast wall of a prison camp in Viñales Valley.

Samuel Carleton knew that in his nub of a pencil there were no more words. His story had finished itself as stories do. He squinted at the fresh sun. Behind his jaundiced eyes he heard the tall miner's voice speaking over his black wet shoulder to Esther Slone half asleep behind him. The miner driving old Henry's best team did not know the girl's name.

"Tomorrow when the sun comes up, the whole world starts new."

TEN

SAMUEL CARLETON SURVEYED THE CARNAGE IN FRESH CLEAN
daylight. All of the murdered Spanish prisoners and all of the Voluntarios who had died assaulting the stockade were gone. Rebels
moved casually about the compound. With only one Spanish regular and only two Voluntarios still alive, the Cubans had little to do
but sip rum-laced coffee. Early Friday morning sun shone brown
on long splashes of dried blood along the stockade walls. Carleton
wondered how the makeshift fortress could bleed. Then he saw
one of the rebels carrying a dead Spaniard slung over his back like
a sack of beans from the officers' mess. The Cuban dragged the
corpse up one of the ladders propped against the upper catwalk
of the stockade wall. The rebel heaved the body over the top into
the heap of old dead and new dead, throwing more food upon the

banquet table of the repulsive blue land crabs, "demons to the nerves," the writer called them, and the turkey vultures with their grotesque red heads on the far side of the camp wall.

When Rosa came to Carleton's side, she looked down at the writer's anguished face and tugged at his shoulder until he turned away from the bleeding wall.

"The child comes quickly now."

"I don't know about such things," the American said gravely. "I was the youngest of fourteen children. Little wonder that my mother lost her mind after my father died."

Rosa returned to María. The American stood and leaned against a barrel beside the officers' hut where Francisco stood.

"It is quiet now," said the priest. "I must go outside to do my work."

"I would not," Manuel said. "There may be more Spaniards coming."

"There are Spanish souls outside, Manolo," Francisco said, looking away from the Cuban's thin face where the sunken eye sockets, cheek bones and whiskered chin were as sharp as broken glass.

Manuel waited for Francisco to walk alone into the sunlit clearing and for the stockade's heavy timber doors to close behind him.

"Vultures do not eat souls," Manuel laughed toward Alfonso.

A black-faced Cuban from Manuel's men interrupted Carleton's mental translation of every other Spanish word caught by his English ears.

"Now, Manolo? Father Francisco is gone," the Cuban said earnestly.

"Now, but quickly," Manuel smiled while lifting a rum bottle to his face.

"What comes now?" Samuel Carleton asked in halting Spanish.

"*La corrida*, Perdido. At Santiago de Cuba, you saw the *ruedo*—the bull ring?"

"Yes. I saw it. But it was abandoned because of the fighting."

"You have seen the bulls run, Gringo?"

"Never." Carleton paused to collect his thoughts. "You can shoot a man through the head, but you cannot remove from his brain a love for the bloody death of a bull." He waited for the Cuban to take offense.

"*Muy bien*," Manuel said merrily. Carleton fell into Alfonso when the old man slapped the American on the back. "You understand. Come."

Manuel led Carleton and Alfonso toward the barbed wire pen where the Spanish prisoners had been slaughtered, save one.

Walking in a sweating crowd of two dozen Cuban veterans, Samuel Carleton watched the lone, nameless Spaniard who still paced and waved his arms at only putrid air and who spoke in breathless, jumbled Castilian to no one. The remnant of his regular army officers' linen uniform hung close to his bone-thin legs. To the writer, the last survivor's rags appeared glued to his body by dysentery down to where the shreds of trousers ended at ankles thin as a Mauser rifle barrel and his black-mud caked bare feet. The officer who gave his mind for Spain wore a regulation straw hat. Carleton knew "cannon fever." Among the Marines at Guantánamo he watched his hand write that, "The weariness of the body and the more terrible weariness of the mind at the endlessness of the thing made it wonderful that at least some of the men did not come out of it with their nerves hopelessly in shreds." He recognized the Spaniard's expression of infinite emptiness.

Carleton lagged behind, slowed by the horror of the Spaniard's face—cheeks hollow, gray eyes lifeless, and trousers heavy with brown, red and yellow wetness, the colors the American believed should be used in the new flag of liberated Cuba. The writer stumbled when Manuel reached back to pull him forward by his shirt.

"Here," Manuel said. He gestured to the other Cubans. "Barrera," he laughed and the Cubans dropped to sit cross-legged around three quarters of the pen's perimeter. No one sat near the blood soaked trench latrine.

The Spanish officer noticed suddenly that he was surrounded by jeering, laughing, Cuban rebels drunk or nearly drunk. A week ago, most of these Cubans had been this Spaniard's prisoners. Carleton imagined that the dead-fish eyes looked squarely into his own sockets and clean through the roll call of his memories to the back of the American's skull.

"*¡Montera!*" Manuel shouted, sitting on warm soil beside a half-empty rum bottle.

The officer's wild arms dropped to his side. He looked down at Manuel. The look in the Spaniard's eyes made Samuel Carleton wonder if the officer might actually be blind.

"*Montera*," Manuel repeated. "The hat," he said over his right shoulder to Carleton who sat on Alfonso's left.

When the Spaniard removed his straw hat and dropped it, Carleton saw the short pigtail on the back of his head.

"*Coleta*," Manuel said toward the American. "The *capitán* was a *novillero*—an apprentice bullfighter in Spain."

Manuel pointed to one of his own men who stood and approached the dazed, bareheaded officer. The rebel moved a wood stake with barbed wire around it, forming a gate to the pen. He entered and handed the Spaniard a muddy bean sack. Its seams had been opened to make a bolt of colorless cloth. Morning breeze fluttered the flaps. By instinct, the Spaniard took it in his left hand. The edge of the cloth in his hand was rigid where it had been wrapped around a rough-cut wood stick.

"The *muleta*," Manuel instructed the American.

Carleton nodded dumbly.

"*¡Estoque!*" Manuel called to his man who put a narrow tree branch two feet long into the Spaniard's other hand. To Carleton, it looked like a birch switch from every schoolboy's nightmares.

"*¡Toro!*" a squatting Cuban cried and the sitting rebels joined the mid-morning chorus, "*¡Toro! ¡Toro!*"

The first Cuban left the pen as a stocky, bow-legged rebel stood among the insurrectos seated outside the pen. He pulled two rusty machetes from his belt of hemp rope, entered the pen, and raised a long blade in each fat fist to his temples glistening black with sweat. He faced the Spaniard. Dull even in glaring sunlight, the weapons pointed toward the officer ten paces away.

The bulky Cuban holding the blades ran a filthy bare foot across the dirt. This he did three times without blinking at the Spaniard slouching blurry eyed, hatless, bare feet close together, holding against his sides in one hand a long twig bent at the end and in his left hand a rag sack limp except for the stick in his fist.

"*¡Toro!*" Manuel shouted.

In the pen the Spaniard stood arms down, head cocked slightly toward his right shoulder.

When the machete beside the Cuban's left ear dipped with his head, he ran toward the officer's face but the Spaniard shuffled out of his path. The puffing Cuban skidded to a stop three paces past the Spanish captain. The left blade caught and tore the officer's left sleeve.

"*¡Flojo!*" Manuel laughed toward the Cuban whose blades never moved from his head. "A weak bull," Manuel grinned at Carleton with a jab of his elbow into the American's side.

Samuel Carleton's wide, yellow-eyed stare watched the trickle of blood flowing narrowly down the Spaniard's arm, around his left wrist, and dripping onto the bean sack. The American felt suddenly nauseated but his stomach was hard empty.

The thick Cuban did not lower his blades. He faced the Spaniard with the bleeding arm.

Carleton could not close his mouth and he could not make his
legs stand when the Spaniard slowly raised the red and gray sack
waist high and lifted the twig in his right hand to arm's length
in front of his dripping face. Against his will the writer watched
the officer tilt his head as if sighting down the twig aimed now at
the Cuban's broad forehead. With his left hand he raised the stick
holding the cloth and he flicked it once at the Cuban with machetes apparently growing long and warm from the sides of his head.
Noon sun well above the stockade wall scalded Carleton's eyeballs.
But the American could neither blink nor look away. He wanted
to look away. And he wanted his stunned senses to stop repeating
inside his head the lines he had written two long months earlier,
a now silly and pathetic reflection about "the western man who
chewed tobacco, and yet, in certain poker games, acknowledged
that he dared not turn his head long enough to perform a certain
obligation of men who chew tobacco." Samuel Carleton, like that
westerner, could not turn his head.

The thick Cuban ran again at the Spaniard, who again slid
away from the assault.

"¡Olé!" the sitting Cubans shouted and a dozen rebels on the
catwalk parapet screamed, "¡Olé!"

This time the Cuban passed on the Spaniard's right and new
blood ran from the officer's deeply slashed right forearm.

"Sin vergüenza," Manuel said over his raised fist pounding
the stagnant air in the Spaniard's direction. "This torero is without shame," he said to Carleton who leaned away from the elbow
which did not come.

"¡La hora de la verdad!" Manuel shouted firmly and impatiently. "Time to end this," he said toward Carleton and waved his rum
bottle at the Spaniard.

A light hot wind climbed over the stockade wall and swept the compound. It ruffled the Spaniard's thinning gray hair covering his ears.

Samuel Carleton raised his chin when the Spaniard lifted his. When their eyes met for a heart beat, the American saw a flicker of light in the weary eyes too far and too long away from home.

The Spanish officer turned slightly so his left shoulder faced the panting Cuban. Again the Spaniard raised the twig in his right hand and aimed its bent, trembling tip at the Cuban's face.

The American gasped and raised his hands to his eyes when the Spanish captain suddenly stepped on naked tiptoes through blood and dysentery-fouled mud squarely toward the round rebel who must have hated the Spaniard for generations before either man was born.

The Cubans and Manuel and Alfonso stood shouting when the machete wielding Cuban lunged forward hard, met the Spaniard, and drove his face, his skull, and both blades deep into the captain's chest. When the officer fell backward, the wooden handles of the two machetes stood erect and dull and motionless in the sunlight shining brightly on the sweat dripping from the officer's dead face.

Shouting, laughing Cubans pulled down the pen's fence and all of them crowded around their comrade who had killed the last of the garrison's Spaniards.

Manuel turned around and stepped back to the American— the only man down on the warm earth who was not dead. Grunting, Manuel hoisted the writer to his feet.

"Human agony is not pleasant," the American sighed.

"I have seen worse *cornadas*—gorings—than this one, Gringo." Manuel grinned and his grizzled face glowed red in full sunlight. "That one," he gestured over his shoulder toward the dead officer, "that one knew this was his *despedida*—his last performance in the ring. In the end, he behaved well," Manuel nodded thoughtfully.

Two rebels dragged the officer by his bare muddy ankles toward the stockade wall, leaving the corpse near the closed gate. The writer watched and he remembered the body of a dead boy in Greece killed by a Turkish bullet in the chest. "This dead young Greek had nothing particularly noble in his face," he wrote nineteen months ago. "They had lifted the body and laid it to the rear in order to get it out of the way." So with the dead Spaniard dragged by his naked feet.

Carleton staggered to his place beside the officers' mess where he sat without looking up or toward the stockade's entrance latched tightly with leather thongs. He pulled the pages from last night bearing witness in tight clear handwriting to the last of Esther and George. Reading quickly, he drew large Xs through his last five pages.

Pecos trotted to his side. His floppy ears perked forward toward Carleton and his dog tongue hung wetly from his open mouth with dog greeting. The writer looked up with narrowed yellow eyes blank and cold. With wolf senses which humans cannot imagine, Pecos felt the ice crystals in his friend's soul, sucked in his tongue, lowered his ears, and sulked away with his black nose nearly touching the ground.

The writer carved a fresh pencil point and he assaulted his last blank sheets of charred paper. He knew that his pencil had no more story in it so he drove the wood stick roughly across the empty page with the cold resolve of a colonel prodding an exhausted wide-eyed regiment uphill over open ground against an impregnable front of stone battlements.

Samuel Carleton found George in the mine where he crouched on his left hand and knees in darkness. His right arm ended at a tight shoelace above where his right hand had lived for 22 years.

That hand lay buried now half a mile away under a wall of coal. Sitting back on his haunches, he cradled his handless arm to his chest. On each side, men walked past him, their legs making little waves in black water at their knees like fast ships cutting the sea with their bows.

George raised his left hand. He felt a voice in his dry throat but he did not recognize its sound.

"Help me."

None of the walking fast shadows stopped. Davy lamps and little oil lamps on cloth caps dimly glowed in a long line against each wall of the black tunnel. To George's bloodshot eyes the passing lights above him resembled the red, eyelike gleam of hostile campfires set in the low brow of distant hills.

"Help me. Someone."

Still no one stopped his steady march through black water knee deep and rising.

But Samuel Carleton's pencil stopped. If George Fleming did not know the sound of his father's voice, the writer did. The writer knew and loved the voice of old Henry best of all. Reading the new words bled from the dead pencil, Carleton heard inside his head old Henry's voice as a boy in Yankee blue, remembering "the red, eyelike gleam of hostile campfires set in the low brow of distant hills." Furious that he had stolen from old Henry whose voice three years earlier had allowed Samuel Carleton to enjoy briefly the mysterious thrill of reaping the full harvest of The Writers' Life, he drew a violent line through the stolen words and started over.

To George Gordon's bloodshot eyes the lights above him passed like heavy, steam locomotives with their single bright eyes cleaving narrow white holes in a long black tunnel.

"Please help me."

Crouching in the new underground river flowing from Mahaney's shattered wall, George felt the icy water flowing under his armpits. Raising his face, he reached for a wall timber with his good left hand which slid down the slippery damp wood.

With every nerve on fire, George crawled toward the unseen entrance of the shaft. On his knees and one good arm like a three-legged dog, he followed the yellow head lamps and lanterns. Legs splashing beside him made wakes which drove oily water over his neck and into his bleeding mouth which had tried to eat a shovel handle. He spit out the mountain's cold black blood with his own blood and pushed on, limping on his left palm, which jagged rocks sliced to the bone.

The Mahaney shaft floor shivered under his bloody hand and bleeding knees. He recognized a spasm of the mountain's beating heart. But she had no soul and she could crush him, drown him, burn him alive, or smother him with poison gas according to her soulless whim.

"Get up, boy, or move out of the way," said a hoarse voice.

George felt a hand grab his thick belt and jerk him to his feet. Standing feebly, he was surprised that the water lapped only at his bare bruised knees.

The tall miner moved without releasing George's belt and he felt himself half pushed and half carried. Stumbling and holding his mutilated arm in his left hand, he looked at the miner called Scovel who held him erect. The face was coal black and its features were lost in the dim light.

"Thank ...".

George disappeared into a dip in the shaft floor. Holding his breath, he reached forward with both hands but he had only one.

Exposed wrist bones burned white hot on the shaft floor. His boots pushed off the sunken ground and his head popped above the water. He pushed and pulled his body forward until he felt dry earth with his left hand.

Crawling and choking on swallowed water, he felt no hand on his belt. He grabbed a wall timber and pulled himself up one palm width at a time. He felt his fingernails ripping away from skin and bone. Pain radiated down to his bowels. Standing now with his forehead against the cold wet wall of stone, George vomited on his mountain.

He turned and commanded his legs to keep pace with the men breathing hard around him. Only in short dim arcs of swaying lanterns and head lamps could he see stooped shoulders and gaunt blackened faces.

For all the times he had been in the company of these dark faces and for all the years he had journeyed into their world, he understood now with startling clarity that he knew nothing. Their breath-holding black world and his were Earth and Moon—so close and yet, so utterly other.

Someone laughed loud and hard ahead. George looked up and saw a dim yellow hole in the dark shadows.

His wife's voice inside his head and little Jimmy like a vapor at her side forced his shaking legs forward step by step.

But George Fleming whimpered, "Esther," before the sudden darkness crushed him and all the lamps went out in one long foul breath from that mountain which cursed him.

Outside the mine in a cool June night, the cries of two women drew Esther's face to the Mahaney shaft entrance. Proud of her tearless eyes, she saw a short man and a tall one stumble out of Mahaney Pit. When they were rushed by their shrieking women and children, the miners dropped a burden they were dragging. After embracing their sobbing families, the two men bent over, picked up what they had left in the black mud, and together they pulled something toward the police cordon.

Esther saw them dragging a body by its ankles. One boot and sock were gone and the bare foot was coal black. Close to the Dunbar Coke guards who stepped wordlessly aside, she recognized George Gordon's up-turned face, his blue-gray eyes and mouth open.

An ancient, hump-backed man with a miner's face hobbled to George. The old face looked carved from the same stone as every Civil War statue standing on every town square in the country, north or south. He knelt beside the corpse, closed its dead eyes, and laid his tattered hat upon its face.

Esther walked slowly to the body and she came down on both knees. The old man disappeared into the crowd behind her. Esther uncovered the face. It was still George Gordon, only wet and coal black. She winced when she saw two forearm bones freshly pink at the ragged right sleeve.

Without a tear, she wiped George's forehead with the hem of her skirt. Then Charles Slone's only child leaned forward and kissed old Henry's son on the clean gray place she had made.

Samuel Carleton blinked and looked at his hot pencil and the hand holding it. Alfonso's amputated right hand had been proven innocent after all. But the writer's hand had already killed Maggie whom he loved and then old Henry whom he loved most of all. Now he had killed Henry's son, his only son. Samuel Carleton threw his pencil squarely into a nearby fire in the warm Cuban earth. He still had the arm which had been celebrated by the Syracuse University baseball team. He managed to gain admission to Syracuse seven years ago only because his mother's uncle, Reverend Jesse Peck, had helped to create the school—the same great uncle who had declared that "novel reading is a crime." Carleton lasted six months before fleeing to New York City to become a newspaperman and writer. He looked up from his murderous hand when he felt Francisco at his side.

"In the name of God," the priest shouted in Spanish with a visible shudder. "Manuel!"

"We have no *mulillas*," Manuel said in Spanish to Francisco. The old Cuban shrugged with an empty bottle of rum in his fist which he pointed at two Cubans who had picked up the dead Spaniard by the ankles to drag his body through the gate. "No mules," he said in English to Carleton.

Gunfire on two sides stopped the priest's response somewhere between his brain and his trembling lips. The Cubans dropped their bloody cargo outside and pulled the gate closed as they dived into the stockade.

"They're coming back! Spaniards to the south and west!" Alfonso shouted.

Rifle and pistol fire intensified in the noon air, misty and calm. The American stood at the officers' hut. Little flecks of palm pulp flew from the pointed tops of the stockade timbers. Numbed by rum and fever, Carleton held out his hand and caught the splinters like falling snow. One fragment landed heavily and stung his dirty fingers. He looked down and saw a revolver's soft lead bullet flattened against the sliver of wood. He looked up when he felt a firm arm touching his elbow.

Alfonso pushed his uncle with his left hand and Carleton with the stump of his right arm. The boy pushed the stumbling American and the priest into the three-sided pigsty.

"You hide here," Alfonso said breathlessly to Francisco and Carleton where Rosa leaned over María, now wrapped in a filthy wet blanket. "There are many Spaniards this time. Maybe twenty-five."

Francisco resisted and pulled away from Alfonso's grip.

"I must stop this madness," the priest shouted above the cracking gunfire all around them. He hesitated, touched his sister's cheek, then ran toward the center of the compound where rebels were kneeling and aiming their Mausers at the top of the walls, where Spanish irregulars were clawing their way over the pointed palm trunks. Rosa's mouth was too dry from fear of the guerilla troops to answer and she stood trembling and watching as her brother ran between the riflemen. He pushed down the hot rifle muzzles of several rebels who moved sideways and resumed firing. No one dared raise his weapon toward the priest. They slithered out of his way.

"Stay inside," a new voice shouted above the rising tide of fire. Manuel had run over to the little shed. "Señora, there are many Spaniards now. Get in the back of the shed and stay out of sight. The Lost One will protect you and the girl when the child comes."

Carleton could not follow the Spanish of the fast-talking Manuel. But the word "perdido" registered as did the tone of contempt which carried it. The American gently pushed Rosa into the ankle-deep pig excrement, turned, and stumbled breathless back into the haze of early morning fog and gunfire. Alfonso followed Manuel, leaving Rosa hunched over María who kicked off the blood and water soaked blanket and pulled white knuckled on the backs of her naked knees and screamed.

Samuel Carleton ran coughing and wheezing in the footprints of Manuel. The old rebel stopped and turned. A smile lit the Cuban's dirty face.

"Where do you run, Perdido?" Manuel shouted above the thunder of their tiny war.

The grinning question in English stopped Carleton. He leaned forward, placed his hands upon his flexed knees, and panted hard toward the moist ground. He looked up with his half-closed eyes without raising his head. He could not think of an answer. But he remembered dead old Henry as a boy in his first battle. "He finally concluded that the only way to prove himself was to go into the blaze, and then figuratively, to watch his legs to discover their merits and faults." So Carleton looked at his legs.

A red-faced rebel rushed toward Manuel and handed him a

Mauser. Manuel took it, laughed once at the gasping gringo and ran firing toward the south wall.

Carleton stood frozen in the center of a maelstrom. Spaniards were scaling the walls on three sides and were firing down into the camp. Firing into the air, rebels were crouching behind water barrels and sacks of beans and rice. There was no smoke from the smokeless powder in the stolen, Spanish Mauser cartridges. Francisco was running through the camp like a man possessed, pleading for peace. The American looked down at his legs. He waited. And he stood there while bullets were thudding into the dirt, raising little mounds of red soil inches from his boots.

Manuel turned around twenty yards away, looked hard at the American, and then burst out laughing. He was laughing so loud that close to him rebels stopped firing and turned to face him.

When Manuel grimaced with pain, the American's legs finally moved one step. The rebel dropped his rifle and fumbled at his shirt. Carleton blinked when he saw Manuel holding up both hands. His thick farmers' hands were dripping dull red.

Shaking where he stood as rebels bumped him in their passing, Carleton looked hard at the old campesino's face. Carleton's dry eyeballs saw Manuel grow taller and his face became white and his gray hair became shaggy blond. The old man's black eyes softened into warm blue. Breaking into a smile, the suddenly tall Cuban pulled open what was now a wrongly blue blouse, opened just enough for the gringo to see, as if only Samuel Carleton were meant to see it like some unclean secret shared by boys.

The Cuban waited for the writer to recognize the ragged red mess on the man's side. Carleton heard only Henry Fleming's voice inside his throbbing head: "As the flap of the blue jacket fell away from the body, he could see that the side looked as if it had been chewed by wolves."

Looking at Carleton, the old rebel's face blackened and he

shrank as his shirt became filthy linen. Manuel smiled, shrugged his shoulders, and crumbled to the ground.

In the center of the compound Carleton stood protected by the same divine messengers who had spread their wings wide around Francisco running unscathed among the still living rebels.

"Gringo!" Manuel shouted on his hands and knees. He looked up with the eyes of a wounded animal. "Yanqui!" The rebel eased his shattered body to the ground, but he never took his gaze from Carleton's aghast face. "Help me," Manuel begged. When he reached out his bloody hand toward the writer, Carleton with all his heart reached toward Manuel. But still, Carleton's distant and unreliable legs refused to move.

Manuel looked up from where his chin touched the bloody ground. He raised his head, lowered his hand, and smiled. Blood dribbled through the gaps between his teeth.

When Manuel nodded without taking his stare from the American's wide yellow eyes, Samuel Carleton shivered. The Cuban lowered his face to the dirt. Face down, he spread his arms wide on the ground and breathed hard once. Then he lay motionless. Pecos ran to his master and he licked his dead face.

Carleton did not feel the running Cuban rebel who smashed into his side. The American found himself panting on the ground and wondering, How precisely did I get here?

For half an hour, the American remained flat on his belly. With his brave heart pounding inside his head, he tried desperately to stand. He was surprised at the heat radiating from the blood-soaked Cuban ground. He moved his head from side to side. He saw bleeding rebels falling and bleeding Spaniards falling. The sun exploded over the top of the stockade's eastern wall when the firing trailed off, leaving behind only the groans of the wounded.

Carleton closed his eyes and thought of sleep. He remembered a line from one of the stories which lived inside his sweating throbbing head. "The eels of despair lay wet and cold against his back." He did not open his eyes when strong hands jerked him to his feet.

"Are you hurt?" Francisco asked.

"I don't know," the suddenly standing American stammered as he blinked and focused. He saw Cubans move among wounded Spaniards and aim their rifles toward the earth and fire through uplifted, pleading Spanish hands.

The priest released his grip on Carleton's arms and he walked toward Manuel. Pecos sat motionless beside him. Francisco knelt and rolled Manuel over. He reached into the dead man's bloody shirt and pulled out something shiny. Standing, the priest returned to Samuel Carleton, reached for the American's hand, raised the palm, and laid a gold pocketwatch over the thin, nicotine-stained fingers. Francisco walked away and knelt down beside three Cubans, wounded and soon to die. The priest lowered his face and Carleton could hear him praying in Latin.

Carleton collected his wits and studied the sudden peace of Saturday noon. With all the Spaniards dead or murdered, only groaning wounded rebels broke the quiet with ghastly bubbling gurgles from pierced lungs.

Alfonso found the American standing dim-eyed in the center of the bloody compound.

"You have had your battle, Gringo."

"My last," Samuel Carleton sighed. "I am done with death like this."

"You will turn all of this into words on paper?"

"If I can, Alfonso."

Carleton surveyed the sunlit charnel house of the new dead and the still dying. He and Alfonso looked toward Manuel. Flies feasted on the dried blood around Manuel's nostrils and the flies covered his blood-browned hands.

"That old man is the revolution," the boy said with a strange smile.

"I suppose so."

"You know nothing of Cuba, Gringo."

Carleton faced Rosa Montoya's son. The American's expression was a question.

"That old man sold my uncle to the Spaniards," Alfonso said. "The Spanish garrison was waiting for Manuel to deliver Uncle Francisco to them. Manuel wanted the bounty offered for the famous rebel priest."

"But Manuel said he loved Francisco. I heard him say it."

"He did love him," Alfonso laughed. "But, Gringo, this is Cuba."

"Does Francisco know that Manuel betrayed him?"

"No."

"Will you tell him?"

"No," the boy soldier said softly.

Alfonso and Carleton watched Francisco move among the dead and wounded. The priest's knees were red from kneeling in the bleeding mud beside Cubans and Spaniards. He prayed without discrimination for mercy upon these gasping whimpering sinners now and at the hour of their deaths which was mostly now. They watched him dribble bread crumbs into bloody open mouths while administering the Latin *viaticum* Eucharist.

Before Samuel Carleton could collect his fever-heavy thoughts, Rosa's son walked away. Carleton stood coughing and he watched the little dog who guarded still his dead friend. For an instant he remembered the scruffy little dog Booth who followed bravely at the heels of black Sergeant Horace Bivins of the all-black 10th Cavalry. Booth spent puppyhood on the former Little Bighorn battlefield out West. After the Americans had charged San Juan Hill on July 1 and the firefight was over, Carleton had found Booth sitting patiently beside the body of Sergeant William Slaughter of the Tenth's G Troop. The loyal dog did not abandon his friend until the litterbearers came for the black trooper's corpse. The dog's loyalty unto death and the soldier's blood had already flowed onto the writer's stack of dirty paper. In the blink of his yellowed eyes, Carleton saw Booth dissolve into Pecos panting beside Manuel.

Smoke and ground fog settled over the compound like a cloud sent by Francisco's God to heal the blood-soaked Cuban earth scarred now with little clods of soil raised by bullets and by desperate fingernails. Carleton turned toward the pigsty. He could not see past its open side which looked like a black tunnel entrance against the stockade wall behind it. One long wet scream rolled from the shed. A heartbeat later, he heard tiny lungs cry for their first gulp of free Cuban air, free for the first time since the sails of Columbus had climbed out of the island's eastern horizon.

INSIDE THE SHED, ALFONSO STOOD OVER HIS MOTHER. ALFONSO carried a warm Mauser rifle in his surviving hand. Rosa huddled in dried pig droppings. She had wrapped the wet blanket around the girl and the son at her breast. The older woman laid her hand on the covered infant and she leaned over María Teresa. Rosa Montoya sang softly in the gloom.

> *Durme, durme, mi almo donzello*
> *Durme, durme sin ansia y dolor*
> *Heq tu esclava que tanto desea*
> *Ver tu sueño con grande amor*

Rosa looked up with tearfilled eyes.

"Do you remember hearing this at my own breast, my son?"

"No," Alfonso said with a voice dry and empty. "There won't be any more attacks. They're all dead. Spain is dead. I have nothing left now."

"You have a son, Alfonso. And now I have a grandson. María

calls him Victor after my husband and your father."

"Your grandson—if he is—will know only new masters who will soon look like your gringo."

"Alfonso," María Teresa whimpered. She pulled down the blanket and fleas jumped like tiny flecks of black pepper. She exposed the infant's head still wet with his mother's water and blood. "Your son, Alfonso. I swear."

"Perhaps," said Victor Delgado's soldier son.

Rosa gently rolled the child away from his mother's blue-veined breast. Kneeling, Rosa turned the red wrinkled face toward Alfonso. The newborn opened his eyes for an instant.

"Look," Rosa said to her son towering above grandmother and child. "Already he has *los ojos del sufrimiento* like you, like your father and Paco, and all of our fathers in Spain. Look, Alfonso." Rosa turned the tiny face back to the breast and covered him.

Alfonso stood blinking down at the women and the little head no bigger than his surviving fist tightly clenched.

"Thank God you are safe, Alfonso." Rosa said. "What about Paco and Samuel?"

"Uncle is busy sending souls to heaven. Your gringo is alive out there somewhere, too. Uncle Paco's God protects fools and cowards."

"Samuel is no coward," Rosa said softly. "He tries. He has much courage but even his courage is sick with fever. Now we can all go home and become a family again. There is still time."

"María is not my family, Mother. The only family I had cut off my hand, whored with Spanish officers, or became a priest for the men trying to kill me. I am a Spaniard. Alhambra and the great suffering are ancient history. I never became a Cuban peasant like you and Father. I will go home to Madrid with the others when the Yanquis bring the boats for us. I will carry father's name, Delgado, with me. When my king comes of age to take the Spanish throne,

I shall fight for him."

Rosa looked down at the ground. She sat cross-legged where long-ago-eaten pigs had rested.

"I thought it was a killing hand," Rosa said through tears running down her face and making tiny riverlets of sweaty grime. "I thought I had made you a killer."

"I am only a soldier," the boy said. "God go with you, Mother. And especially with Uncle Paco." He looked down at the girl with the almost black, tear-stained face. "And with you and the child."

Alfonso shifted the weight of the heavy rifle. He lifted it out of the crook of his arm and wedged its stock under his armpit. He held the Mauser with his good hand, muzzle downward, and steadied it with his stump. He could hardly see his mother's face in the shadows.

Rosa was driven backward by the concussion of the blast which exploded inside her son's head. Brain tissue slapped her hard in the face and she grabbed her stinging eyes where bone fragments scratched her face. The boy's skull vaporized into a warm cloud of melting flesh.

Samuel Carleton was standing in the center of the camp when he heard the single report of the Mauser. He recognized its peculiar thunder. He thought he could even hear the strangely musical whine of its heavy bullet prone to tumbling in the thick Cuban air.

The American ran toward the pigpen. He could taste blood on his lips as his wind came hot and wet from his decomposing lungs. Each running stride sent white-hot pain up his spine. His swollen liver slammed hard against his ribs. Carleton skidded to a stop in the blood-wet mud and sunshine outside the dark pigpen. He stumbled the last two paces and stopped beside Francisco.

The priest still squinted over the sights of the Mauser which he had lifted only to protect his Rosita from a Spaniard in the dark and stinking gloom.

ELEVEN

"All is lost, Perdido."

Rosa Montoya stood in their room at Mary Horan's boarding house. On the bed, María Teresa nursed Rosa's grandson, eight days old. Rosa watched Carleton packing two dirty shirts and three bottles of warm beer into a bean sack. He gently pushed into the sack a muddy book, *Soldiers of Fortune*. Inside the well worn cover was a kind note scrawled by Richard Harding Davis, the most famous American war correspondent in Cuba. He also saved copies of fragments of his book manuscript etched through tattered sheets of Rogers Carbonic Paper.

"Then you will stay in Havana?" the American asked through a cough.

"Yes. My husband is buried here. And so will my dear son and my only brother. The fighting and the fever were just too much even for Paco's great soul. Manuel's men said they will help me bring their bodies back from the valley in the spring because Manolo loved Paco, too." Carleton stepped close to Rosa and she laid her head upon his sunken chest. "Oh, Perdido, tonight is Noche Buena. Can't you stay with us until after Christmas?"

"My ship leaves this afternoon. I don't know when I'll get another one. My New York *Journal* is very upset with me for filing only sixteen dispatches since I came to Havana in August. I don't think they will pay my fare if I wait another day since I sent my last report to the cheap bastards on November 9. I'm sorry."

Rosa wept. The girl looked down at her son.

When they had returned from the country, no one asked any questions about the Spanish officer found dead on the stairs two weeks ago when Rosa and her little family had fled the city. No one asked; no one cared.

Samuel Carleton fumbled with his little sack of worldly possessions. He reached into his pocket, toyed with his cold pipe, and left it there. Rosa looked at the little table of Mauser cartridge boxes where a ragged saddlebag lay among dirty linen and well chewed pencils.

"I can carry that for you," Rosa said. She pushed away from the American and wiped her darkly puffy eyes with her sleeve.

Carleton picked up the leather bag which had belonged to one of Manuel's troop. He opened it and pulled out a pile of muddy, frayed paper secured with a filthy piece of string. The edges of the thick stack were torn and ragged as if nibbled by mice. He held the paper in both hands as gently as he would carry María's newborn child. He handed Rosa the heavy manuscript written in ink and pencil, fever and passion.

"Samuel Carleton is not my real name, Rosa. I used that name in Jacksonville, Florida, and here when I stayed at the Hotel Pasaje last August. My real name is on these, my book and a new story written in the country. I dedicated the book to you for loving me. In Spanish," he smiled tightly. "And to the memories of Francisco and Alfonso. When the Americans come in three weeks, maybe you can sell them. Once, my name was worth something."

Rosa wiped her eyes. She took the bound paper and studied it through the tears streaming down her face.

"This is all that I am," he said softly. "Only the written words survive."

Looking older than his 27 years, the fragile writer with the rotting teeth embraced the woman, hard. He picked up his sack and knelt to gently touch María's face. Then he opened the door and walked toward the stairs.

Behind him, Rosa stood barefoot in the doorway. Her gringo paused on each step to catch his breath.

"Go with God, Perdido," the woman whispered. Behind her, María Teresa breathed, "*Vaya con Dios*," toward her suckling infant.

The American writer walked slowly into Christmas Eve, 1898. Saturday afternoon sunshine warmed his yellow cheeks. He listened to the sound of La Habana Vieja's narrow alleys under his worn-out shoes as he made his way to the harbor and the sea. He had booked passage to New York City on the ship *City of Washington*—the same ship which had evacuated him from Cuba in July under the yellow fever flag. Seven weeks later he had shuffled into Havana and into Rosa's warm bed.

The correspondent and storyteller did not look back through the blinding tropical sun in a purple sky heavy with the scent of Old Havana which always smelled like "old straw" to his pen. He only stopped once—at Machina Wharf to stand head bowed, hands folded, lips quivering silently at the rusting wreck of *Maine*. Opening his eyes and turning his head he expected to feel Rosa at his side. But Rosa was not there and he stood alone.

After his ship and the winter sun disappeared in the west, Rosa Montoya de Delgado fed Stephen Crane's words one page at a time into the potbellied stove to keep her grandson and María Teresa and Pecos warm till morning.

Taps

The honored dead of Stark County, Ohio, 1898

8th Ohio Volunteer Infantry

Sgt. Clyde B. Crubaugh, Alliance

Pvt. Frank Eckley, Canton

Pvt. Frank Gibler, Canton

Pvt. Frank J. Hagaman, Canton

Pvt. Charles Harbet, Canton

Pvt. James B. Heacock, Alliance

Pvt. David F. Hoshour, Canton

Cpl. William R. Knowles, Alliance

Pvt. Guy G. Kosht, Canton

Capt. John A. Leininger, Canton

Pvt. James L. McGrath, Canton

Pvt. Charles Mitchell, Canton

Pvt. John O. Patterson, Alliance

Pvt. Ora N. Royer, Alliance

Cpl. Charles E. Tarner, Canton

Pvt. John G. Treuthardt, Alliance

Capt. Henry L. Willis, Canton

Pvt. Edward S. Wingerter, Canton

NOTES

FRONTISPIECE

1. "That was all it was to him ..." William Faulkner, *Absalom! Absalom!* NY: Vintage International, Random House, 1936, 1986, 1990, Pages 201-202.

2. "What's the use of not being wounded..." Ernest Hemingway, *A Farewell to Arms.* NY: Charles Scribner's Sons, 1929; Book of the Month Club edition, 1993, Page 182.

ONE

1. Sinking of the cruiser *Maine*: Dierks, 17-19; Blow, 31, 38, 102, 107, 109, 114-115, photo of Colón Cemetery funerals in Blow at Page 256; O'Toole, 30-31, 126 (citing 268 dead); Keller, 38 (citing 260 dead);

Samuels, 90, 92-93, 97, 106-108, 161, 163, 250 (citing 252 seamen and Marines killed outright with 15 more dying later from their wounds).

2. Crane's father, uncle, and grandfather were Methodist ministers: Benfey, 25-26.

3. "... only a little ink more or less." From Stephen Crane, "War is Kind," No. 79 in Crane's *The Black Riders and Other Lines*: Katz, 544.

4. "None of them knew the color of the sky." This is Stephen Crane's most famous opening line from his short story "The Open Boat." Colvert, 277; Katz, 360.

5. Commodore sinking which resulted in Crane's short story, "The Open Boat": Berryman, 155-165, 165-166; Brown, 69-74; O'Toole, 78-79; Milton, 137; Benfey, 185-192; Davis, 178-181; Katz, 331 (Note 1).

6. "He resembled a man on a sinking ship ...". From Stephen Crane, "One Dash-Horses": Bergon, 40.

7. Stephen Crane moves into Mary Horan's boarding house on September 1, 1898. The sources are in dispute as to whether the boarding house was owned by a Mary or Martha Clancy or a Mary Horan. Advocates for Martha Clancy's include Brown, 439; Berryman, 227; Milton, 356-358; Benfey, 252-255; Bowers, 500. While these sources seem unanimous that Crane lived at Martha Clancy's, Linda Davis at Page 280 is the principal source for arguing that Martha Clancy's was really Mary Horan's lodging house. Stallman, at Page 425, also argues that Crane did live at Horan's but disguised her as "Mary Clancy" in his short story, "The Majestic Lie." This author accepts the conclusions of Davis and Stallman. See also Bloom 9, 12.

8. "... red-hot wire.": Crane, 258.

9. "Historians are, as a rule, unsentimental." From Stephen Crane, "Not Much of a Hero": Bergon, 151.

10. "... looked like a collection of real tropic [sic] savages ...". Crane, 256.

11. "[T]here was a strange effect of a graveyard ...". From Stephen Crane, "Experiment in Misery": Colvert, 253; Katz 160; noted Benfey,

60.

12. "He had blindly been led by quaint emotion ...". From Stephen Crane, "A Mystery of Heroism": Colvert, 264.

13. "He starves and he makes no complaint ...". Crane dispatch from Cuba, dateline 27 June 1898: Bowers, 147, 489.

14. "The battle was like the grinding of an immense and terrible machine ...". Stephen Crane, *The Red Badge of Courage*: Katz 238.

15. Spanish warship *María Teresa*, beached and destroyed by U. S. Navy, 3 July 1898: Keller, 182, 188; Blow, 347; Dierks, 138-140; O'Toole, 333, 335.

16. "No man should be called upon to report ...": Stephen Crane quoted by Richard Harding Davis in 1897: Davis, 193.

17. U. S. Marines with Stephen Crane land at Gauntánamo Bay, Cuba, singing "It'll Be a Hot Time in the Old Town Tonight," 10 June 1898: O'Toole, 248; Blow, 291; Trask, 140; Milton, 303, 305; Brown, 280-281.

18. U. S. landing on beach at Daiquiri, Cuba. Surf and pier at Daiquiri: Alger, 97; Kennan, 154; Dierks, 83, 153. Landing craft: O'Toole, 265-267; Keller, 122-123; Kennan, 79; Alger, 79; Bradford, 115. Landing troops sing "Hot Time": Jones, 100.

19. Drowning horses at Daiquiri landing zone: Brown, 307; O'Toole, 266-267; Dierks, 85; Keller, 126; Post, 110.

20. Theodore Roosevelt sketch: Mason, 88; Blow, 273, 276, 287; Keller, 63; Kennan, 99; Langford, 56, 103, 106-109, 145, 194; Downey, 70-71; Roosevelt, 60, 221; Jeffers, 147.

21. "Camp Hungry" at Sevilla, Cuba: Feuer, 35.

22. Theodore Roosevelt kills a Spaniard on San Juan Hill: Roosevelt, 139. Theodore Roosevelt gloats and shows off dead Spaniard he killed, which William H. Harbaugh calls "one of those desecrations of the human spirit that will forever bar him [Roosevelt] from the immortality of Jefferson, Lincoln, and [President Woodrow] Wilson." William Henry Harbaugh, *The Life and Times of Theodore Roosevelt.*

NY: Collier, 1961, 1966, Page 107. "Crowded hour" of Lt. Col. Roosevelt: Roosevelt, 126.

23. Theodore Roosevelt's revolver salvaged by his brother-in-law, William S. Crowles, USN, from *Maine*: Jeffers, 111, 236.

24. Lt. Jules Ord, killed San Juan Hill: Cashin, 173-174. Portrait of Lt. Ord: Goldstein, 115.

25. William "Bucky" O'Neill, killed San Juan Hill: O'Toole, 310-311, 313-314; Trask, 241-242; Jones, 178; Jeffers, 231; Roosevelt, 123-124.

26. "[O]ne could have sworn that the man had great smears of red paint ... reaching dignity": Stephen Crane dispatch from Greece, dateline 10 May 1897: Bowers, 29, 450.

27. Richard Harding Davis' recurring sciatica pain: Langford, 148-149, 188, 191; Downey, 139.

28. Pvt. Stovall and heroic black troops: Cashin, 169, 171, 189.

29. 9th U. S. Cavalry called "Nigger Ninth": Johnson, 38.

30. That Cubans stole U. S. Army food: Jones, 193.

31. U. S. troops use ants to eat the lice from their clothes: Post, 256.

32. "... a fleet of red-hot stove lids." Stephen Crane on flees in Greece, dateline 1 May 1897: Bowers, 16, 423.

33. Pubic lice called "Rough Riders": Blow, 370.

Two

1. Riots by pro-Wyler Voluntarios in Havana, January 1898: Dierks, 16; O'Toole, 20, 111; Samuels, 48-49.

2. That Stephen Crane had blue-gray eyes: Davis, 230.

3. "I came into Havana without permission ... But no one molested me.": Stephen Crane dispatch, dateline Havana, 28 August 1898: Bowers, 188, 503.

4. Governor-General Valeriano Weyler and concentrado detention camps: Blow, 29; O'Toole, 56-58, 84; Milton, 84; Trask, 8-9;

Keller, 13; Millis, 59;

5. "Catch any Spaniard in a lie ...": Stephen Crane dispatch, dateline Havana, 4 November 1898: Bowers, 211, 507; quoted at Stallman, 434.

6. Stephen Crane 5 feet, six or seven inches tall, and 120 pounds: Berryman, 21, 24; Benfey, 164. (Stephen Crane's bad teeth noted elsewhere: Davis, 121.)

7. "To a woman, war is a thing ...": Stephen Crane dispatch from Greece, dateline 26 April 1897: Bowers, 267, 523.

8. General Shafter's sickly condition in Cuba: O'Toole, 299, 327-328; Trask, 234, 250; Blow, 311, 328; Keller, 172-173; Alger, 174-176.

9. "... with a kind of slow rhythm ...": Crane, 170.

10. Black trooper carried a tired dog after San Juan Hill and Caney battles: Nankivell, 83.

11. Army surgeons, July 1-3, 1898: Kennan, 114, 139-140. Field hospitals: Milton, 343; Keller, 171; Trask, 295.

12. "Through the door of the hospital ...": Stephen Crane dispatch, dateline Greece, 1 June 1897: Bowers, 63, 460.

13. Santiago civilians evacuated, 5 July 1898: O'Toole, 344; Trask, 287; Keller, 176, 202-203. Crane present: Brown, 393.

14. 6 July 1898, first confirmed yellow fever case: Trask, 324; review of symptoms for malaria and yellow fever, and treatment: Kennan, 320; Keller, 201; Blow, 371 (puts first yellow fever case on July 10).

15. Siboney yellow fever: Mason, 252. Spreading yellow fever epidemic among U. S. Troops, July and August, 1898: Kennan, 158, 160, 213; O'Toole, 348; Trask, 329-330, 332, 579 (Note 24).

16. General Shafter stopped military funerals as bad for morale: Cosmas, 255; Post, 260; Feuer, 115.

17. "... that extraordinary wail of mourning ['Taps'] ...": Stephen Crane dispatch from Puerto Rico, dateline 5 August 1898: Bowers, 176, 496.

18. 8 July 1898, Stephen Crane evacuated with yellow fever by hos-

pital ship: Benfey, 252; Brown, 432 (note); Milton, 346; Berryman, 225; Bowers, 492-493; Davis, 267-268.

19. "bank of flowers" and "[T]hrough this lane there passed ...": Crane, 306-307 (syntax changed).

20. "I know nothing ...": Stephen Crane dispatch from Cuba, dateline 24 June 1898: Bowers, 143, 487.

21. "I was a child ...": Stephen Crane, quoted at Benfey, 245; Davis, 253.

THREE

1. "It is an axiom of war ...": Crane, 19.

2. "The advantage of international complication ...": Stephen Crane dispatch from Greece, dateline 1 May 1897: Bowers, 15, 423.

3. "Plans for truces ...": Stephen Crane dispatch from Greece, dateline 22 May 1897: Ibid., 557, 459.

4. "a man becomes another thing ...": Stephen Crane in *Red Badge of Courage*: Katz, 214.

5. "Most wounded men ...": Stephen Crane dispatch from Greece, 10 May 1897: Bowers, 22, 424.

6. Siboney is burned 15 July 1898: Kennan, 162.

7. Black "immunes" replaced white troops: Trask, 326. Black 24th Infantry moved to Siboney, 16 July 1898: Trask, 326; Alger, 449-450; Keller, 208; Cosmas, 257; Gatewood, 103; Fletcher, 43. Since the sources vary on the number of 24th Infantrymen who became sick, the author used Fletcher's statistics.

8. "A curious feature ...": Theodore Roosevelt: Roosevelt, 199. Servant Marshall also sick: Ibid., 219.

9. Black troops and segregation at Tampa, Florida, staging camp, June 1898, and banned from "whites-only" public stores: Gatewood, 43, 50.

10. "... plenty of bourbon for the white men ...": Post, 53.

11. "The colored infantrymen ...": Tampa *Morning Tribune* of 5 May 1898, quoted at Gatewood, 47-48. Tampa racial tension between white citizens and black troops, June 1898: Ibid., 48-49. Tampa racial disturbance and shooting of black troops by white troops, 6 June 1898: Ibid., 52-53.

12. U. S. Navy troop ship *Concho* segregated by race, 8 June 1898: Nankivell, 69; Fletcher, 34; Gatewood, 55; Johnson, 24-25. *Concho's* segregated coffee pots: Johnson, 25.

13. Daiquiri, Cuba, landing when two men drown: O'Toole, 269-269; Trask, 214; Wheeler, 75; Jones, 4-5.

14. General Shafter's history leading black army troopers: Carlson, 31-32, 37, 45, 52-55, 61, 75-87, 115.

15. Sgt. George Berry of black 10th Cavalry, 1 July 1898: Gatewood, 59; Jeffers, 234; Roosevelt, 129.

16. Racism after the war: Gatewood, 103, 112-113. October 10, 1898, murders of 10th Cavalry troopers in Huntsville, Alabama: Fletcher, 11.

17. United States casualties, Cuba and Puerto Rico, June-August 1898: Alger, 454; Trask, 335; O'Toole, 17, 375; Millis, 353, 367. The sources vary slightly in the numbers. Training camp casualties: Keller, 241; Trask, 160.

18. "When all has been said and done ...". Stephen Crane dispatch, dateline 4 September 1898: Bowers, 190, 503.

19. "My pen is dead." Stephen Crane letter to Nellie Crouse, 18 March 1896: Benfey, 169; Stallman, 1898; Cady and Wells, 54 (by permission of the publisher).

20. Stephen Crane's dog "Sponge" in England: Benfey, 4, 13-14, 17, 19-20, 257, 260, 270 (Crane portrait with Sponge: Plate 26); Berryman, 235, 239, 258-260; Milton, 376-377.

21. Cora Stewart, also known as Cora Taylor: Langford, 186, 188; Bloom, 104; Berryman, 168, 171, 178, 180; Benfey, 202-203, 206; Milton, 160-161, 166-168; Downey, 138-139; Davis, 174-176. Location of Hotel de Dream, Jacksonville: Davis, 176.

Four

1. "I cannot help vanishing ...": Stephen Crane (probably 1896), quoted at: Benfey, 42; Davis, 150; Stallman, 201, 421. Syntax changed.

2. "I thought they were all shooting at me ...": Stephen Crane, "The Veteran": Katz, 325.

3. "[I]n my first battle ...": Ibid., 324.

4. "I have faced death ...": Crane, 270.

5. "[T]he only man who has any business ...": Stephen Crane dispatch, dateline 4 November 1898: Bowers, 213, 508.

6. "From a distance ... it was like a game ...": There are two versions of this dispatch from Greece by Stephen Crane, dateline 10 May 1897. Ibid., 20, 424.

7. "... dreamed all his life ...": Stephen Crane, *Red Badge of Courage*: Katz, 192.

8. Death of Dr. Gibbs. "I thought this man would never die ... I wanted him to die." Crane, 238; Benfey, 244-245; Blow, 291-292; Milton, 303-304. Portrait of Dr. Gibbs, Goldstein, 73. The quotation is from Crane's *Wounds in the Rain*. Although *Wounds* has Dr. Gibbs dying all night from his head wound, Crane did write a battlefield dispatch, dateline 12 June 1898, in which he has Dr. Gibbs dead in only ten minutes: Bowers, 129, 484.

Five

1. "War is death." Crane, 254.

2. "[A] fight at close range ...": Ibid., 189.

3. "war the red animal ...": Stephen Crane, *Red Badge of Courage*: Katz, 213.

4. "It requires sky ...": Stephen Crane in "Flannery and his Short Filibustering Adventure": Katz, 347.

5. "I write what is in me." Stephen Crane, quoted at Davis, 137.

6. "The lives of some people ...": Stephen Crane, letter to Nellie Crouse, 31 December 1895: Cady and Wells, 30 (by permission of the publisher).

7. "I work better at night ...": Stephen Crane, quoted at Davis, 61, 67; Stallman, 60, 107.

8. "His face ceased instantly ..."; death of Henry Fleming, the fictional hero of *Red Badge of Courage*, and Henry's grandson Jim: Stephen Crane, "The Veteran": Katz, 326.

9. "It was a beautiful sound ...": Stephen Crane dispatch, Greece, dateline 10 May 1897. There are two, slightly different versions of this dispatch: Bowers, 20, 24, 424.

10. Edward Marshall, reporter, wounded at Las Guásimas: Blow, 303; O'Toole, 279; Davis, 259; Bowers, 145.

11. Stephen Crane fired by New York *World* and hired by New York *Journal*: Berryman, 226; Brown, 432; Milton, 354-355.

12. "red sickness." Stephen Crane, *Red Badge of Courage*: Katz, 318.

13. "dust on a butterfly's wings." Ernest Hemingway, *A Moveable Feast*. NY: Charles Scribner's Sons, 1964; Book of the Month Club edition, 1993, Page 147.

14. "... crack like hot stones." Stephen Crane, *Red Badge of Courage*: Katz, 223.

15. 10th Cavalry whistles "Star-spangled Banner" on the march, 30 June 1898: Cashin, 90.

16. Signal Corps hydrogen-filled balloon beside river and above U. S. troops: Keller, 151-152; O'Toole, 282, 287; Alger, 154. Trask erroneously calls the balloon hot-air powered, 239. Balloon draws Spanish fire at Aguadores River: O'Toole, 305-306, 310-312.

17. "... a fat, wavering, yellow thing ...": Crane, 12.

18. That Stephen Crane was at the crossing of the Aguadores River and at Bloodly Brook: Milton, 330.

19. Bloody Brook/Bloody Bend: Mason, 186; Keller, 153, 157;

O'Toole, 311-313; Wheeler, 53; Feuer, 51.

20. Black troops' heroism at Bloody Brook/Bloody Bend: Fletcher, 40; Cashin, 178, 272.

21. "... a miserable huddle at Bloody Bend ...": Crane, 277.

22. "heat, dust, rain, thirst, hunger and blood." Stephen Crane dispatch from Siboney, dateline 27 June 1898: Bowers, 147, 489.

23. "soft, mellow, sweet ..." cooing of doves: Crane, 104.

24. "... the Spanish guerilla calling ...": Ibid., 99.

25. "I have never heard ...": Ibid., 242.

26. "They wound along this narrow winding path ...": Stephen Crane, dateline 24 June 1898: Bowers, 143.

27. "Soldiering at its best ...": Stephen Crane dispatch, dateline 4 November 1898: Ibid., 213, 508.

28. "[T]he Mauser is a fine weapon." Stephen Crane dispatch, 4 September 1898: Ibid., 191, 503.

29. German-made, Spanish-issue Mauser's bullet: Feuer, 64.

30. "... frightful tearing effect ...": Stephen Crane dispatch, 14 June 1898: Bowers, 131, 485.

31. "Bullets began to whistle among the branches ...": Stephen Crane, *Red Badge of Courage*: Katz, 218.

32. "... as if one string ...": Stephen Crane on Mauser rifle sound, dispatch, dateline 22 June 1898: Bowers, 137, 487.

33. "When the wounded men dropped ...": Crane, 101-102.

34. Las Guásimas engagement, 24 June 1898, noting Jenkins, Capron, Fish, Haefner: Jones, 116-117 (giving the number of Rough Riders deployed as 423), 127, 129, 131-132, 134, 290, 301; Roosevelt, 39, 104, 106, 239, 266; Jeffers, 154, 214-215; Feuer, 27; O'Toole, 271-278; Alger, 104-105, 108; Mason, 171-172, 176-177; Wheeler, 19, 26, 33-35; Trask, 220-221; Dierks, 89-91; Blow, 301-302. Several accounts of Henry Haefner's heroism spell his name "Heffner" and some of the sources list his hometown as Gallop, New Mexico, or Marissa, Illinois.

35. Las Guásimas engagement: Richard Harding Davis as medic;

Pvt. Dawson; and Hamilton Fish's pocketwatch: Downey, 154-156; O'Toole, 277; Langford, 200; Jones, 132, 294; Jeffers, 212, 214.

36. "... frightful field sport." Stephen Crane dispatch, dateline 22 June 1898: Bowers, 140, 487.

37. Las Guásimas engagement casualties and burials on battle-field: Wheeler, 22, 29, 40; Dierks, 92; Alger, 110; Trask, 222; Milton, 314-316; Keller, 132; Kennan, 101; Jones, 143 (Note 1), 144-145; Roosevelt, 79, (portrait of Sgt. Hamilton Fish, Page 94), 108-109, 239; Jeffers, 216-217. Photo of mass grave of dead Rough Riders and photo of grave of Allyn K. Capron, Jr., USA: Goldstein, 94-95. American wounded sing: Keller, 131, has them singing "America." Brown, 319, has them singing "My Country 'Tis of Thee."

38. "Hang all war stories." Stephen Crane, letter to Nellie Crouse, 5 February 1896: Cady and Wells, 46 (by permission of the publisher).

39. "I am simply a man struggling with a life that is no more than a mouthful of dust to him." Stephen Crane, letter to Nellie Crouse, 18 March 1896: Cady and Wells, 54 (by permission of the publisher).

Six

1. "The sky was bare and blue ...": Crane, 185.

2. "Seconds, minutes, were quaint ...": Ibid., 143.

3. "... eyes deep as wells, serene ...": Stephen Crane, "The Price of the Harness," quoted at Halliburton, 148. That Crane always loved horses: Bloom, 21; Halliburton, 108; Berryman, 132.

4. "I adore dogs." Stephen Crane, letter to Lucius Button, 15 December 1892. Cady and Wells, 7 (by permission of the publisher). Crane's love for dogs: Ibid., 63; Berryman, 23, 189.

5. Sketch of the Tampa Bay Hotel, 1898: O'Toole, 230; Milton, 269-270; Blow, 285; Kennan, 2; Chidsey, 98; Jones 50-51, 55. For a photograph of the hotel, see Plate 24 at Jones, 138, and Jeffers, 149, Plate F.

6. Tampa, FL, army camp's "Noah's Ark" and "Restaurant": Jones,

54, 71-72; Post, 85-86.

SEVEN

1. "In his eyes ...": Stephen Crane, "The Blue Hotel": Katz, 423.

2 "... the flesh over his heart ...": Stephen Crane, *Red Badge of Courage*: Katz, 211.

EIGHT

1. "The land was very empty ...": Crane, 138

2. Phrase "up-turned face" from Stephen Crane's short story, "The Upturned Face": Colvert, 272 and noted at Bloom, 145, 149.

3. "The wind raised the tawny beard ...": Stephen Crane, *Red Badge of Courage*: Katz, 212.

4. "[W]ar is a spirit ...": Crane, 39.

5. "... brown bodies sticking out ...": Stephen Crane dispatch, dateline 22 June 1898: Bowers, 132, 486.

6. "It was the Americans alone who stormed ...": Stephen Crane dispatch, dateline 4 November 1898: Ibid., 213, 508.

7. "... the Cuban back of the firing line stole ...": Stephen Crane writing in England, dated April 2, 1899: Ibid., 227, 509.

8. Maggie "blossomed in a mud puddle ...". Stephen Crane, *Maggie, Girl of the Streets*: Katz, 20.

9. *Maggie, Girl of the Streets,* self-published by Stephen Crane in 1893, using pen name Johnston Smith: Davis, 59; Benfey, 64; Halliburton, 63.

10. "... souls did not insist upon being able to smile." Stephen Crane, *Maggie, Girl of the Streets:* Katz, 62.

11. "trashy literature," Stephen Crane's father: Davis, 14. "nauseous descriptions ...," Stephen Crane's father: Bloom, 42. "Total abstinence ...," Stephen Crane's father: Stallman, 15. Crane's father's distaste for

all novels: Davis, 8; Benfey, 40.

12. "Under the trees of her dream-gardens, there had always walked a lover." Stephen Crane, *Maggie, Girl of the Streets*: Katz, 23.

13. "[W]ith these fevers comes ...": Crane, 334. Verb tenses changed.

14. Richard Harding Davis at Delmonico's restaurant, New York City: Langford, 70; Downey, 20, 91. For classic portrait of Davis (dapper, as ever) with Lt. Col. Theodore Roosevelt, spring 1898, see Blow, 256, Plate J.

15. Stephen Crane's fingers stained with nicotine from hand-rolled cigarettes: Stallman, 45, 92.

NINE

1. "It seemed that the dead men ...": Stephen Crane, *Red Badge of Courage*: Katz, 225.

2. Cuban prostitutes paid with Mauser ammunition: Post, 132.

3. "[T]he apparition of Reuben McNab ...": Stephen Crane, quoted Davis, 265; Stallman, 392.

4. "Cuba," Theodore Roosevelt's mascot dog of the Rough Riders: Roosevelt, 221.

5. Thesis that pro-Wyler Voluntarios sank *Maine*: Samuels, 48, 152-153, 306-307.

6. "A .44 caliber revolver ...": From Stephen Crane, "One-Dash-Horses." Bergon, 34.

7. "Samuel Carleton" walking stockade parapet while smoking and oblivious to Spanish gunfire and dreaming of someone else doing a similar display is drawn from the historical record. Standing and smoking casually, Stephen Crane twice exposed himself to Spanish fire atop San Juan Hill, 1 July 1898, during the battle: Blow, 321-322; Downey, 160-161; O'Toole, 321; Brown, 361; Berryman, 223; Langford, 202; Milton, 331; Benfey, 251.

8. "Down in the mystic, hidden fields ...": Stephen Crane, "The

Dark-Brown Dog," published posthumously, 1901: Katz, 86.

Ten

1. "... demons to the nerves ...": Stephen Crane on Cuban land crabs: Crane, 97.

2. Stephen Crane's mother suffers nervous breakdown by 1880s standards in about 1886 and was termed insane during her later years: Mentioned only by Benfey, 36-38. Crane's mother bore 14 children. Four siblings died in childhood before Crane was born when his mother was 45 years old. His father died in 1880; his mother died in 1891, orphaning Crane at age 14. Ibid., 32, 34, 36, 38.

3. "You can shoot a man through the head ...": Stephen Crane dispatch, dateline 7 August 1898: Bowers, 178, 497.

4. "The weariness of the body ...": Crane, 179.

5. "... the Western man who chewed tobacco ...": Stephen Crane dispatch, dateline 17 October 1898: Bowers, 205, 505.

6. "[H]uman agony is not pleasant." Stephen Crane undated dispatch from Havana: Ibid., 201, 505.

7. "This dead young Greek had nothing ...": Stephen Crane, dispatch from Greece, approximate dateline 10 May 1897: Ibid., 39, 450.

8. "The red, eyelike gleam ...": Stephen Crane, *Red Badge of Courage*: Katz, 190.

9. "... novel reading is a crime." Jesse Peck, quoted at Davis, 14.

10. "He finally concluded that the only way to prove himself ...": Stephen Crane, *Red Badge of Courage*: Katz, 201.

11. "As the flap of the blue jacked fell away ...": Stephen Crane, *Red Badge of Courage*: Katz, 246. This famous description of the death of Jim Conklin, the "Tall Soldier," and the wound like wolf bites may have been borrowed by Crane from the Civil War writings of Ambrose Bierce: Benfey, 116.

12. "... the eels of despair ...": Stephen Crane, "Five White Mice":

Bergon, 65.

13. Dog "Booth" guards body of Sgt. Slaughter: Cashin, 326. See Page 323 for an etching of the famous scene. Sergeant Horace Bivins and his dog, Booth. Ibid., 61.

ELEVEN

1. The number of newspaper dispatches cabled or mailed by Crane from Havana between September and November 1898 is drawn from Bowers, *Collected Works*.

2. Stephen Crane leaves Havana for New York on 24 December 1898. From there, he returned to England, Cora Stewart, and his three beloved dogs Sponge ("Spongie" to Crane), Flannel, and Ruby. He died from TB and his tropical diseases 18 months later. Crane's farewell with close British friend, novelist Joseph Conrad, and death of Stephen Crane: Benfey, 4, 13-14, 17, 19-20, 257, 260, 270 (Crane portrait with Sponge: Plate 26); Berryman, 235, 239, 258-260; Milton, 376-377; Stallman, 345. The biographers of Crane agree with his Christmas Eve departure from Cuba with one dissenter. Stallman has Crane leaving Cuba on 17 November 1898: Stallman, 438, 442.

3. Stephen Crane living at Havana's Grand Hotel Pasaje in August 1898: Stallman, 414; Davis, 278.

4. Stephen Crane leaves Havana for New York City on ship *City of Washington*: Davis, 291.

5. "old straw" odor of Havana: Crane, 203.

6. Note on Crane's fictional, last visit to hulk of sunken *Maine*: The wreck was raised, floated out of Havana Harbor, and sunk off Cuba in deep water in March 1912. That same year, a ten-foot steel section of *Maine*'s bridge was dedicated as a war memorial in Canton, Ohio, hometown of President William McKinley and of his second Secretary of State William Day. The fragment of *Maine* remains on display at Canton's Veterans Memorial Park: Gary Brown, "Remember

the *Maine*," The Repository; Canton, Ohio; 10 February 1992, Page D-1.

7. "Samuel Carleton" used by Stephen Crane as an alias at St. James Hotel in Jacksonville, Florida, in 1896: Benfey, 185; Davis, 173; Milton, 125-126.

8. "Taps": Dead of 8th Ohio Volunteer Infantry: Hard, Appendix 2.

SELECT BIBLIOGRAPHY

Alger, Russell A., *The Spanish-American War* (1901). Reprinted, Free-port, NY: Books for Libraries Press, 1971.

Bergon, Frank, Ed., *Western Writings of Stephen Crane.* NY: New American Library, Signet Edition, 1979.

Berryman, John, *Stephen Crane.* NY: William Sloane Associates, The American Men of Letters Series, 1950.

Bloom, Herald, Ed., *Stephen Crane.* NY: Chelsea House, 1987.

Blow, Michael, *A Ship To Remember: The Maine and the Spanish-American War.* NY: William Morrow, 1992.

Bowers, Fredson T., Ed., *Stephen Crane, Reports of War: The Works of Stephen Crane*, Vol. IX. Charlottesville, VA: University of Virginia Press, 1971.

Bradford, James C., Ed., *Crucible of Empire: The Spanish-American*

War and its Aftermath. Annapolis, MD: U. S. Naval Institute Press, 1993.

Brown, Charles H., *The Correspondents' War: Journalists in the Spanish-American War*. NY: Scribner's, 1967.

Cady, Edwin H. and Lester G. Wells, Eds., *Stephen Crane's Love Letters to Nellie Crouse*. NY: Syracuse University Press, 1954. Excerpts reprinted by permission of the publisher.

Carlson, Paul H., *"Pecos Bill": A Military Biography of William R. Shafter*. College Station, TX: Texas A & M University Press, 1989.

Cashin, Herschel V., et al., *Under Fire with the Tenth U.S. Cavalry*. NY: F. Tennyson Neely, 1899; reprinted, NY: Arno Press, 1969.

Chidsey, Donald B., *The Spanish-American War*. NY: Crown, 1971.

Colvert, James B., Ed., *Great Short Works of Stephen Crane*. NY: Perennial Library, Harper and Row, 1968.

Cosmas, Graham A., *An Army for Empire: The United States Army in the Spanish-American War*. Columbia, MO: University of Missouri Press, 1971; reprinted, Shippensburg, PA: White Mane Publishing Company, 1994.

Crane, Stephen, *Wounds in the Rain* (1900). Freeport, NY: Books for Libraries Press, 1972.

_____, *The Works of Stephen Crane, Vol. IX: Reports of War*, edited by Fredson T. Bowers. Charlottesville, VA: Rector and Visitors of the University of Virginia, 1971. Excerpts reprinted by permission.

Davis, Linda H., *Badge of Courage: The Life of Stephen Crane*. NY: Houghton Mifflin, 1998.

Dierks, Jack Cameron, *A Leap to Arms: The Cuban Campaign of 1898*. Philadelphia, PA: Lippincott, 1970. Note: Great care must be taken with this volume. Many of its dates for historical events are wrong.

Downey, Fairfax, *Richard Harding Davis and His Day*. NY: Scribner's, 1933.

Fletcher, Marvin, *The Black Soldier and Officer in the United States Army, 1891-1917*. Columbia, MO: University of Missouri Press, 1974.

Feuer, A. B., *The Santiago Campaign of 1898: A Soldier's View of the Spanish-American War*. Westport, CT: Praeger, 1993.

Gates, John M., *Schoolbooks and Krags: The United States Army in the Philippines, 1898-1902*. Westport, CT: Greenwood Press, 1973.

Gatewood, Jr., Willard B., *Black Americans and the White Man's Burden, 1898-1903*. Urbana, IL: University of Illinois Press, 1975.

Goldstein, Donald M., Katherine V. Dillon, J. Michael Wenger, and Robert J. Cressman, *The Spanish-American War: The Story and Photographs*. Dulles, VA: Prange Enterprises/Brassey's, 1998.

Halliburton, David, *The Color of the Sky: A Study of Stephen Crane*. NY: Cambridge University Press,1989.

Hard, Curtis V., *Banners in the Air: The Eighth Ohio Volunteers and the Spanish-American War*, Robert H. Farrell, Ed.. Kent, OH: Kent State University Press, 1988.

Jeffers, H. Paul, *Colonel Roosevelt: Theodore Roosevelt Goes to War, 1897-1898*. NY: John Wiley and Sons, 1996.

Johnson, Edward A., *History of Negro Soldiers in the Spanish-American War*. Raleigh, NC: Capital Printing Company, 1899; NY: Johnson Reprint Corporation, 1970.

Jones, Virgil C., *Roosevelt's Rough Riders*. Garden City, NY: Doubleday, 1971.

Katz, Joseph, *The Portable Stephen Crane*. NY: Penguin Books, 1969, 1977.

Keller, Allan, *The Spanish-American War: A Compact History*. NY: Hawthorn Books, 1969.

Kennan, George, *Campaigning in Cuba* (1899), facsimile edition, Port Washington, NY: Kennikat Press, 1971.

Langford, Gerald, *The Richard Harding Davis Years*. NY: Holt, Rinehart, and Winston, 1961.

Mason, Gregory, *Remember the Maine*. NY: Henry Holt & Company, 1939.

Millis, Walter, *The Martial Spirit*. Cambridge, MA: Riverside Press, 1931.

Milton, Joyce, *The Yellow Kids: Foreign Correspondents in the Heyday of Yellow Journalism*. NY: Harper and Row, 1989.

Nankivell, John H., *History of the Twenty-fifth Regiment, United States Infantry, 1869-1926*. NY: Negro University Press, 1927, 1969.

O'Toole, G. J. A, *The Spanish War: An American Epic 1898*. NY: W. W. Norton, 1984, 1986.

Post, Charles Johnson, *The Little War of Private Post*. Boston, MA: Little, Brown, 1960.

Roosevelt, Theodore, *The Rough Riders* (1902). NY: DaCapo Press, 1990.

Samuels, Peggy and Harold Samuels, *Remembering the Maine*. Washington, D.C.: Smithsonian Institution Press, 1995.
(Author's note: This volume should be the standard text on the mystery of who destroyed the battleship *Maine*.)

Stallman, R. W., *Stephen Crane*. NY: George Braziller, 1968.

Trask, David, *The War with Spain in 1898*. NY: Macmillan, 1981.

Wheeler, Joseph, *The Santiago Campaign* (1898), facsimile edition, Port Washington, NY: Kennikat Press, 1971.